P9-CRZ-291

AN EVIL HOUR

Also by Jill McGown

A Perfect Match

AN EVIL HOUR

Jill McGown

St. Martin's Press
New York

Library of Congress Cataloging-in-Publication Data

McGown, Jill.
  An evil hour.

  "A Thomas Dunne book."
  I. Title.
PS3563.C365E9   1987   813'.54   87-4398
ISBN 0-312-00592-X

First published in Great Britain by Macmillan London Limited.

First U.S. Edition

10 9 8 7 6 5 4 3 2 1

'Thou's met me in an evil hour'
Robert Burns, 'To a Mountain-Daisy'

AN EVIL HOUR

ONE

Annie Maddox looked in the mirror, and reached for make-up to try to disguise the fact that she had been crying. Tears of anger, of dismay, had puffed up her eyes, and still her breath was coming in little shuddering sobs. But she was under control now, as she worked quickly to repair her face.

The anger had been at him, at his presumption; the dismay at herself and her reaction.

Annie was coming up to forty, dark and slim. She reminded herself of her years as she looked in the mirror, feeling as wretched as any fifteen-year-old who had just cut off her nose to spite her face. But she had been right. It was over, and it ought to stay that way.

She glanced at the clock. Ten past five – Linda would have taken over from Sandra on reception, and she ought to apologise to Sandra for leaving her to cope on her own. She might just catch her. Taking a deep breath, she walked quickly through the sitting room, and opened the door, almost bumping into Mr Grant as he stepped out of the lift.

'Oh, I'm sorry,' she said.

'Not at all,' said Grant.

James Grant owned the Wellington Hotel. He was in his late fifties, a large, heavy-jawed man, with almost black hair, even more slicked back than usual today. His wife was on an extended visit to her family, and he had closed up their imposing house on Amblesea's sea front to move temporarily into the hotel.

It was a situation that Annie viewed with deep misgiving,

because not only was he neither staff nor guest – as witness his use of the staff lift – but it seemed to Annie that in his wife's absence Grant was making a determined, twinkling, avuncular play for her.

The Wellington Conference Complex had been conceived and built by Grant, who already owned a dozen other hotels and nightclubs along the South Coast, not to mention quite a lot of London.

He had also built most of the new shopping centre, as well as practically everything else that had gone up in Amblesea, a success rate that had given rise to suspicion and speculation in the town. The allegations had been dropped, but Grant's heart never seemed to be in it again, and he had gone into semi-retirement with his ex-beauty-queen wife.

Annie had managed the Wellington since it had opened, three years ago. She was normally bright and efficient and vigorously in control of what was at last becoming a very successful enterprise indeed. But right now, she felt far from bright.

Grant had retired to his room after a large Sunday lunch with instructions that he was not to be disturbed; Annie could wish that she had done the same.

'I just came down to check the time of the disco this evening,' he said.

'It starts at eight,' she said, unable to conceal her surprise at the question. The disco was what was going to usher in the new year at the Wellington. It had not occurred to Annie that Grant would be in the least interested.

'Ah,' he said. 'You think I am too old for disco dancing?'

'Everyone's too old for disco dancing,' she said, with a fair approximation of a smile. 'I was just going to check with Sandra that everything's ready.'

Grant stepped back to allow her to go first down the corridor, catching her up again in order to reach the door a fraction ahead of her, and open it, standing back with a little bow.

'Linda?' Annie said. 'Is Sandra still around?'

Sandra, still very much the new girl – though, Annie had been gratified to notice, quietly efficient – appeared from the staff room. 'Did you want me, Mrs Maddox?' she asked.

'I'm sorry,' Annie said. 'I lumbered you with all this disco nonsense.'

'Oh, that's all right,' she said, a little shyly, still.

'Thanks anyway,' Annie said.

'Are you taking calls now, Mr Grant?' Linda asked.

'What? Oh – yes. Have there been any?'

'No,' Linda said.

They all laughed, and Annie suddenly felt very alone. She wished she hadn't been such a bitch to Gerald. She wished he had stayed. She wished he had never come.

'Mrs Maddox here thinks I'm too old to go to the disco tonight,' Grant said, twinkling like mad.

'Not a bit of it,' Annie said, determinedly joining in. 'I'm looking forward to your break-dancing exhibition.'

'I only do that in the street,' he countered. 'I had hoped you would oblige.'

'She probably could,' Linda complained, joining in the rather stagey chit-chat in which they were indulging.

Linda and Annie had grown up together, and Linda had been the first person Annie had asked for when she needed staff for the Wellington. It had always been going to be that way round, as it had always been written in the stars that Annie would keep her athletic figure while Linda's would spread to more comfortable proportions. And that Linda would feel obliged to dye her mousy hair blonde, while Annie's came dark and shining, like her eyes. It didn't bother Linda.

Grant looked out of the big glass doors. 'Has it stopped raining?' he asked.

'I think so,' Linda said.

'I hope so,' said Sandra. 'Or I'll get soaked.'

'Where do you have to go?' Grant asked.

'The new flats,' Sandra said. 'You know – out where the prefabs used to be.'

'I will drive you,' he said expansively. 'We can't have you

walking home.'

'Oh, no – really. I didn't mean—'

'Not another word.'

'Well – thank you.'

She allowed herself to be shepherded out, and Linda and Annie exchanged glances.

'She's old enough to take care of herself,' Linda said.

'She's not that many years older than Christine,' Annie argued.

'Which is old enough,' Linda repeated. 'Anyway – maybe he'll forget you now that he's clocked Sandra.'

Grant's fondness for the opposite sex had become all too apparent during his stay at the Wellington. But he was more than old enough to be Sandra's father.

'She won't take any nonsense from him,' Linda said reassuringly.

Grant appeared in the doorway, with Sandra in tow.

'My car is gone,' he said.

Annie stared at him. 'What?' she said.

'Gone. It isn't there.'

'It can't be gone!' Annie said. 'I saw it there myself, not—' She looked at her watch. 'Not two hours ago.' She had in fact closed Grant's boot, which he had left ajar; she thought this was not the best time to mention it.

Grant walked slowly to the desk. 'Mrs Maddox,' he said. 'There are fourteen cars on the entire car park. My car is not one of them.'

'When did you leave it?' Linda asked.

'Lunchtime,' he said. 'About one o'clock, I suppose.'

'Ten past,' Sandra said. 'You gave me back the lift key.'

Grant had moved in some creature comforts from home, and had been using the service lift. 'I stand corrected,' he said. 'Ten past one.'

'It was there at three fifteen,' Annie said again, helplessly.

'Well,' said Grant. 'It's not there now.'

'Who else came in or out, Sandra?' Annie asked.

10

'Not many people,' she said. 'Mr Grant, of course. And you – you went out to get something from your car.'

'My sweater,' Annie said. 'That's when I saw your car,' she told Grant.

'And the gentleman who was visiting you,' Sandra said. 'Then just Linda – oh, and Jimmy. The disco,' she explained to the blank faces. 'That's all.'

Annie sighed. Today was impossible.

Grant was in Annie's sitting room, a thin cigar in one hand and a brandy in the other, when the door opened, and Christine and Pete came in.

Christine was Annie's daughter, and just nineteen. Annie might have had no role to play in her creation; everything – her fair colouring, her blue eyes, her strong-mindedness – she had got from her father. Pete was unaccountably Christine's boyfriend. He was twenty-seven, an unemployed ex-soldier, attractive in an unkempt, gipsy-like way, and pleasant enough, Annie supposed.

'We've come to see if we—' Christine broke off when she saw Grant. 'Oh,' she said. 'I'm sorry.'

He smiled tightly, but graciously.

'Mr Grant's car's been stolen,' Annie said.

'I am sorry,' Christine said. 'Where was it?'

'Here,' Annie answered for him.

Christine bit her lip. 'Oh dear,' she said. 'When was it taken – do you know?'

'Well, it was there at quarter past three,' Annie said.

Pete looked slightly uncomfortable. 'We'd better go,' he said to Christine.

'But I wanted to ask Mum—'

'It'll keep. She's busy.'

Christine gave in, and Pete hustled her away.

'I just don't like him, that's all,' Pete said.

Christine sat down on the bed, and looked up at him. 'You

11

don't even know for certain,' she said.

'Don't I?' Pete's face was flushed.

Sometimes, Christine felt more like his sister than his girlfriend. More like his mother. She put out her hand, and he took it, sitting beside her on the bed.

'I thought you were over Lesley,' she said, gently mocking him.

'It is over,' he said.

'Looks like it.'

He smiled. 'I'm sorry,' he said. 'Why do you put up with me?'

Christine had answers, but she couldn't articulate them. She loved Pete; she loved his eyes, darker blue than hers. She loved his mouth – that was what she had noticed first about him. She stroked the little silky hairs on the back of his hand as she thought these things that she had never told him, and never could. Now and again, she had told him the things she didn't love about him; the fact that he wouldn't get a job and stick to it, his lack of common sense, his obsession with Lesley.

'Why can't you forget her?' she asked. 'She's gone now.'

Pete looked at his hands, at her hand holding his. 'It was just seeing Grant,' he said.

'If you're going to be like this every time you see him, perhaps you'd better not come here.'

His eyes widened. 'What do you mean?'

'I mean, I'll come to the flat while he's staying here, if you'd rather.'

She was gratified to see him relax a little. He had misunderstood, thought that she meant not see him any more, and it had worried him. That, at least, was a step in the right direction.

'There's no need,' he said.

'You can hardly avoid him,' she said. 'He's always hanging round Mum.'

'Poor Annie,' said Pete, standing up. 'I think maybe I should just go,' he said. 'Do you mind?'

Chris did, but she didn't say so. 'I'll come with you, shall I?' she asked.

12

Pete hesitated. 'No,' he said. 'No – I'll just go. I'll be back for the disco.'

'Pete—'

'I'll be back,' he said.

Tom Webb appeared at the open sitting-room door.

'Annie.' He nodded to her, his face grave. 'I understand that someone has reported a stolen car.'

'Mr Grant's car,' Annie said, with a nod in Grant's direction. Tom was a policeman, but he was a detective superintendent; not, Annie would have thought, the most likely person to be concerned with a stolen car. He was based at Harmouth, the big port just ten minutes along the coast from Amblesea.

'Mr Grant?' Tom turned to him. 'We've met before. Webb, Harmouth CID.'

Grant frowned. 'I have given all the particulars to the police,' he said.

'Yes, sir, I know.'

'Then might I suggest that you look for my car rather than talk about it?'

His accent was more noticeable than usual, Annie thought. He liked to think that he didn't have a foreign accent at all. His homeland had been devoured by war and politics; he had fought behind enemy lines before he was out of his teens, and had come to Britain after the war, still a very young man. He had taken British citizenship, and a British name, in an attempt to wipe out all that had happened to him. His brush with the authorities earlier in the year had brought it all back to him, and Tom wasn't Grant's favourite person.

'That's just it,' Tom was saying. 'We have found it. In an office car park a few streets away. Just off High Street, in fact.'

Grant looked up at him. 'You don't seem very happy about it,' he said. 'Is it a write-off?'

'No,' Tom said. 'But it is damaged.'

Which meant that it was a write-off as far as Grant was concerned, Annie thought. She had never seen anyone who

13

spent money like he did. He boasted of having made three fortunes and spent two, and she could believe it. Grant had started out after the war, demolishing the blitzed buildings in London, and constructing new ones in the belief that land in London would become very valuable. He had been right.

'Still,' he sighed. 'At least you have found it.'

'Yes,' Tom said, slowly.

'Does it go? Can I collect it?'

'It goes,' he said. 'But I'm afraid it's having to stay with us for a while.'

'Why?'

'It's just possible that it was connected with another more serious incident.' Tom glanced at Annie. 'Another taxi driver,' he said. 'Stabbed this time, and his money stolen. He was found down at the old prom.'

'Oh, how awful.' Annie sat down. 'Is he badly hurt?'

Tom nodded. 'They're operating,' he said grimly. 'But they don't hold out much hope.'

'And in what way do you think my car was involved?'

'It probably wasn't,' Tom said. 'But it's a possibility.' He sat down. 'We'd just like to make certain of the details. When did you last see it, Mr Grant?'

'At about ten past one, I'm told,' he said. 'I normally park right outside, but it was raining, so I parked it in the covered area on the other side of the car park.'

Tom nodded. 'It had the key in it,' he said reprovingly.

'A bad habit,' Grant agreed.

'You're lucky it didn't turn up in Glasgow. Today of all days.'

'I saw it after that,' Annie said. 'At about three fifteen.'

'So it went missing between three fifteen and five fifteen?'

Grant and Annie nodded in agreement.

'Who was on reception?'

'Sandra,' Annie said.

'Oh, yes. The new girl. Where is she now?'

'She went home. I asked her who she'd seen, but it didn't help.'

'If you can let me have her address, someone will pop round to see her.'

The phone rang, and Annie picked it up.

'It's for you,' she said, handing it to Tom.

'Webb.' He listened without speaking. 'Thank you,' he said, after a moment, and replaced the receiver.

'The taxi driver,' he said. 'He died, half an hour ago.'

Pete walked through the rain, into the Wellington's car park. He glimpsed Sandra as she went in, and that meant it was almost ten; she was starting later because of the disco.

Sandra and Linda were talking, and Christine was waiting for him behind the desk when he walked in.

'You look good,' he said.

'Where have you been?' she asked. 'I've been ready for an hour and a half.' She lowered her voice. 'You weren't going to come, were you?'

No, he hadn't been going to come. He had sat and told himself how Christine would be better off without him altogether. But he had come.

'It goes on until after midnight,' he said. 'We'll have plenty of time.'

'That's not the point,' she said.

'Oh, come on,' he answered, putting his arm round her, aiming a kiss, but failing to land it as she pushed him away.

'Don't,' she said, pushing open the corridor door.

In the privacy of the staff corridor, she allowed herself to be kissed.

'Chris,' he said. 'Would you do something for me?'

'Yes,' she said, without hesitation, then turned away from him, embarrassed, as the sitting-room door opened.

Annie smiled. 'Hello, Pete,' she said. 'She'd just about given you up.'

'I know,' he said. 'Are you on your way to the disco?'

Pete offered an arm each to the ladies, but they couldn't get

15

through the door like that. Somehow his occasional efforts to be smooth never really paid off.

'. . . *for auld lang syne*.' Annie and Linda, arms linked, sang lustily, not so much from *joie de vivre* as from the certainty that they were the only people present who were actually singing the right words. The intrusive 'for the sake of' had been expunged from their rendition by a couple of Scottish soldiers one very memorable New Year's Eve in their teens.

As they uncrossed their arms, Christine, on Annie's other side, allowed herself to be given a peck on the cheek by her mother, and in return kissed the air somewhere behind Annie's right ear.

They toasted one another and the new year just before a torrent of sound made them all wince – even Christine, Annie noticed, despite her nineteen years. Pete took Christine on to the floor, as balloons cascaded down, and Annie moved away from the loudspeaker, but it didn't make any difference. The music still pounded in her ears, music no longer. Just sound, noise, and a racing pulse beat. The coloured lights played round the room and hurt her eyes. She didn't have to stay; she could go back into the quiet of her own room and feel sorry for herself. But through the smoky, flickering gloom, she could see Christine and Pete as they danced, and she knew she had to stay. It would worry Christine if she left, and she couldn't spoil everyone else's night.

She turned to the tap on her shoulder to see Linda mouthing something at her. It took her a moment to realise that she wasn't mouthing, she was speaking. Yelling, even. Annie fine-tuned her ear to catch the words.

'I just said are you all right?' Linda repeated.

As ever, Linda had been the one who had listened to Annie's woes.

'Yes, thanks,' Annie bellowed back. 'I'm fine.' The music stopped abruptly, and her last word was proclaimed to the gathering. She glanced round, aware that everyone must have heard, but no one seemed to have noticed.

In the brief lull, Christine and Pete walked through the crush

16

to the emergency exit, and went out into the night.

'Are they having problems too?' Linda asked.

'Difficult to tell with Christine,' Annie said.

Linda's own love life was apparently fairly free of trouble, but he was away, so she was on her own too. 'Come on,' Annie said. 'Who needs men?'

They joined the dark shapes on the dance floor as the throbbing music – the same music, for all Annie knew – began again.

Outside in the chilly night, Chris propped the door open with the fire extinguisher.

'Well?' Pete said.

Christine shivered. Pete had his leather jacket on; she wasn't dressed for this weather. She looked up at him. She had never imagined moonlight and roses. She wouldn't have expected violins. But a proposal bellowed in her ear over bass guitars and balloons bursting was one she had to be certain she had heard.

'Marry you?' she said doubtfully. 'That was what you said?'

'No,' he said. 'I asked where the gents' was.' He put his arms round her. 'Will you?' he asked.

Christine wasn't so sure that she didn't prefer things the way they were. 'Some day,' she said. 'If you still want me.'

'I'll get a job,' he said. 'A proper job.'

Maybe, Christine thought. But that wasn't what was stopping her jumping at marriage to Pete. Pete got by, somehow, on Giros and casual labour. She could put up with that. But where did you go when you wanted to be alone?

'Say you will,' he said. 'We don't have to put a date on it.'

Christine couldn't really see what difference it made to him, but she was aware of her lack of romance, and assumed that it did. 'Yes,' she said. 'I will. One day.'

He pulled her up on tiptoe, and they sealed the bargain.

'Are you coming back to the flat tonight?' he asked.

'No,' she said. 'I think I ought to stay. Mum's had a rotten day.'

It was an odd way to start off their more permanent

17

relationship, she thought, as he walked away into the wet, dark night. She rolled the extinguisher back from the door, and went back into the hot, noisy disco.

'No joy,' Lancaster said, straightening up as Webb came in, answering him before he had asked the question. 'Can't tie it in.'

Tom Webb sighed. 'Fingerprints?' he asked.

'Lots,' Lancaster said, scratching his beard. 'On the driver's door, nearside rear, boot, bonnet, and windscreen. All just the owner's, and someone wearing gloves.'

Just the owner's. A nice glib phrase that clearly knew nothing of the diplomacy and cajoling that had gone into getting James Robert Grant's fingerprints. The man was paranoid about the police. Possibly with good reason, Webb thought, in view of the bribery business.

'What about the damage?' he asked.

'Can't match any of it for certain. Grant's car had been bashed into walls by the joy-riders. I could tell you the kind of wall it was, but that's about all.'

'Any point in hanging on to it?' Webb asked.

'No,' Lancaster said.

Twelfth Night. Annie looked up at the decorations, for once glad that it was time for them to come down. She would be glad to see the back of this most unfestive of festive seasons.

She was serving behind the bar in the Iron Duke because of the tummy bug that everyone but her seemed to have caught.

Tom Webb was looking reflectively into his pint. 'At least he can have his car back,' he said. 'That should please him.'

'He's got a new one,' Annie said, pleased that her prediction had come to pass.

'Has he, by Jove?' Tom whistled. 'Quick work.'

'Oh, it's not a *proper* car,' Annie said. 'Just an off-the-peg runabout.'

'There wasn't all that much damage to his old one.'

'Not good enough for our Mr Grant,' Annie said.

18

'Nothing's good enough for your Mr Grant,' Tom said. 'God, he's a miserable bugger.'

Annie smiled. 'He isn't really. But he's got a thing about policemen.'

'This policeman's got a thing about him.' Tom swilled the beer about in the bottom of his glass. 'I remember the fuss he made when I couldn't place his accent. He was a British citizen, he was a taxpayer, I don't know what all. I was only being sociable.'

'He's from somewhere that ended up in Russia,' Annie said vaguely. 'I think he was in a prison camp. He says he had to fight Germans just so the Russians could win.'

'Before he was old enough to eat solids. I know,' Tom groaned. He had obviously been treated to the same speech. 'But that's not my fault.'

Annie laughed. 'He's all right,' she said. 'But I wish he'd go home, all the same.'

'Back to Russia?' Tom asked, finishing off his drink.

'No! Just back to his own house, and out of my hair.'

'Oh, yes – he's staying here, isn't he?' Tom pushed his glass across the bar. 'While his wife's away?'

'She's supposed to be off visiting her family,' Annie said. 'There are those who reckon she's left him.'

Tom looked round, as though he might be overheard. 'Where is he?' he asked.

'At the head office,' Annie said. 'Board meeting.' Safely in London, out of the way, so she and Tom could talk about him. It wasn't a very nice thing to do, she thought fleetingly. 'He said he would make a weekend of it,' she said, refilling his glass.

'Oh yes?' Tom answered. 'You'd think he'd be content with the one he's got. If he has still got her.'

Annie smiled. 'I know,' she said, thinking of the one-time Miss Butlin's Holiday Camps, now considerably more elegantly eye-catching in her forties.

'But she's not twenty-five any more,' Tom said.

'Neither am I,' said Annie. 'It doesn't put him off.'

'So I've heard.' He winked. 'I'm told that you're quite high on his list.'

'Anything in skirts,' Annie said.

There was nothing Tom liked better than a good gossip. He had made it to superintendent despite his appalling lack of discretion – or perhaps, Annie thought, because of it. He discussed things readily and openly, and people found that they responded in kind. He'd only been at Harmouth for eight months, and Annie thought that he would already have learned a lot of things that way.

He was in his forties, single, and attractive; Annie was mildly disappointed at his lack of interest in her, and slightly surprised. Not because she thought she was God's gift to men, but because she was presentable, and on her own. So was he, and she had had high hopes when he had first arrived, alone in a town where he knew no one. But though he liked her, and often spent whole evenings chatting to her, he had a depressing tendency to treat her like one of the boys.

Short of wearing a notice that said I Have No Intention of Trapping You into Marriage, Annie had exhausted her womanly wiles long ago.

'Was his car involved in that taxi–driver business?' she asked.

'Don't think so.' Tom sipped his beer. 'The taxi had some slight damage at the front. We thought whoever nicked Grant's car had maybe banged into the taxi, and when the driver got out to inspect the damage – wallop.' The last word was accompanied by a graphic demonstration. 'He gets a knife stuck in him, and his money stolen.'

'But?'

'A million buts. But we can't conclusively match up the damage. They'd been bashing Grant's car into walls, by the look of things. And then some joker at Harmouth station says he noticed that the taxi's indicator was bust when it dropped a fare at ten to five.' He shook his head. 'And the broken pieces were found by the building site. On that side of the road.'

Annie looked enquiringly at him.

'That suggests that it happened when the taxi was coming *from* Harmouth. If the porter's right, then it must all have happened earlier on.'

Annie shook her head. 'So you're no further forward?'

'We are following a number of lines of enquiry,' Tom quoted, with his spokesman's voice. 'We know sod all, Annie.'

'A hundred pounds,' she said. 'What would make anyone do that for a hundred pounds?'

Tom wiped froth from his lips. 'Drink,' he said. 'Drugs, glue sniffing – you name it.'

All the other attacks on taxi drivers had taken place in Harmouth; that sort of thing just didn't happen in Amblesea.

But it had.

TWO

The dark winter tide came rolling in, and the pebbled beach gleamed as the waves withdrew and quietly came again. In the calm cold darkness of a January evening, the sea was docile. But the elements were not always so benign; jutting out into the water was what had once been Amblesea's pleasure pier, all but torn in two by raging seas. The structure stood like a monument to the past, defiantly pointing a ragged, accusing finger at the Continent.

Tonight, the water flowed around the timbers with a whisper, edging closer to Annie as she stood watching it, her face expressionless. She leant back against one of the supports, the dark wood staining the crisp whiteness of the shirt she wore. Reluctantly she pushed herself away from the pier, and walked slowly along the shore, the incoming tide running almost to her feet before she moved away from it, and back towards the sea wall. She started to climb the steps, but turned suddenly and sat down, bent over as if she were in pain.

Slowly, she straightened up, and looked with sadness at the desolation. She could just remember what it used to look like when she was a child, and had come on holiday as hundreds of Londoners used to do. Some of the buildings had been long gone even then, demolished in a wartime bombing raid intended for Harmouth. What Hitler had started, the council had finished, levelling the ground for use as a makeshift coach park in the kiss-me-quick fifties. But one by one, the seaside attractions had failed to attract, and one violent night the pier had been damaged and closed to the public.

'Annie?' Tom Webb's voice startled her. 'What are you doing here?' he asked.

'Just sitting,' she answered, turning dark, troubled eyes towards him, then back to the sea.

He frowned. 'Are you all right?' he asked.

'Yes, thank you, I'm fine.' Her voice was flat and bleak.

She looked at him again, at the tough good looks that were just beginning to show the effects of his hearty appetite for pub snacks and beer. He looked cold, concerned, and curious.

'It's a bit cold to be out without a coat,' he said in almost comic understatement as fine snow began to fall.

She nodded slightly.

'And—' He crouched down to be on her level. 'And the tide's coming in, Annie,' he said. 'Why don't you let me take you home?'

'Home?' she repeated, her normally expressive eyes looking at him blankly.

'The Wellington.' Tom looked puzzled.

'It's an hotel,' she said.

'Yes,' he agreed. 'Did something happen?'

She shook her head slowly.

He put out a hand to touch the greenish brown smears on her back, and looked along the shore. 'Were you with someone?' he asked. 'Has someone been bothering you?'

'No,' she replied.

'Tell me what's wrong, Annie. I might be able to help.'

But again, she shook her head.

He smoothed back his hair, a habit he had when perplexed. 'I can't leave you here,' he said, putting a firm law-enforcing hand on her elbow, and straightening up. 'You can't stay here,' he repeated firmly. 'Come up now.'

She did as she was told, with his guiding hand on her arm. She was shivering.

'You'll catch your death,' he said.

It had come on the tea-time news.

'*The body of Mr Gerald Culver, MP for Eastham and Foley, was*

23

found early this morning, in the hallway of the luxury block of flats in which he had his London home. Police say that they are treating Mr Culver's death as murder, but they have not yet released details. Mr Culver was forty-three, and leaves a wife and two children. As Junior Minister for . . .'

Annie had stared at the screen in bewildered disbelief, and had turned and left the room, left the hotel, to go anywhere. Somewhere she could be alone. And now she stood by the railings, her hands clasping the cold metal. Tom Webb gripped her arm, and she knew what he was afraid of.

'I'm not thinking of drowning myself,' she said, and she felt him relax his hold on her. 'I just have to think about something,' she added.

He let go, and removed his overcoat. 'Here,' he said, draping it round her shoulders. 'Let me drive you ho—' He smothered the word. 'Back to the hotel,' he said.

But Annie just pulled the coat closer about her, and leant her elbows on the railings.

She had come to watch the world obey natural, immutable laws. The tide would ebb and flow, the sun would rise, constant and inviolate. No one could rip that from her.

'He's dead,' she said aloud.

'Who's dead?' Tom asked cautiously.

She looked at him. 'Just someone I know,' she said.

'I'm sorry.' Tom put his hand on her shoulder. 'Please let me drive you back, Annie.'

She shook her head.

Gerald had come back to her, and she had sent him away. Now he was dead. Murdered.

Murdered. The word was unreal, theatrical.

'He was—' Her lips came together in an effort to say the word, but she couldn't.

The water already covered the bottom step, and was rising to the next. Annie nodded slowly. 'I'll come with you now,' she said.

'Good girl,' Tom sighed with relief, as she allowed herself to be guided away, across the deserted waste ground.

They didn't speak on the short drive through the town. Tom glanced at her now and then, but he didn't ask any more questions. He pulled into the Wellington car park, and came into the hotel with her.

Christine darted to the door as Annie arrived. 'Mum?' she said anxiously.

'I'm all right,' Annie said quickly. 'I'm all right.'

'I think she's had some bad news,' Tom said.

'I know,' Christine said.

'Thank you.' Annie slipped off Tom's coat. 'I'll be fine now – thank you.'

'Well – if you're sure.' Tom handed her into Christine's custody. 'A hot drink and bed, if you ask me,' he said.

'We'll take care of her,' Linda said from reception. 'Don't worry.'

Linda began to arrange for tea, and Annie allowed Christine to steer her into the sitting room. For a moment, neither of them spoke.

'He's dead, Chrissie,' Annie said.

'I know,' Christine said helplessly. 'I know.'

'Who would do a thing like that?' Annie asked, hunched up again with the pain she'd felt on the steps.

Christine shook her head. 'Why didn't someone ring you?' she asked. 'Why did they let you find out like that?'

'You know why,' Annie said dully. 'I'm Gerald's guilty secret.'

Christine looked uncomfortable as they were both reminded of her initial hostile reaction to Gerald. 'Sorry. I didn't—' She was interrupted by a knock on the door. 'That'll be the tea,' she said hastily, obviously relieved not to have to continue the conversation, and she opened the door to Linda.

Annie's hand shook as she picked up the cup and saucer, and Linda took the saucer away.

'Thank you for not telling Tom,' Annie said, holding the cup with both hands.

'Do you want anything else?' Christine asked. 'A brandy or anything?'

Annie smiled. 'No,' she said. 'Thank you.'

She was so like her father. There was the same instinctive shying away from emotion, the same practical approach to a situation which couldn't be altered, but might be eased. And that wasn't helping, because she had lost Eddie, too. Not a violent death, but just as sudden, just as devastating.

Annie watched Christine and Linda, each trying to help, and she wished with all her heart that they would just go away. But they didn't; they operated a kind of shift system so that she wasn't alone, taking it in turns to man both the desk and her until Sandra came on at nine. They plied her with cups of tea, and spoke of anything but Gerald.

'Perhaps you should try to sleep,' Linda said, as Christine came in again.

Annie seized the simple solution which had not occurred to her. 'Yes,' she said. 'I think I'll take Tom's advice, and go to bed.'

At last, they were leaving.

'Don't forget we're here if you need us,' Linda said.

'I won't.'

'Are you all right?' Christine asked, pausing in the doorway. 'Do you want anything?'

Yes, Annie thought. I want to scream. But she gave Christine a half-smile. 'I'm sorry I went off like that,' she said. 'I didn't mean to worry you.'

'I didn't think you were going to do anything,' she said.

'Tom Webb did.'

Christine nodded. 'You're sure you don't want me to stay?'

'I just want to be on my own, that's all.'

Christine understood, and left. But Linda still hovered anxiously.

'Do you think you'll sleep? I've got sleeping pills if you'd like one.'

'No, thank you.'

26

Annie needed so badly to be alone, and Linda wouldn't let her.

'I'll be all right,' she said again, firmly, and Linda went at last.

Annie gave a short sigh, and quietly turned the key in the lock. She checked the windows, switched off the lights, and slowly walked through to the bedroom.

She didn't put the light on; she closed the curtains on the ghostly brightness of the snowy night, and lay in the dark with only the fist-clenching pain for company.

It wasn't the same as when Eddie died. Then, she had been so aware of the empty side of the bed, strange after seventeen years of marriage. But it had been a long time since she and Gerald had shared a bed, and there was no immediate sense of loss.

Just pain. The pain of knowing that she had hurt him, that the last words she had spoken to him had been harsh and unkind. He had come back, saying that he'd missed her, and she had turned him away, quickly, before he could start it all up again.

She had to face the pain, to force herself to believe that he was dead. She couldn't comfort herself with ritual. She couldn't go to his funeral, and watch them bury him as proof that he was dead. She had to take a newsreader's word for it. Now, he was dead. There were no tears. Just pain and memories, and a darkness that seemed to last for ever.

Except that it couldn't. The tide had come in, and the sun would rise, even on this despairing night. The sun would rise.

But it was a long, long time coming.

THREE

Ex-Det. Insp. Harry Lambert was an exiled Geordie who smoked too much, drank too often, and didn't eat often enough. He walked up the wide steps to the flats, hands thrust in the pockets of his zipper jacket. Harry never looked quite warm enough; women had a tendency to buy him sweaters and scarves. His fair, fine hair, never his best feature, was receding rapidly, and the effect of his ever more careful hair-combing had been ruined by the chill wind blowing off the Thames. He was smoothing it down with his hand as the security door clicked open at Mrs Culver's command.

To Harry, a London flat meant part of a house with ill-fitting doors and someone else's furniture. To Gerald Culver, it had meant a riverside view and a six-figure price tag. Culver had been the same age as Harry, but he had used his forty-three years to rather better social and financial effect, taking care, Harry had observed, to marry into class *en route* to the top. Becoming an MP had been virtually automatic – par for the course.

Harry called the lift, which arrived silently, minus the graffiti and the smell of urine that seemed to be built into the design of tower-block lifts.

Harry had never owned any property, had never had a wife, or even a lasting relationship. His legendary temper had caused him to resign his twenty-five-year career, and he was never going to forgive himself for that. But, he thought philosophically as the lift doors opened, he hadn't been stabbed to death. There was nothing like still being alive to make you feel superior to a bloke.

Culver had been happily married, and the father of two teenage children. He had been popular with his employees and his fellow directors, and was obviously missed by his family, his friends, and his colleagues on both sides of the House. He was apparently honest, his finances were strong, he didn't gamble.

There was a low-key suggestion in the papers that it might have been a terrorist killing, but it wasn't really the style of any of the known groups, and no one had claimed responsibility. Besides which, Culver's activities were concerned with state benefits – politically sensitive, perhaps, but as yet the Child Poverty Action Group did not seem to be recruiting assassins.

Culver was from what the papers that morning had called 'humble beginnings', as exemplified by his love of football. He had switched his allegiance from Leeds to West Ham when he moved to London as a young man, and followed West Ham's fortunes to the eccentric extent of actually going to the matches whenever he could, which made him a working class hero, and the papers loved it.

All of this would be making him a headache for the investigating officers, Harry knew. Victims were usually just that, whether they were nineteen-year-old thugs or eighty-year-old pensioners. They were crooked, or violent, or defenceless. They were hitchhikers or informants, security men or prostitutes, villains or unwary schoolgirls. They had usually put themselves, wittingly or unwittingly, in danger.

Culver had been killed in the exclusive hallway of his exclusive address, where he had no reason to think that menace lurked.

Harry stepped out of the lift into the discreetly lit, carpeted corridor where Culver had bled to death. There was no sign now, a fortnight later, that anything so distasteful had ever sullied the interior décor.

The door to the flat was open, but he knocked and waited.

'Come in, Mr Lambert.'

Laura Culver had classic English Rose looks which didn't appeal to Harry, but which the newspapers called beautiful.

Small, slim, and fair, she had the sort of delicate bone structure and fine skin that made her look almost unreal, as though someone had drawn her. Her face was still pale with the grief that she had suffered, but there was a hint of something else. A touch of disappointment, of anger, even.

'You come highly recommended, Mr Lambert,' she said.

'Recommended for what, Mrs Culver?' Harry had no idea why she had wanted to see him, but there had been something about her tone when she had phoned him – an automatic assumption that he would see her as she had requested – that had made him do just that.

'I'm told you were a very good policeman,' she said. 'And I understand you have resigned.'

'That's right,' he answered. 'I was, and I have. But I'm not sure how I can help you.'

'I want some enquiries made,' she said evenly. 'Some unofficial enquiries, you understand.'

Harry shook his head. 'Oh, no, Mrs Culver – I'm not in the enquiry agent business.'

'What business *are* you in, Mr Lambert?' she asked sweetly.

Harry looked at her for a moment, then sighed. 'All right, I'm not in any business. I don't know any other business. I've only ever been a policeman. But I don't intend becoming a private enquiry agent.'

'Mr Lambert,' she said soothingly. 'If I had wanted an enquiry agent, there are dozens to choose from. I don't. I want you. And I'm prepared to pay quite a lot of money to get you. Or do you have private means?'

Harry smiled reluctantly. 'Get me to do what?' he asked.

She nodded slightly, and opened a drawer in the desk behind her, taking out a bundle of letters secured by a rubber band, and handing them to him.

Harry glanced at the writing, which was bold and large; black felt pen on white paper. The envelopes were addressed to Culver at the flat. He raised his eyebrows.

'They're from a woman,' Mrs Culver said, answering his

30

unspoken question. 'They're not in any sort of order. He – he didn't have them all together like that.' She turned to close the drawer, and turned back. 'They were in there.' She waved her hand. 'You can read them.'

Harry drew out the top envelope, and removed the letter.

There was no torrid prose; there were no pet names, no fantasies, no vows of eternal devotion. It was an almost business-like arrangement to meet, and yet it was undoubtedly a love letter, a touching, painfully practical love letter. It wasn't written to be kept, but Culver hadn't thrown it away.

'You didn't know?' he asked, opening the next.

'I had no idea.'

Harry read the next letter, a newsy one about the hotel from which they were written. Gossip, funny stories, and a request. *'Please come soon.'*

'Two years,' Laura Culver said, her voice bitter. 'You wouldn't believe I could be kept in the dark that long, would you?'

'I'm very sorry, Mrs Culver,' Harry said. 'But I'm still not sure what—'

Laura Culver sat down and motioned to him to do the same.

'If I tell the police, the papers will in all probability get to hear of it. And that's why I want you to go there – as an experienced police officer. If you think that there is any reason to believe that this ...' She paused. '... this affair might have a bearing on what happened, then I'll tell the police. But if it needn't come out, then I'd much rather it didn't.'

Harry flipped through the letters as he listened to the prepared and slightly breathless speech. 'All right,' he said, putting them in his pocket. 'I'll do it.' He cleared his throat. 'I do have to ask you some questions,' he said.

'I realise that.'

'I understand from the papers that he was here on his own,' Harry said. 'Was that usual?'

'Yes,' she replied. 'Gerald used the flat during the week. I wasn't often here.'

31

'You would have been at your other house in – Surrey, is it?'

She ignored the note of criticism which was unconsciously present in Harry's voice. 'It is,' she said. 'And that's where I was.'

'So your husband would have felt safe bringing someone here?'

'Yes,' she said, her lips coming together in a tight line.

'I have to ask,' he said. 'If you want me to find out what went on.'

'Quite.'

'But the—' Neighbours seemed like a very downmarket description, Harry decided. 'The other residents thought he was alone? From what I've read.'

She nodded. 'Despite the way they look,' she said, 'these flats have very thin walls. You can hear voices.'

'If he didn't bring anyone here, then he opened the downstairs door in the middle of the night,' Harry said. 'Presumably to someone he knew.'

'Presumably,' Mrs Culver said.

Harry walked to the open door. 'Forgive me,' he said. 'But it happened out here, in the hallway, didn't it?'

'So I believe.' Mrs Culver's control was slipping just a little.

'I'm sorry,' he said. 'But I can't ask for – and wouldn't get – any co-operation from the police. I have to ask you.'

'I understand,' she said.

'Have the police made any—' He almost said *stabs*, for God's sake. 'Have the police got any theories on his injuries?' He looked down the corridor at the lift, and the doorway to the stairs. 'Was he trying to get out?'

'They don't think so,' she said. 'They think he was facing whoever ...' She didn't continue the sentence.

'As though he'd come out to meet them?' He deliberately used the ungrammatical but neutral plural.

'Yes.'

'Would he normally do that, do you know? Or would he just do what you did, and leave the door ajar?'

'Let's say he never rushed out to meet *me*,' she said.

Harry went back into the flat. 'The papers just said "the early hours",' he said. 'Were the police any more definite?'

'Between four and five a.m.,' she answered. 'They say that that's reasonably accurate.'

'Good,' Harry said, almost to himself. 'Good.'

'Good?' she queried.

'An accurate time of death,' Harry explained. 'It really can help.' He looked out at the river, sparkling in the bright, impotent January sun. 'Did they find the weapon?'

'No.'

'Fingerprints? Or wouldn't you know?'

'I'm not sure – they didn't really discuss it. I think they only found Gerald's and the daily's in here. But they did the lift, and the street door.'

Too many there to be of much use, Harry thought. Unless they found him immediately. 'When was he found?' he asked.

'At about seven,' Mrs Culver said.

'By?'

'By the couple across the hallway. But I'd rather you didn't speak to them,' she added.

'As you wish,' Harry said. 'But it would help. And I'd like to speak to the people he knew – people he may have confided in. Friends, colleagues.'

Laura Culver looked less than enthusiastic. 'Can you do that without going into detail?' she asked. 'Without mentioning her?'

'I think so,' he said. 'I can say I'm some sort of insurance investigator, if you back me up. But someone might know something about this woman. I won't mention her first, I assure you.'

She considered for a moment. 'Very well, Mr Lambert,' she said.

'And – just to make sure I've got it straight – my brief is to find out if she can be eliminated from the enquiry?'

She nodded slowly. 'There's something else,' she said, going back to the desk. 'This key.'

33

Harry took it from her. It was a Yale key, smaller than a door key, larger than a filing cabinet key.

'It was in the drawer with the letters,' she said. 'It may have nothing to do with it, of course, but no one knows what it fits.'

'Thank you.' Harry made for the door. 'Just one thing,' he said. 'I suppose the police have asked if you can prove where *you* were, have they?'

'That isn't part of your brief,' she reminded him. 'But yes,' she added, with just the ghost of a smile. 'And as you see, they are quite satisfied.'

'I've no doubt,' Harry said, dropping the key into his pocket.

'We haven't agreed your fee, Mr Lambert.'

'If you call it a lot of money, I'm sure I do,' he said cheerfully. 'We'll talk about it when I report back to you.'

Mrs Culver walked with him to the lift. 'I didn't read them all,' she said. 'There might be something in them that would help you.'

'Yes,' Harry said, patting his pocket. 'Do you want a receipt, or anything?'

'No,' she said emphatically. 'Give them back to her, Mr Lambert.'

'Fine,' Harry said, stepping into the lift. 'Fine,' he repeated, as the doors closed.

Fine, he thought. Harry Lambert, private eye. My God.

'Ah, there you are, Mrs Maddox,' Grant said, at last sighting his quarry as she came out of the kitchen. 'No problem, I hope?'

'No, none at all,' she replied. 'Did you want me?'

He positioned himself carefully in the narrow corridor, so that she would have to be very impolite to push past.

'You work too hard, Mrs Maddox. Do you know what time it is?'

She smiled. 'Yes,' she said. 'But I don't really, you know. I make my own hours – I have time off when other people are rushing around.'

'And what do you do with this time off?' he asked.

She was looking tired, he thought. But very attractive, even with her make-up worn off. Karen always looked quite plain without make-up. He wondered, not for the first time, why he had married Karen, with her head full of nothing but clothes and diets, and her evenings wasted if she couldn't go out somewhere.

Mrs Maddox never seemed to go out.

'Oh, I like going down to the beach,' she said.

'In January?'

'Yes. I think I like it better in winter.' She smiled. 'I don't get much chance to see it in summer, of course.'

'I think you should go out more, Mrs Maddox. The RSC are doing *Taming of the Shrew* at Harmouth Playhouse next month – do you like the theatre?'

'Well, Shakespeare isn't quite my cup of tea,' she said.

'Will you think about it?' He stood aside to let her pass.

'Yes,' she said, and almost scuttled to her own door. 'Thank you.'

But she wouldn't think about it, of course. He had hoped she would like Shakespeare. Her answer was a bit too much like Karen's would have been for his liking.

He took the stairs, and went to his own room. Looking round, he wondered briefly if he gave his patrons enough comfort for their money. Yes, he decided, of course he did.

He pulled off his tie, unbuttoned the top button of his shirt, and thought about Mrs Maddox. She was looking too tired, he thought again. Not like her usual self. Almost too tired to repel his advances, but not quite. Still, he wasn't giving up yet.

He should have married someone like Mrs Maddox, someone with ability, someone who could make her own way. He married the wrong women; he had done it twice.

The first Mrs Grant, a boringly conventional woman of his own age, had died a boringly conventional if early death, and he had left London to live by the sea, in a town ripe for reshaping. He had soon identified a need for a conference complex, and met Miss Butlin's Holiday Camps on her publicity visit, and these

35

unrelated circumstances had shaped his destiny. He had acquired Miss BHC rather more quickly than the conference centre.

But he should have married someone like Mrs Maddox, and perhaps he would, now that Miss BHC was gone.

Yes. Perhaps he would.

The next day, having done some homework, Harry was on his way. Amblesea was an hour and a half from London, if you didn't miss the turn off the motorway, which Harry had, and now he was having to negotiate Harmouth's incomprehensible one-way system. He ran a frustrated hand through his hair as tantalising glimpses of Amblesea slipped away behind him.

He wound down the window and shouted colourful advice to the woman driver who dithered between the lanes; she couldn't hear him, which was just as well. He closed the window as a blast of icy air filled the car. 'Silly bitch,' he said aloud.

After twice going round a clover-leaf junction which was apparently supposed to simplify matters, Harry finally found himself pointing the right way to find the coast road back to Amblesea. Even if you didn't take the wrong turning, Harry reflected, it was a long way to come for a bit of nookey. And he wondered what she was like, the Annie Maddox of the letters that charted the affair from '*Dear Gerald, Thank you for writing back – I wasn't sure you would . . .*' to ' *. . . I've got loads to tell you when you come – please come soon. Love you, A.*'

There weren't many letters, and the last one was postmarked last June.

He picked up speed on the empty road into Amblesea, which must have looked like that since there were roads. There was a sandy grass verge on his left, the cold, choppy sea on his right, and nothing else on the road at all. This was what driving was about.

The desolation of the old promenade area took him by surprise; he could have been on the moon for all the signs of life. The thick rope binding the gates of the derelict pier was new, and the only indication that anyone ever came here.

A sharp, unmarked bend forced him to brake, and he found, to his surprise, a plot of building land with a dozen houses under construction, and a show house. Harmouth, presumably, was overflowing. A notice proclaimed Luxury Homes at Realistic Prices. Past the site, set back from the road, was a large, white-painted house, its solitary splendour slightly marred now. It was clearly a Luxury Home at an Unrealistic Price.

After that, there was nothing again. Just what had been the sea front, now empty spaces where the buildings had been, and an incongruous telephone box in the middle of nowhere. He took the left indicated by the signpost, along a road which bisected a piece of waste ground. He was relieved to find himself heading towards the sort of old-fashioned wooden-fronted shops in which it was something of a surprise to find computers and video games on sale. There were no houses at all here. Just shops and offices. He stopped and asked directions to the Wellington. Carry on, he was told. Turn left at the square, you can't miss it. So he carried on, his window still down, and was very glad to see a pub, despite the pop music which floated out into the streets. He wound up his window as the sleet turned to snow.

Now he could see the square, complete with fountain, and modern shops, and as he turned left, he could see the reason for Amblesea's rebirth. If he had not missed the motorway turn-off, this would have been his first view of the town, not the bleak, deserted promenade.

The Wellington had been built as a kind of extension to the existing shopping arcades, which had been totally pedestrianised and given a face-lift; the 'ample parking facilities' indicated on the roadside notice were reached via a side street.

It was a large, modern, well-designed complex, and was beginning to attract business away from the bigger resorts, Harry had been told by Tourist Information, for his article on conference centres.

As a result, Amblesea's fortunes were on the upturn, and the revamped shopping centre was also attracting visitors in its own right. Originally, the complex had been going to be built on the sea front, but it had been decided that access to the motorway was more useful, and it had been incorporated into the redesign of the main shopping area.

Amblesea District Council, however, could not take the credit for it. It had been built, with not a little opposition from some members of that august body, by one man with vision and hard cash.

And it was managed by Annie Maddox.

Harry took out the letters, now sorted into postmark order, and frowned. Now that he was to meet the author of these dignified love letters, he felt just a little guilty for having read them. And inexplicably angry.

FOUR

'There's a Mr Lambert to see you,' Linda said, over the intercom.

'Lambert?' Annie frowned, unable to place anyone of that name. 'Ask him to come in, Linda.'

She opened the door as he approached.

'In here,' she said, smiling. 'Can I help you?'

'My name is Lambert,' he said. 'Mrs Maddox, is it?'

He was from the North; Tyneside, Annie thought. It was a nice voice.

'That's right,' she said. 'What can I do for you?'

'I've come to talk to you about Mr Gerald Culver,' he said.

Annie's welcoming smile faded. 'If you're the police, I'd like to see some identification, please,' she said.

'I'm not the police.'

'Then I've nothing to say to you,' she replied.

'No?' Lambert drew the bundle of envelopes from his pocket, dropping them with a small thud on the coffee table. 'Recognise them?' he asked.

Annie's eyes widened as she saw the little pile of letters.

'Does it surprise you that he kept them?' Lambert was asking.

She shook her head slowly. 'Not really.' She sat down, her heart sinking. 'Have you read them?' she asked.

'Yes.' Lambert sat opposite her, uninvited.

'Are you a reporter? How did you get hold of these? Who gave them to you?'

He removed the rubber band, and fanned the envelopes like cards. 'His wife,' he said.

'Oh, no.' Annie closed her eyes. 'He shouldn't have kept them.'

'No, he shouldn't,' Lambert agreed. 'But he did. And Mrs Culver isn't very happy. She wants to know what's been going on.'

'So she sent you? You're some sort of private detective, are you?'

'You could say that,' Lambert said steadily. 'When did you last see Mrs Culver's husband?'

'How do I know you're from Mrs Culver?' Annie asked. 'How do I know you're not from a newspaper?'

'You don't,' he said. 'But I do have these letters. Either way, you'd be best not to ignore me.'

'All right,' Annie said.

'You still haven't answered my question,' he said.

'No.'

'Well then? When did you see him last?'

'New Year's Eve,' Annie replied.

'But you didn't tell the police?'

'Why should I? And why didn't Mrs Culver, if she's bothered?'

'She might yet.' He took out a packet of cigarettes. 'Did you and Mr Culver part on good terms?'

'Yes,' Annie lied, but she wasn't prepared for the tears that sprang up.

'Really?' Lambert looked sceptical. 'How often did you see him?'

'Not often.'

'How often is not often?'

His eyes already mocked her, and the truth was that she had seen him twice since last April. She didn't want to tell him the truth.

'Not often,' she repeated.

'You were having an affair?'

Annie sighed. 'Yes,' she said. 'We were. But we didn't see each other very much.'

40

'But he was here less than a month ago – on New Year's Eve, you said.'

'Yes.'

'How long was he here?'

Annie shrugged. 'I don't know,' she said. 'An hour or so.'

'But it takes well over an hour to get here,' he said. 'Surely he usually stayed longer than that?'

'It's none of your business,' Annie said.

'He was murdered.' Lambert let the words hang in the air for a moment. 'His wife didn't have any idea about you, and I want to know how he managed that.' He sat forward. 'So. How much time did he spend here when he did come down? And when did he see you?'

It couldn't hurt, Annie thought. 'Saturdays, mostly,' she said. 'Sometimes weekdays.'

'Saturdays? Isn't that the MP's day off? People like him should spend Saturdays in the bosom of their families.'

Annie raised her eyebrows. 'I don't think he was seeking your approval, Mr Lambert.'

'Just as well,' Lambert said. 'But what I mean is how come he wasn't missed?'

'Football,' she said.

'Football?'

'He was a football fan,' Annie said slowly. 'Some of the northern clubs are a long way away.'

For a moment, Lambert still looked puzzled, and then his brow cleared. 'Oh,' he said. 'I get it. When West Ham were playing away from home, so was Gerald?'

'Sometimes,' Annie said quietly. 'You have to find excuses. That one was as good as any.'

'And sometimes he'd make an overnight stop for the midweek matches,' Lambert said. 'Very ingenious.' He sat back again. 'What if his wife had decided to go with him?' he asked.

'There was no fear of that, Mr Lambert. His wife didn't approve of his working-class pursuits.'

'Is that what you were?' Lambert asked, his voice harsh. He

41

scooped up the letters, and held them up. 'Time off from all the nanny-fixated old school ties and their Sloane Ranger wives?' He let the letters drop, and scatter. 'Pity he had to miss the football. Still, I expect he got to the home games, so it wasn't too much of a sacrifice.'

'Have you finished?'

'No, pet.' He sat back in his chair. 'I've only just started.'

'What do you want to know?'

'New Year's Eve. What happened?'

'Nothing,' she said, frowning.

He offered her a cigarette. When she refused, he shrugged, and lit his own. 'When did he arrive?'

'About half past three. And he left at about twenty past four.'

'Match abandoned, was it?'

Annie didn't reply.

'Let me ask you again,' he said. 'Did you part on good terms?'

'Yes,' she repeated.

'I'll ask around,' he said, a warning note in his voice.

Annie doubted that. Not that it would do him much good if he did, but anyway she assumed that Mrs Culver had hired him to keep it quiet, not to have him asking around.

'He was going to some do,' she said. 'And I was supposed to be working. That's why he left early.'

'I don't believe you,' he said.

'Please yourself.'

'Why did he come, if he couldn't stay?'

'It's none of your business,' she said again. 'If you've nothing relevant to ask me, I suggest you leave.'

Lambert turned his lighter in his fingers, tapping its end on the coffee table each time. 'Something relevant,' he said. 'Did you stab your boyfriend to death?'

Annie barely shook her head.

'Where were you between four a.m. and five a.m. on the ninth of January?'

'Here,' she said. 'In bed.'

'Any witnesses?'

42

Annie's expression didn't change, but the atmosphere was charged with anger.

He stuck the cigarette in his mouth as he gathered up her letters again, his eyes screwed up against the smoke.

'Do you know of anyone who might have wanted to kill your boyfriend?' he asked.

'No,' she answered, as the tears began to fall. 'No. No one would want to kill Gerald.'

'No,' Lambert said, the cigarette jammed in the corner of his mouth. 'No one except whoever stuck a knife in him.' He sighed wearily. 'If you believe all the stuff in the papers, he was kinder than Santa Claus.'

'You can believe the papers,' Annie said.

'Can I?' Lambert said. 'I know what he was up to here, don't I? So what else was he doing that the papers don't know about yet? What was he doing that put someone's back up? Because someone didn't like him very much, did they?'

'Are you enjoying this?' Annie asked.

'It's quite like old times,' Lambert said. He wound the rubber band twice round the envelopes and removed the cigarette from his mouth. 'How did you meet him?' he asked.

'It's none of your business.'

'So you keep saying. But I'm being paid to find out.'

'Then find out from someone else.'

Lambert put the letters away.

'I have to go back to Mrs Culver,' he said. 'She wants to know if she has to tell the police about you. If you're uncooperative, it's no skin off my nose. I'll just tell her that you might have something to hide, and she'll send Scotland Yard down to see you. That'll mean reporters, and . . .'

'What difference does it make how we met?'

'I want to know what his business was down here in the first place,' Lambert explained.

'All right. I'm sure it's good for a laugh,' she said. 'Amblesea had a cup run. West Ham came here, and Gerald came with them. He happened to stay here, and we met.' She stood up. 'Do

43

you have any more questions?'

'Yes,' he said, getting to his feet. 'Did West Ham score too?'

Annie raised her eyebrows. 'You're not a very nice man, are you, Mr Lambert?'

'No,' he agreed. 'Not like Gerald.'

'Not very,' Annie said.

He smiled frostily, and left. Annie sank down into the chair as the door closed, and buried her face in her hands.

FIVE

Do you want to get done for speeding, next? the voice in Harry's head asked him as he drove through the town, towards the pub. He braked dangerously, and put on his lights, as fog began to blur the edges of the buildings.

Do you think she did it, or what? No, of course he didn't think she'd done it. She looked as if she hadn't slept since it had happened. Anyway, the grapevine said it had been professional. Terrorist style. No, she had nothing to do with it. But Amblesea might have. He hadn't finished with Amblesea, or Annie, come to that. But he'd let her stew for the night, and wonder what he was going to do. She might know something about Culver that she was keeping quiet about, after all. But no, she didn't do it.

Then why were you needling her all the time? What was it all about? She made him angry, Harry thought, taking out his cigarettes and flipping open the top. He pushed a cigarette into his mouth, switched hands on the steering wheel, and conducted a search of his clothing for his lighter. Culver was too good to be true, and those letters proved that Annie Maddox had loved him with an accommodating, forgiving love that made Harry angry.

Maybe, the voice persisted. *But that's no reason for you to tear into her like that.*

Harry swore viciously as his lighter failed to turn up. He could see it. He 'had a picture', as an Italian girlfriend of his used to say. A picture of his lighter sitting just to the right of the fruit bowl on Annie Maddox's coffee table.

Psychological? the voice in his head asked smugly, as he searched for somewhere to turn the car round.

★★★

45

'Mr Lambert?' The receptionist looked warily at Harry as he came into the foyer.

'Is she in?' he asked, pointing at the door.

'If you mean Mrs Maddox,' she said coldly, 'she isn't available.' Her voice still held the South London accent that was all but gone from Annie's.

He smiled at her. 'Only, I left my cigarette lighter in her sitting room,' he said.

She slid open her drawer and picked out a slim gold lighter. 'Is this the one?' she asked.

'That's it!' He smiled again.

She was a tall, well-built blonde. Harry liked tall, well-built blondes.

'Do you smoke?' he asked, offering her his packet.

'No, thank you.'

'Do you mind if I—?'

'Be my guest.'

Harry leant on the desk. 'That's better,' he said, exhaling smoke with the words. 'I can think now. I can't think without a cigarette.'

She pushed the ashtray towards him.

'Pity she's not here,' he said. 'There was just one more thing I wanted to ask her.'

'Perhaps I can help,' she said.

'Well – we're making enquiries about Mr Gerald Culver. You know, the MP. We understand that he was an occasional visitor here.'

She shook her head.

Harry smiled. 'Is there a Mr Maddox?' he asked.

'He died,' she said.

'Did he?' A little whistle escaped Harry. 'She's none too lucky, by the sound of things.' He flicked idly through one of the local newspapers piled up on the desk. DRIVER'S WIDOW HITS OUT, a headline read. 'How did her husband die?'

'He just suddenly died,' she said. 'Brain haemorrhage, they said.'

46

Thirty-eight-year-old widow Anne Fowler yesterday hit out at what she called the 'couldn't-care-less' public, the article began.

'How old was he?' Harry asked.

'Thirty-six.'

He let the page fall shut. 'Now, that's what I *call* unlucky,' he said. 'When did it happen?'

'Just over three years ago. Not long before she came here.'

'Can I have your name?' Harry asked.

'Linda Benson,' she said.

Harry crushed out his cigarette. 'How long have you been here, Linda?'

'Today?'

'No,' Harry said, with exaggerated patience. 'How long have you worked here?'

'Eighteen months,' she said.

'Let's try again, then, pet. I understand that Mr Culver used to be a fairly regular visitor here.'

'Was he?'

'Yes,' Harry said, through his teeth. 'I believe he visited your Mrs Maddox.'

'Did he?'

'I would like to ask you some questions about his visits here.'

Linda looked quite baffled. 'I'm sorry,' she said. 'I know nothing about any visits.'

'I don't know who you think you're helping with your refusal to co-operate,' Harry said heavily.

Linda sighed. 'And I don't know who you think you're kidding,' she replied.

He grinned. 'Myself,' he said, disarmingly.

Linda turned as the corridor door opened, and Annie Maddox appeared. 'It's Mr Lambert,' she said.

'Yes, so it is. I thought you'd left, Mr Lambert.'

'Came back for this,' he said, holding his cigarette lighter between his forefinger and thumb.

'I'm so glad you've got it back. Now perhaps you'd like to leave?'

47

He dropped the lighter into his pocket. 'I'd rather have another word with you, if I may.'

She looked quickly at Linda, then back at Harry. 'Come in,' she said, holding the door.

He followed her down the corridor, back into her sitting room. 'I seem to have got off on the wrong foot with you,' he said, as Annie closed the door. 'I usually find I hit it off with women, too.'

'Do you?' Annie asked coldly.

'Not this time,' said Harry. 'Obviously.'

'Is this what you wanted to say?'

'No – I was just—'

'Then please say whatever it is quickly. I'm extremely busy.'

A slow smile spread across Harry's face. 'Oh, yes. There must be at least half a dozen people here.' His eye fell on a snapshot stuck behind a vase. Gerald Culver smiled confidently at him.

'This is the way your boyfriend liked the place, isn't it?' Harry asked, holding up the photo. 'Half empty? Is that why he didn't come in the summer?'

She reacted to his bit of deduction, and he felt as pleased as a schoolboy. 'Please put that back,' was all she actually said.

'The letters,' he said, although she had not asked for an explanation of his uncanny powers. 'They were only written in summer.' He put the photo back as requested, and turned to face her. 'Close season, of course.'

Annie walked to the door, and opened it. 'Goodbye, Mr Lambert,' she said.

Harry felt very angry when he looked at Culver's smiling face, then at Annie Maddox and the eyes that burned with too little sleep. He strode across, and pushed the door shut with a bang. 'It's me or my ex-colleagues in the Murder Squad,' he said. 'Which do you prefer?'

Annie didn't speak, but she walked away from the door.

'You said something earlier,' Harry said. 'About having to work when he was here.' He took out his cigarettes. 'What did he normally do if that happened?'

'It didn't normally happen. But if it did, he didn't do anything much. He'd have a drink, or a game of snooker, or something.'

'He came here to play snooker, did he?'

Annie eyed him impassively. 'That's probably closer to the mark than you think,' she said, her face expressionless.

Harry stood up, made to walk to the door, then stopped as though he had just remembered something. 'Oh yes,' he said, turning. 'Mrs Culver said to let you have these.'

He drew the bundle of letters from his pocket. 'I almost forgot,' he said, putting them down on the coffee table. 'And this.'

The key dropped on to the letters, and she looked up quickly.

'It does belong to you, I take it?'

'Yes.'

'Does it open this door?' he asked, and held up his hands before she said it again. 'I know. Mind my own business. But it occurs to me that if he had a key to your place, maybe you had one to his.'

'I didn't.'

No, thought Harry. You wouldn't.

The letters, no longer private, lay on the table, and she had made no move to touch them. She was naked in those letters, Harry thought angrily, and the bloody fool hadn't even had the sense to get rid of them.

'Any chance of calling off your watchdog?' he asked.

Annie affected not to understand.

'Linda,' he said. 'You've got a very loyal staff.'

'Linda's a friend of mine,' she said.

'Well, I'd like to ask her some questions. She won't answer them unless you say she can.'

Annie's eyes remained on him as she reached over and pressed the button on the intercom.

'Reception.'

'Mr Lambert's just coming along, Linda. He wants to ask you some questions.'

There was a silence, then a crisp 'All right.'

Harry inclined his head slightly. 'Thank you.'

'I'm not afraid of your questions, Mr Lambert.'

'I thought it was none of my business.'

'Mrs Culver didn't know Gerald as well as she thought she did,' Annie said, opening the door. 'Perhaps I didn't either.'

Harry walked along to reception, and Linda turned as he opened the door.

'What do you want to ask me?' she said.

Harry smiled. 'What time do you get away?' he asked.

There was a suspicion of a smile. 'Nine,' she said.

'Will you come for a drink with me?'

'No, thank you.' She seemed to be going to leave it at that, but then she expanded. 'I'm meeting someone,' she said. 'Sorry.'

Harry leant on the desk. 'How well did you know Culver?' he asked.

'Just to chat to,' she said.

'Did he ever meet anyone here? Business meetings, that sort of thing?'

She shook her head.

'What happened if Annie was busy when he came?'

'He'd pass the time with whoever was on reception, or go in for a drink or something,' Linda said. 'But he didn't often come on spec.'

Harry glanced into the bar, not yet open for business.

'What about New Year's Eve?' he asked. 'Did you see him?'

'No. Sandra was on duty when he was here.'

'When's she on duty again?'

'Tonight. She takes over from me.'

The corridor door opened, and Harry unconsciously straightened up, to present as good a picture as possible to the very pretty blonde who emerged.

'You must be Mr Lambert,' she said, sounding so like Annie that it made Harry smile.

'This is Christine, Annie's daughter,' Linda said.

'Hello,' Harry said. 'Have you been warned off me?'

'No. Mum says you're trying to find out what happened to Gerald.'

'More or less,' Harry agreed, as the shutters were noisily pushed up in the bar. 'Would you like to help me?'

She shrugged slightly. 'Is Pete here yet?' she asked Linda.

'No, I haven't seen him.'

'Would you like a drink while you're waiting?' Harry asked.

'Yes, all right.' She glanced at Linda. 'Tell Pete where I am when he comes,' she said. 'I don't think I'll be much use to you,' she told Harry.

'Never mind,' Harry said. 'It's a good excuse to have a drink with you.'

She drank tonic water, as it turned out, so she didn't even cost him much. Harry offered her a cigarette, which she took.

'Thank God,' he said. 'I was beginning to think I was the only smoker left.'

'I don't smoke much,' she said. 'Pete keeps trying to make me stop.'

'Pete's your boyfriend?'

'Yes.' She looked at her watch.

'Late?'

'He always is. We're not going anywhere in particular.'

'Do you work here?'

'Yes,' she said. 'Relief work – I stand in for other people on their days off.' She smiled. 'So I do anything and everything.'

'Does that mean you're sometimes on reception?'

'I cover for Sandra on Monday, and Linda on Thursday. And weekends twice a month.'

'Weekends?' Harry leant forward. 'Saturday's when Culver usually visited your mother, isn't it?'

She stiffened slightly. 'Sometimes,' she said.

'How did you feel about that?'

She didn't answer, and Harry let it go.

Pete walked over to the table where Christine sat with Lambert. 'Hi,' he said. 'Sorry I'm late.'

'This is Pete,' Christine said. 'Only an hour or two late.'

'Harry Lambert,' he said. 'Pleased to meet you. What can I get you?'

Pete warmed to him. 'A lager,' he said. 'Thanks.'

'Can I get you another?' he asked Christine.

'No, thanks. I'm fine.'

Pete watched him as he made his way to the bar. 'What's he like?' he asked.

'He's quite nice,' Christine said. 'He used to be a policeman. Scotland Yard.'

Pete pulled a face. 'I've had enough of policemen,' he said.

'One long cool lager,' Lambert said, when he arrived back. He sat down. 'Cheers,' he said.

Pete lifted his mug, slightly suspicious of Lambert's friendliness.

'Did you know Gerald Culver?' Lambert asked him.

'No,' said Pete. 'I knew about him, but I never met him.'

'Were you here on New Year's Eve?' he asked Christine. 'When Culver came?'

Christine glanced at Pete before she replied, and Pete wished she hadn't because he saw Lambert noticing.

'Yes,' she said. 'But we didn't see him.'

'Oh.' Lambert seemed unconcerned. He twisted his glass backwards and forwards between finger and thumb. 'Did you know he was here?' he asked. 'At the time, I mean?'

Pete saw a little frown of puzzlement on her brow as she answered. 'No,' she said slowly. 'I didn't find out until the evening. Why?'

'Oh, it just seemed odd. Since he and Pete had never met. I'd have thought you would have taken the opportunity to introduce them.'

'I might,' she said.

'He didn't stay long, did he?'

'No,' she said. 'He had some function in London.'

'So your mother said.'

'Then why are you asking Christine?' Pete asked, suddenly

aware of what Lambert was trying to do.

'It's what's known as double-checking,' Lambert said easily.

Pete put down his glass. 'Just so long as we're all clear on that,' he said.

Christine looked slightly flustered.

'I'm just trying to find out who murdered the guy,' said Lambert.

'But I don't know when he came and went,' Christine said. 'What's the point in asking me?'

'I want to know if your mother told you the same things she told me,' he said.

'Are you accusing Annie?' Pete said, dropping his voice to a whisper.

'I have to know if I'm being given the whole story, that's all.' He turned back to Christine. 'Did she tell you she'd had a fight with Culver?' he asked.

'She – she didn't tell me anything,' Christine said.

Poor Chris, Pete thought. She had never told so many lies in her life. As she looked at him, her eyes went to the doorway, and he could see the dismay. He didn't need to turn round.

'Ah, Miss Maddox,' Grant boomed heartily. 'Is your mother still in the building, do you know? She's not in her room.'

'I don't know. I'm sorry,' she said.

'Ah well, never mind. I don't believe we've met,' he said to Lambert, holding out his hand. 'James Grant.'

'I've been hearing about you,' Lambert said. 'Very nice place,' he added, looking round. 'I'm Harry Lambert. Pleased to meet you.'

They shook hands, and Grant went off to boom heartily at someone else.

'I didn't know Mum was going out,' Christine said. 'She must be avoiding him.'

'She's probably hiding under the bed,' Pete said. 'Though on second thoughts, maybe it should be somewhere less suggestive.'

'It's like that, is it?' Lambert said.

'He'd like it to be,' said Christine, with a smile.

Lambert finished his drink. 'Ten past nine,' he said, standing up. 'I have to go and talk to – Sandra, is it? – on reception.'

'Sandra, yes.'

'Thanks for your help. I'll maybe see you around.'

He walked off, and Pete let out a sigh of relief. 'Do you think Annie did tell him about the row?' he asked.

'I don't know. But I'm sure I wasn't going to.' She pursed her lips. 'It's too late now to go anywhere,' she said.

'Oh, I don't know,' he said. 'I can think of somewhere.' He leant across to kiss her, to annoy her, to get pushed away.

'People will see!' she said.

He grinned. 'Let's go to your room, then,' he said. 'Where people can't see.'

She stood up, and he followed her out of the bar.

'Chris,' he said, once they were in the staff corridor. 'You couldn't let me have a fiver, could you? Just till I get my money.'

'You already owe me ten!'

'I know,' he said. 'But I'll give you a fiver this Thursday, and ten next.'

The lift doors opened, as did her purse.

Why couldn't he feel about her like he had about Lesley? Pete took the fiver, and pushed it into his pocket. She was worth ten of Lesley, he knew that. And somewhere in the future, he really did have a dream of being married to Christine, of providing for her, of having children and dogs and cats. A dream he'd never had with Lesley.

He even liked Christine's mother, though it probably wasn't reciprocated.

Lesley wouldn't have pushed him away if he'd tried to kiss her in the bar. A bit more pushing away wouldn't have done Lesley any harm. Lesley, telling him she was leaving. Lesley, refusing to come to the phone. Refusing to see him.

The lift arrived, and Christine took out her door key. 'Before we go in,' she said, looking up at him. 'I just want to be sure you know it's me you're with.'

He coloured slightly. 'Sorry,' he said. 'You're right – maybe I shouldn't come here while Grant's here.'

'Maybe you shouldn't.' She still hadn't unlocked the door.

'I've blown it again, haven't I?'

'I'm not having you thinking about her all the time you're with me.'

'No,' he said, as the lift doors slid shut behind him, and the lift went whining down. 'Will you come over tomorrow?'

She nodded her reply, and he took the stairs.

Harry Lambert was still talking to Sandra as he got to reception. He called good night as Pete passed, but Pete didn't really hear him until it was too late to reply.

'He just looked a bit cross,' Sandra was saying. 'You know.'

'As though they'd had words?' Harry asked.

'Yes. At least, that's what I thought.'

'And did you see Mrs Maddox?'

'No. She didn't come out.'

Grant passed, going up the wide staircase, and raised a hand to them.

'At least someone's speaking to me,' Harry said. 'What's he like?'

'Mr Grant?' Sandra took a moment before replying. 'I like him,' she said.

'I hear he's a bit sweet on Mrs Maddox,' Harry said.

'Oh, no. I don't think so. His wife's left him. I think he's just a bit lonely.'

'Right, well – thanks, Sandra. I might see you again some time.'

'I hope so,' she said.

Harry drove back that night, through the driving rain on the motorway, having to concentrate on every inch of the road.

It was after midnight when he parked in the yard of the builders, bumping in past the sign that said it was a private car park, and the gates were locked at six every night. He locked up the car and splashed through the puddles that had gathered in the uneven side street.

Inside, he surveyed his fridge unenthusiastically, and poured himself a scotch instead.

Possibles. Annie, if they had had a big enough row about something. Grant, if he was taken with Annie and happened to be a homicidal maniac. Christine, even, if her silence *re* Culver was read as murderous rage.

All highly improbables, but possibles.

Pete? Christine said he'd been in the commandos. He'd be handy with a knife. He was quick to rise to Annie's defence – and he wasn't all that much younger than her.

He smiled to himself. Given that anyone could be a psychopath, then anyone could have killed him. Including his own wife, though she would hardly have drawn his attention to her motive by sending him to see Annie.

Linda, Sandra, Sammy the barman. No doubt if he dug deep enough he'd find out that Culver had failed to say please or thank you or have one yourself at some time; the fact was that none of these people seemed to have the slightest reason for killing the man.

Except Annie, he told himself. Perhaps she was tired of playing second fiddle. Perhaps Culver had used her once too often.

Then he thought of the letters, and remembered just how prepared Annie was to play second fiddle. He felt angry again, and certain that whoever killed Culver, it wasn't Annie Maddox.

SIX

In the undeniably gracious surroundings of the Culvers' Surrey house, Harry presented himself to his employer.

Mrs Culver took the typewritten report from his hand, and read it through, though he had already told her what was in it. Now and then her eyebrows came together in disapproval – Harry wasn't sure whether this was at Annie's behaviour, his style, or Francie's typing. This last had only cost him a small box of Black Magic, so he couldn't quibble.

'But you haven't given me your recommendation, Mr Lambert,' she said, removing her reading glasses. 'Do I give the police this information or not?'

Harry rubbed his chin thoughtfully. 'It depends on—' Another photograph of the smiling Gerald Culver met his gaze. He was haunted by photographs of the man. This time he was holding a glass up to the camera. Harry looked closer, and advanced upon it.

'Is there something wrong, Mr Lambert?'

'No, no. Nothing wrong.' He took the photograph off the bookcase. 'This isn't a black eye your husband's got in this picture, is it?' he asked, his voice light, in order that he could shrug it off if it turned out to be a grease stain on the photo.

'Well—' said Laura Culver.

'Is it?' Harry asked again, disbelievingly.

'Yes – but he said it wasn't anyone's fist.'

'But you thought it might be?' Harry put the photograph back on its shelf. 'When was this, Mrs Culver?'

'New Year's Eve,' she said. 'New Year's Day, by then. We

57

were at a dinner. He'd been at some sort of charity football match in the afternoon, and I saw a mark on his face when he came home. Later on, it turned into quite a bad bruise – well, you can see.'

Harry nodded.

'So I asked what had happened. He said he'd hit his face when the train suddenly swayed, but he was being very ... very *cagey* about it.'

'Are you saying you didn't believe him?' Harry asked.

'I suppose I am,' she said. 'I think there was some trouble at the match. Oh, I know it was for fun and all that, but that doesn't seem to make much difference these days. I always worried about that – people throwing things, and so on. It annoyed him. He said if there were any hooligans at matches, they threw things at the referee, not him. So you see, if there had been trouble that afternoon, he wouldn't have told me.'

No, Harry thought, I'll bet he wouldn't.

'So,' she said briskly, putting away her memories. 'What's your verdict, Mr Lambert? About this woman, I mean. Is it worth telling the police?'

'No verdict, Mrs Culver. My opinion is that you should perhaps let me carry on asking questions. That way, if Amblesea's a wild goose chase, at least the police won't have wasted time on it.'

A faint smile appeared on Laura Culver's lips.

'All right, Mr Lambert,' she said. 'We'll do it your way.'

Harry picked up the photo again. 'Could I get this copied?' he asked. 'It might help.'

She consented, and he waved cheerfully enough as he drove off down the drive. Even optimistically. But he was going to get very, very tired of looking at the slightly merry, slightly bruised Gerald, raising his glass to the camera. Very tired indeed.

'I think you ought to hear this, sir.'

Webb raised an eyebrow at his inspector, who jerked his head at the door as he handed him a file.

The young, eager constable, who had already passed his sergeant's exams and still didn't look old enough to be a policeman, came into the room.

'Do you mind if I leave PC Gordon to it?' the inspector asked, with the tiniest of winks.

'Sure,' Webb said, sitting back and contemplating Gordon.

'Sir,' he began. 'I have—' He cleared his throat. 'I have someone who gives me information now and then.'

'Have you?' Webb said. 'But you're not CID. I hope you're not in here to claim expenses.'

'No, sir. The thing is, he's given me good tips now and then about what's going—' The word 'down' quivered on his lips, but he wisely bit it back. 'On,' he said.

'And what is going on?'

'Do you remember Peter Ainsley, sir? We had him in over the last cabby – the one in the summer.'

No, Webb didn't remember Peter Ainsley. They had had everyone in over the last cabby. The bottom of the barrel had been scraped clean.

'Yes,' he said.

'Well, I saw him hanging round the Wellington the day the car went missing off the car park.' He pointed to the file. 'It's in there,' he said helpfully. 'When I approached him, he went into the hotel, and I decided not to follow.'

'No law against going into an hotel, constable.'

'No, sir. And as it was some hours prior to the car being stolen, we had no real grounds for suspicion.'

'But?' Webb presumed that the crux of the matter was about to be reached.

'It seems that he was at the Wellington disco that night, sir. I couldn't go because it was too expensive – but he was there. And Ainsley doesn't work, sir.'

'Is that it?'

'No, sir. As it happens, I saw him earlier on New Year's Eve – at lunchtime. He was at the Anchorage, and he couldn't even stand his round.'

The Anchorage. A big, bawdy dockside pub in Harmouth, in which it was hard to imagine the constable being inconspicuous.

'As it happens?' Webb said. 'Do you frequent the Anchorage?'

'No, sir.'

'How come your informant only told you about the disco now? It was almost a month ago.'

'He didn't know of my interest in Ainsley until today.'

'Your interest?' Webb said, turning the pages of the file. 'Have you been following him?'

'No, sir. Not following. Keeping an eye on him.'

'Why?'

'I didn't like his attitude when we brought him in before.'

'Mm.' Webb closed the file. 'I don't suppose he liked yours.' He looked at the fresh-faced youth, brim-full of eagerness. He had never been like that, he was sure.

'And this morning,' Gordon continued, 'I spotted him hanging round the Wellington car park again. I didn't approach him this time.'

The Wellington car park. Webb wished the constable could have been a little less enthusiastic. He didn't want Grant's car dragged back into this enquiry just when he thought he'd got rid of it.

'He's been done twice for taking and driving away,' the constable said. 'And got a not guilty on aggravated burglary – someone used a knife.'

Webb nodded. That was presumably why they had brought him in the last time.

Webb was beginning to see Grant as some sort of judgement on him. The man had even moved into the hotel so that he couldn't enjoy a quiet drink without being aware of his presence. And now, just when he'd thought he'd seen the last of him, up pops an eager beaver with this Peter Ainsley.

'Shall I bring him in, sir?'

'On what charge?' Webb asked wearily.

'To help with enquiries?'

'He wasn't seen at the Wellington immediately before the car went,' Webb said, counting on his fingers.

'No, sir, but—'

'His prints weren't found on Grant's car, or the taxi.'

'No, but—'

'He has never been convicted of violent crime.' Webb stopped. 'Have you a shred of evidence to connect him with either offence?' he asked.

'Just that he was broke that lunchtime, and spending that evening. And that I did see him on the car park that morning, and that he was suspected of involvement in attacks on cab drivers.'

Webb didn't speak.

'I'd want to know where he got the money from, if . . .' He tailed off.

'If you were me,' Webb said. 'If you were CID – do you want to do CID work, Constable?'

'Oh yes, sir. I've applied—'

'Then don't argue with senior officers.'

'Sorry, sir.'

Webb opened the file again. 'Who was Ainsley with at the Anchorage?' he asked.

'A couple of lads. And a blonde – very pretty.'

'Expensive?' Webb asked, relieved to find that he did have some outside interests.

'No,' he said slowly. 'Just an ordinary girl, I'd say.'

'*Have* you been following him around? Why were you at the Anchorage?'

'I had just seen my mother-in-law off at the station. She'd been with us for Christmas.'

He was married. This child was married. Webb felt very old.

'I was walking back to the car, when I saw him getting out of a mini-van. I just thought I'd see what was what.'

'And what was what?'

'He was just a passenger, and the van checked out.'

He must have been really upset. No faked tax disc, no bald tyres. Not stolen, not suspect. What a blow.

'The inspector seemed to think it was worth checking out,' Constable Gordon said. 'Do you, sir?'

It probably was worth checking out. Ainsley wasn't the sort of customer the Wellington attracted, so why was he hanging about there? But Webb didn't want to get any more involved with Grant than he had to, and Flash Gordon was going to make him do just that.

'Leave it with me,' he said.

But he couldn't put it off for ever.

'No one would want to kill Gerald Culver.'

If one more person said that to him, Harry might just jump off a roof.

'But someone did,' he said to the smooth, middle-aged man who had made the statement.

He was the last in a long line of successful politicians, go-getting businessmen, and polished civil servants whom Harry Lambert, insurance investigator, had interviewed. They had all said the same thing. No one would want to kill Gerald Culver.

'Someone did,' Harry repeated.

'Yes, I know. But I think it must just have been a madman. Someone who was going to kill whoever he happened to meet.'

'But Culver let him in,' Harry said patiently.

'Perhaps not,' said the other man. 'Perhaps someone else let him in. He could have rung anyone's bell.'

'If someone else let him in, then he wasn't out to kill the first person he met, was he? He was out to kill Culver.'

'Yes, well. I can't see where it makes a difference to the insurance, to be honest.'

'Well,' Harry said. 'It helps to have someone charged, convicted – you know.'

The man frowned. 'Does it?' he asked.

'Red tape,' Harry assured him. 'There's a lot less if it's cut and dried.'

'Well, I'm sorry I can't help you.'

'He didn't go in for . . .' Harry shrugged. 'Oh, I don't know. Shady business deals, women friends, that sort of thing?'

'No. Gerald was just what he seemed. A friendly, honest, hard-working man. He didn't have *enemies*, Mr Lambert. No one would want to kill Gerald Culver.'

Harry left, sorry that Culver was dead. Because *he* wanted to kill him.

SEVEN

Harry dozed in a chair, having finally given up chasing down non-existent leads and up blind alleys. It was now his opinion that Mrs Culver could forget that Amblesea and Annie Maddox ever existed, because, like everyone else, they seemed to have had damn all to do with murdering her husband. Hardly anyone in Amblesea even knew him by sight, never mind who he was, and his friends all said the same thing – Gerald Culver was a nice man. And no one at all knew any reason why anyone could possibly have wanted to murder him.

So Harry had given up his temporary and well-paid job and was snoozing, dreaming of his bank manager, who was refusing to let himself be arrested for employing an Alsatian dog in a police uniform.

A bell rang. It was a police car. No, it was an alarm clock. It was the *dog*, of *course* it was the *dog*.

Harry blinked awake, his mind still desperately trying to retain the fast disappearing threads of his dream as though his life depended on it. His throat was dry, and the phone was ringing. These were the realities. There probably wasn't an Alsatian dog in a policeman's uniform. Perhaps he'd dreamt that.

'Yes. Lambert.'

'Harry?' A woman's voice.

'Mm.'

'You sound awful. Are you sober?'

'Yes, unfortunately. Who's that?'

'Barbara.'

Barbara Briggs, crime reporter of this parish.

'Barbara,' he said, pleased to hear from her. 'What can I do for you?'

'Maybe I can do something for you,' she said.

'You always do something for me, pet.'

'Same here, bonny lad.'

Harry smiled.

'I hear you've gone private,' Barbara said.

'Not any more. The trail, as they say in the best movies, has gone cold.'

'Perhaps not.'

Harry tensed up. 'What do you mean?'

'I have some information that might be of interest to you. Can we meet?'

'We can. Eight o'clock for dinner and debriefing?'

'I'll look forward to it.'

The candle flickered in the maroon brandy glass, giving a pink sheen to Barbara's straight brown hair. She smiled enigmatically at him over her prawn cocktail.

'Well?' he said.

'A stringer rang the paper this morning,' she said. 'He said that a woman had been murdered in Watford. Which I expect is unusual,' she said, 'and is certainly unfortunate, but not, I imagine, entirely unheard of.'

She ate some prawns, clearly enjoying both them and the suspense. Harry was determined not to ask again, and watched each careful spoonful as it was raised to her lips.

'What was odd,' she said, 'was *how* she died. Apparently—' she tantalisingly addressed herself once more to her starter, then relented with a grin. 'Apparently she answered her door in the middle of the night, and got stabbed to death for her pains.'

'Now, that *is* odd,' Harry said. 'You're right.' He persuaded a piece of melon on to his spoon. 'I am interested.'

Barbara smiled, a slow, wide, quite devastating smile. 'Oh,

Harry,' she said. 'That's not it. There's much more to it than just that.'

'Is there? Go on, then.'

But Barbara had finished her prawns, and eaten a goodly portion of her lamb cutlets, before she vouchsafed any further information.

'I went there,' she said. 'As you say, it was odd.'

'Decidedly.'

She chewed carefully, thoughtfully. 'This is very good,' she said. 'Don't let yours get cold.'

Harry picked up his knife and fork again. 'I'm glad you're enjoying it,' he said. It was no more than he deserved; he had dangled information just out of her reach when the boot had been on the other foot.

'The similarity to Mr Culver's demise was what had excited my stringer's attention,' she said. 'And mine – and, needless to say, the attention of the police.'

'It would.'

'Quite. But such a *lot* of attention. I couldn't get near the house for them. And they weren't your ordinary everyday George Dixons, either.'

'No?' Harry tried to sound uninterested as he cut up bits of steak.

'No. *They* were there because she was a clerk.'

'A clerk?' Harry repeated.

'With the Ministry of Defence.'

Harry stopped chewing. 'Well, well, well,' he said.

'So, while the MOD police and Scotland Yard were chasing each other's tails, I popped in to see her next-door neighbour.'

She smiled briefly, then made a serious assault on the rest of her lamb cutlet.

Harry caught her wrist. 'And?' he said.

'And I learned that she was married to a merchant seaman who was away from home a lot, she had no children, and she had handed in her notice to the Min. of Def.' She shook off Harry's hand. 'And I want to finish this,' she said.

66

'You can eat and talk at the same time, you know,' Harry said.

'It's rude.'

'Your mother would forgive you, just this once.'

'And I discovered something else.'

Harry closed his eyes. '*What*, for Christ's sake?'

'That she knew Culver.'

'Did she?' Harry said. 'Culver wasn't Defence, though, was he? He was something to do with Social Security.'

Barbara nodded. 'She'd met him, all the same.'

'Are you sure?' Harry asked.

'Quite sure. So are the police.'

'Oh.' Harry's enthusiasm waned slightly. 'They know, do they?'

'Oh, yes. They interrupted me just as I was getting into my stride.' She took a sip of wine. 'One of them was really quite offensive.'

Harry smiled.

'So,' she said. 'That's what I'm offering, Harry. The name and address of the victim, and her very informative next-door neighbour.'

'Right,' said Harry, picking up his unused table napkin, and searching his pockets for a pen. 'Fire away.'

'I'm not giving this information away, Harry,' she said quietly. 'I'm selling it.'

Harry looked up, his mouth slightly open with surprise. 'To me?' he asked incredulously.

'If you want to buy it,' she said.

'What's the matter? Are you hard up?'

'Never mind why. Are you interested?'

Harry put the top back on his pen, and shook his head. 'No,' he said. 'I'll buy a copy of the paper instead.'

'It won't be in the paper.'

'There'll be enough for me to work on.'

'There won't be anything. Think about it, Harry. He had the contacts, and she had possible access to so-called sensitive information about national security. What does all that add up to?'

'D-notice,' Harry said, sitting back with a smile. 'You've got a scoop and you can't publish it?' He shook his head. 'All right,' he said, and reached into his jacket for his wallet. 'How much?'

'Five hundred pounds,' she said, without blinking.

Harry stared at her, then laughed. 'You're joking. I haven't got that kind of money.'

'Mrs Culver has.'

'Maybe so, but Mrs Culver didn't employ me to find out who killed her husband. My job with her is finished.'

'That's all right then,' Barbara said, arranging her last neat forkful. 'You won't need this information.'

'Look – I do. I want it. I haven't got five hundred quid, though.'

'Yes, you have,' she said.

'I'm unemployed, in case you hadn't noticed. I haven't got that kind of money to give you. My God, when I think of the number of times I've—'

'Yes?' she said, looking up quickly. 'The number of times you've what, Harry?'

He drew out his cheque book. 'All right,' he said. 'All right. But I won't forget this in a hurry.' He wrote the cheque in angry stabbing movements, tore it out, and pushed it over to her. His pen poised over the napkin, he waited.

'Before this has even cleared?' she said, reaching across and taking the pen from his hand.

Harry didn't believe this was happening to him. 'You—' he began, and abandoned it. 'Just you be thankful we're in a restaurant,' he said.

'Oh?' she murmured, as she wrote. 'Watch it, bonny lad. The price goes up if you threaten me.'

'I don't know what you—' He broke off as she handed him the names and addresses, neatly printed on the back of his cheque. 'What's this?' he asked, frowning.

'The first one's the victim. The other one's her neighbour, and where you've to meet her,' Barbara said. 'She's expecting you – I told her she could trust you.' She handed him his pen.

'Why have you given me back my cheque?'

Barbara smiled. 'I didn't want your money, Harry.'

'Then what the hell did you want?'

'I wanted to know how badly *you* wanted that information.' She leant forward, and poured herself some more wine. 'I think there's a big story here, and it isn't about spies. So do you, but you'd never have admitted it.'

Harry nodded, folded the cheque, and put it in his wallet. He had been conned.

Barbara lifted her glass. 'You know something about all this that the police don't know,' she continued. 'That's the only reason that you would be prepared to take on private enquiries.'

Harry smiled, and turned his attention to his cold steak. 'Maybe,' he said.

'You think you can beat the boys in blue to it,' she said. 'And so do I.'

'Thank you for the vote of confidence,' he said. 'But why aren't you off chasing up leads yourself?'

'I don't investigate crimes,' she said. 'I report them.'

'And the rest,' Harry said scornfully.

She treated him to another smile. 'I don't know what questions to ask,' she said. 'Neither do the police. But you do, don't you?'

'Maybe.' Harry felt that her confidence might be a little misplaced.

'So all I want is a promise. If it's a big story, and if it's your story, let me get there first?'

'Done,' he said, and lifted his glass to hers.

Barbara looked in her bag for her key, shifting her stance a little so that light from the street lamp assisted her. 'Got it,' she said.

'Good,' Harry said, his hands in pockets, moving slightly from foot to foot. 'I'll be off then – thanks for the info, and the indigestion.'

69

'Aren't you coming in for coffee? You look frozen.'

'No, thanks. I'd best be off.'

She put the key in the lock. 'Does this mean that I've had all the debriefing I'm going to get?'

Harry smiled apologetically. 'Well, you know. Early start – I've got to get to Watford in the morning.'

'You make it sound as though you have to hack your way through equatorial rain forests,' she said. 'Half of Watford has to get into London. I shouldn't think everyone's celibate as a result.' She smiled. 'Who is she, Harry?'

'Who's what?' Harry looked offended at the very idea.

'The beautiful Mrs Culver? I can imagine her fancying a Geordie lad . . .'

'No, of course not!'

'There's no need to make her sound like one of the ugly sisters,' Barbara said.

'There's no one.'

'So I've just lost my charm?'

'No, I—' He sighed. 'I just don't think we should get involved again,' he said.

'Harry Lambert, you've never been involved with anyone in your life. Least of all me.' She turned her key in the door. 'You're smitten,' she said with a grin. 'Aren't you?'

'I'm going,' he said, and walked quickly away.

'Be good,' she called from the closing door as he got into the car.

Be good, he thought sourly. He didn't have much option. A bird in the hand, he told himself crossly, is worth any number in Amblesea who can't stand the sight of you.

'Sorry,' Lancaster said. 'But I did tell you there was no one we knew.'

Webb tried to look disappointed, but he was just relieved. The taxi had yielded dozens of prints, none of which matched Ainsley's.

'It's been two years since Ainsley did anything,' Webb said.

'But he has been involved in violent crime.'

'Even if he did take the car,' Lancaster said. 'You won't be able to prove anything on the taxi driver.'

'No, ' Webb agreed. 'But we might be able to prove that the car *didn't* have anything to do with the taxi. That would help.'

'Well, if he did take the car, why did he?'

'To impress his girl? Because it was sitting there with the keys in it?' Webb shrugged.

He'd much sooner forget it. He wanted Lancaster to say that Grant's car had nothing to do with the murder anyway, and so what if Ainsley was seen at the Wellington that morning? So what? A known car thief, already suspected of an attack on a taxi driver. At the scene. Spending money he didn't have earlier in the day.

Whether it was for questioning or elimination, he had to speak to Ainsley. And if that meant renewing his acquaintance with Grant, that was tough.

He couldn't put it off any longer.

Mrs Thomas had lived next door to the Wrights for years. She was still shocked by what had happened, but she had answered so many questions that a few more wouldn't hurt, she told Harry.

He didn't know what Barbara had told her, but she seemed to think he was police, and Harry didn't disabuse her of the idea.

They were meeting in a burger bar swarming with the luncheon-voucher brigade. Canned music played 'Winter Wonderland' as they spoke over two paper mugs of tea.

'Now, I understand that Mrs Wright knew a Mr Gerald Culver,' Harry said.

'Oh – I don't think she *knew* him,' Mrs Thomas said. 'Not really. But she had met him.'

Harry sat forward a little. 'When did she mention this?' he asked.

'When it was in the papers about his being killed. I had

popped in for a cup of tea and a chat – you know. She gets – got – a bit lonely, with her husband away all the time. At least he was home for Christmas – practically the whole holiday, so that was something, wasn't it? You're having to get him off his ship, aren't you? Poor man, I don't really know him very well, with him always being away.'

'No, you wouldn't. Anyway – you were in there for a cup of tea, were you? When she . . . ?'

'Oh yes. And the evening paper came. She just looked at it as she brought it in, and she said, "Oh dear, I've met him." And she showed me the paper. It was about him having been found dead.'

'Did she seem worried about it?'

'Worried? How do you mean?'

'Alarmed,' he said. 'Frightened.'

'No, nothing like that. Just sad, I'd say.'

Harry nodded. 'Now,' he said. 'you're sure that *that* was what she was looking at? There wasn't anything else on the front page that she might have been talking about?'

'I'm sure. Because I said did she mean the MP, and she said yes, he'd been murdered, and how awful it was. And she said that he was a really nice man—' She broke off as Harry groaned. 'What's wrong?' she asked sharply.

'Nothing,' Harry said wearily.

She gave him an old-fashioned look, and carried on. 'And she said that he'd given her something,' she said.

'Given her something? What?'

'I don't know.'

'You mean she wouldn't tell you?' Harry asked.

'No – that's not what I meant. How it happened was that she said what a shame it was and things, and then she said, "He gave me—" and the phone rang. She picked it up, and it was Stan ringing from goodness knows where. So I just told her I was going, you know – well, she wouldn't want me hanging about. She hardly ever got a call from him.'

'And you never asked about it again?'

72

'No, because I didn't see her for a couple of days. Not to speak to. And by that time we'd both forgotten about it. I don't think I'd ever have remembered, if . . .' She blinked hard.

Harry sighed. 'Don't upset yourself, pet,' he said.

'Sorry.'

'No. I'm sorry. But I have to ask questions.'

'Of course you do,' she said, reaching in her bag for a paper handkerchief and blowing her nose.

'It was unusual, was it, for her husband to ring her?'

'Not unusual,' said Mrs Thomas. 'Just not very often, if you know what I mean. I think he rang once they were in port somewhere.' She looked at him closely. 'Do you think you'll get him?' she asked, still tearful. 'Do you?'

It was a long time since Harry had felt a real twinge of conscience. He didn't like it. 'Oh, yes,' he said. 'Someone will. Don't you worry.' He took out the photograph of Culver, and handed it to her. 'Have you ever seen him?' he asked. 'With Mrs Wright, I mean?'

She shook her head, and dived into her bag again. 'Miss Briggs said you'd want this,' she said, and handed Harry a photograph. 'It's her,' she said. 'We were just messing around.'

Rosemary Wright was striking a model pose, but it was a good, clear picture.

'Thank you,' Harry said. 'I'll get it copied and let you have it back.'

'There's no need.'

Harry put the photo in his pocket together with the one of Culver. 'Did Mrs Wright go into London much?'

'Now and again,' she said. 'Shopping, or the theatre sometimes. Not all that often.'

'Recently?'

'Not that I know of.'

'Right. Well – thanks for your help. I'm sorry if it upset you.'

He stood up, arguing with himself. It was over. He'd told Mrs Culver to forget it, and so should he.

'I don't suppose,' he said, a little too loudly, as if to force

73

himself into the rest of the question, 'I don't suppose Mrs Wright had any connection with a place called Amblesea?'

'I don't know if you'd call it a *connection*,' she said, and Harry sat down again.

'They went there for a few days last August. Rosemary really liked it – she said they might look for a house there.'

EIGHT

Annie walked back from the old prom, where she had gone to be alone, to watch the sea. The shops and offices were closing, and the streets were emptying. When she got to the hotel, Linda was on reception. It occurred to Annie that Linda could substitute for the sun moon and stars if ever they let her down.

'Hi,' Linda said, as Annie picked an evening paper from the pile.

'Hello,' Annie said. 'I am going to go in there, put my feet up, and read the paper for half an hour.'

Linda looked shifty. 'There's mail,' she said, pushing a small pile of letters over the counter.

'Mail?' Annie said. 'Where on earth did you get mail from at this time of day?'

'Second post,' Linda said. 'Someone must have forgotten to give you it.'

'You mean Sandra forget to give me it,' Annie said. 'She's been miles away lately. Something more important on her mind, I expect.'

She picked up the letters and went into the sitting room, opening them as she went.

She frowned at the one in her hand, and started again. Then she checked the envelope, but it was indeed addressed to the manager. She read it again.

Dear Sir,

Further to our discussions earlier this month, I am pleased to confirm that we are now in a position to present Phase I of our

75

development plan to Amblesea District Council.

I am therefore writing to confirm our reservation of the Waterloo Room for three days, the 15th, 16th, and 17th of February, for a private, invitation-only exhibition of photographs, models, and plans as discussed.

The invitations will be extended to all the Town and County Councillors, to Council executives, local traders, and of course the Press, which we estimate to be in the region of . . .

Annie had never discussed any such thing with anyone. 'Damn the man!' she said aloud, and went marching along to reception.

'Is Mr Grant in?' she demanded.

Linda turned to check the keys. 'No, sorry,' she said. 'He's out. What's the matter?' she asked.

'Read that!' Annie stood and fumed while Linda read it. 'He's done it again!' she said, as soon as Linda looked up. 'I know nothing about that – I could already have booked the Waterloo for all he knows!'

'Have you?' Linda asked.

'No! But that's not the point, is it?'

'Well,' Linda said soothingly. 'It isn't as bad as it might have been.'

'Isn't it? I wish I had. At least then he'd know he can't *do* this sort of thing! Who's managing this place? Him or me? If he wants to do it, that's fine by me!'

'It's just as well he's out, if you ask my opinion,' Linda said. 'Don't go steaming up there and talking yourself out of a job, Annie. Think about what you're going to say.'

Annie took a deep breath and let it out slowly. 'You're right,' she said. 'But it's no good, Linda. He's always doing it. "By the way, I booked a party of twelve into the dining room tonight. Friends of the Earth – it might be vegetarian."'

'He *didn't* say that!' Linda laughed.

'He did!' Annie snatched up the letter. 'You tell me the *minute* he comes in,' she said.

'Don't you think you should maybe leave it until tomorrow morning?' Linda ventured. 'You know, business hours and all that?'

'No I don't!'

She went back into her room, banging the door. Business hours! Fat lot he cared about business hours. All his business was done over large brandies.

Minor alarms and excursions in the kitchen occupied her until just before six, by which time she had vented some of her spleen on the vegetables that she had had to wash and prepare because of the flu which had depleted the kitchen staff. She was having her second go at putting her feet up and reading the paper when the intercom buzzed.

'He's just gone up to his room,' Linda said. 'He seems to be in a bad mood.'

'I don't give a damn what sort of mood he's in,' Annie said.

'Come in.'

Annie, slightly out of breath from her cross refusal to wait for the lift, opened Grant's door.

Grant was just switching on the television. He smiled. 'Mrs Maddox,' he said. 'What can I do for you?'

'I received this letter,' she said, holding it out.

His eyes darted over the contents, and he nodded. 'Ah, yes,' he said. 'It's about the promenade area. Property developers who want to build on it.' He sat at the dressing table. 'They want to give the whole place a—'

'Mr Grant!' Annie interrupted. 'The point is that I know nothing about it.'

'Is there a problem?' he asked.

'Things have to be done,' she said. 'I have to know what sort of exhibits they'll have – what kind of space they'll need. It has to be organised—'

'And is there a problem?' he repeated. 'Are you saying you can't do it?'

'No – I'm saying that I should have been *told*.'

'It slipped my mind,' he said.

'Slipped your mind? They should have been speaking to me in the first place!'

'Should they?' His manner grew stiff and formal, and a little foreign, as it always did if he was crossed. 'Do I have to remind you, Mrs Maddox, that I own this hotel?'

'And you employ me to manage it! We can't both do it. What if I'd booked the room out?'

'Mrs Maddox – do I gather that there is no problem at all about this booking?'

Annie gritted her teeth. 'There's no problem about the booking,' she said carefully. 'There is a problem about your doing my job.'

'On the evidence of the Waterloo Room, I seem to be doing it rather more successfully than you,' he said.

'Oh, are you? Then maybe you'll roll your sleeves up and start chopping vegetables tomorrow night! If you want to do my job, Mr Grant, you go ahead and do it!'

'Mrs Maddox, there really is no need for you to speak to me in this—'

'Excuse me,' Annie said, abruptly shushing him with an outstretched hand, as she saw Gerald's photograph on the TV. She turned up the volume.

'. . . *just three weeks ago, in his London flat. Terrorist involvement has still not been ruled out, according to a statement issued today by Scotland Yard.*

'*In Eastham and Foley, Mr Culver's parliamentary constituency, it has been decided that the by-election . . .*'

'I'm sorry.' Annie turned the volume down again. 'I interrupted you.'

'You have an interest in that story?' he asked, his voice puzzled.

Annie nodded.

'A personal interest?'

'Yes,' Annie said. She looked up. 'Mr Culver and I were—'

78

she began, her voice defiant. But she flushed and dropped her eyes. 'Mr Culver and I were friends,' she said quietly.

'Friends?' Grant repeated.

She looked at him again, and sighed. 'More than that.'

'Are you saying you were lovers?' he asked quietly.

'Yes,' she replied.

Grant looked stunned. 'Do the police know?' he asked.

'No.'

'But they'll find out,' he said. 'And the newspapers. Some of them are just waiting to find out something like this.'

'I know.'

'People *must* know,' he said. 'He was a well-known man – people must have seen him.'

'You didn't,' she said, and sat down. 'He wasn't well known, anyway. Not until he was dead,' she added bitterly.

'Did you meet him here? Was he a guest?'

Annie nodded.

'He was a guest at this hotel,' he said. 'How do you suppose that will look if it comes out? The papers will really like that.'

'Yes,' she answered. 'I'm sorry.'

'You had no right to get involved with a guest, Mrs Maddox.'

'No.' She looked away. 'I'm sorry,' she said again. 'I know how you must feel. And I can't promise they won't find out,' she added miserably. 'I can't. I should have told you before.'

Grant nodded. 'Yes,' he said, and sighed. 'I'm very sorry – you must have been through a great deal.' He smacked his hands on his knees. 'And you are quite right,' he said, suddenly brisk and loud again.

'Sorry?' Annie said.

'I shouldn't be here, getting in your way.'

'Does this mean I'm not fired?' she asked.

'My dear Mrs Maddox, I don't want to fire you. I want to ask a favour.'

'Oh,' Annie said.

'You are quite right,' he said again. 'I should not be trying to do your job.'

'I think I was perhaps a little—' she began, but he shook his head.

'No,' he said. 'You were right. And I think it's time I moved back into the house. I'll move back within the next few days, I promise.'

'Oh, Mr Grant, I really didn't mean to drive you away—'

'My wife will be home soon,' he said. 'It's time I moved back.'

'And the favour?' Annie asked.

'Let me take you to dinner one evening,' he said. 'Somewhere very exclusive, very expensive, and not a bit like a conference hotel.'

Just when she thought he had given up. 'Well,' she said. 'It's very kind of you, but—'

'I know,' he said. 'You don't feel you should go out enjoying yourself. But you've been through a great deal, Mrs Maddox, and I haven't helped, getting under your feet. I think an evening off, away from this place, would do you the world of good.'

Annie smiled. He obviously thought anyone who had the nerve to shout at him must be suffering some sort of breakdown. 'You really don't have to,' she said.

'I know I don't have to,' he said. 'But I would be most grateful if you would accept.'

'Thank you,' she said. 'It would be lovely.'

NINE

'Mrs Maddox has got someone with her,' Linda said, immovably.

Harry looked at his watch. The drive had made him hungry. 'Can I get something to eat here?' he asked.

'The dining room's stopped serving breakfast,' she said. 'But the restaurant's open.'

Harry looked puzzled. 'What's the difference?' he asked.

'The restaurant's self-service,' she said.

'Fine. And if you could tell Mrs Maddox that I'm here, and that it's important, and she should see me as soon as she's free.' He turned away, then back. 'Ever see her here?' he asked, showing her Rosemary Wright's photograph, but she shook her head.

In what it pleased them to call the Wellington Boot, shiny coloured photographs showed him what he could eat in case he couldn't read. There should be a law, he thought grimly, against calling places like this restaurants.

'Hamburger,' he grunted, refusing to give it its silly name. 'And coffee.'

He sat down on a plastic moulded chair at a plastic moulded table, and began to eat his plastic moulded hamburger.

He was actually enjoying it when he became aware of a presence at his elbow.

'Important enough to interrupt your breakfast?' Annie asked.

'Just finished.' He popped the last of the hamburger in his mouth and washed it down with coffee. 'Is there somewhere more private?' he asked.

'Of course,' she said.

He followed her back along to reception, and through to her sitting room.

'Do you know a Mrs Rosemary Wright?' he asked, as soon as the door was closed.

'No.'

'That's her.' Harry handed her the snapshot.

'I still don't know her,' Annie said. 'Should I?'

'Your boyfriend did.'

Annie sighed. 'I didn't know Gerald's friends.'

'Not a friend, I don't think. More of an acquaintance.'

'I don't know any of them, either.'

'But there's a good chance that she met him here,' Harry persisted.

'Here?' Annie frowned a little. 'At the Wellington?'

'Probably. In Amblesea, anyway, and he didn't go anywhere else, did he?' He lit a cigarette. 'She says he gave her something.'

'Gave her what?'

'That's what I hoped you'd tell me.'

'I've never heard of the woman,' Annie said impatiently. 'When did she meet Gerald?'

Harry shrugged. 'I can't be specific – but she was in Amblesea on holiday during the last week in August.'

'Did she stay here?' Annie asked.

'No. You're too expensive – she stayed at one of the guest houses.'

'I thought I would have recognised her if she'd been a guest,' Annie said, with professional concern. 'But anyway – if that's when she was here, she didn't meet Gerald, because he wasn't.'

'Total recall?' Harry asked, with exaggerated surprise. 'And I thought we'd have to get hold of West Ham's fixture list.'

Annie ignored the jibe. 'He wasn't here,' she said firmly.

'Are you sure?'

'I'm very sure.'

Her eyes held his, but he could always win that game. She dropped her gaze.

'I saw Gerald in July last year, and didn't see him again until New Year's Eve,' she said.

'July?' Harry repeated. 'Pre-season friendly, would that be?' he asked.

Annie got up.

'Don't let's have the showing me the door routine,' Harry said. 'How come you didn't see him all that time?'

Annie's dark eyes were on him, and the animosity had been replaced by a kind of detached curiosity, as though she were examining a new and rather unprepossessing species of pond life.

'He thought we should call it a day,' she said simply, without emotion. 'He came specially to tell me that on a very sunny day in July.' She sat down. 'When I was least expecting it,' she added.

In response to her *please come soon*, Harry thought. It was the first sign she had given him that Gerald wasn't perhaps a full-time knight in shining armour.

'So what happened?'

'He just turned up on New Year's Eve,' she said. She was trying too hard to sound casual.

'But he could only spare you an hour?'

'So she didn't meet Gerald in August last year,' Annie said, changing the subject rapidly. 'Not in Amblesea.'

'But I don't believe in coincidence,' Harry said.

'She could be lying,' Annie said.

Harry shook his head.

'Such faith – I didn't know you had it in you. What's she got that I haven't?'

'A death certificate,' Harry replied with studied carelessness, seizing the feed line.

Annie went pale. 'What did you say,' she asked automatically, though she had obviously heard him.

'She was found dead, lying in her hallway, stabbed,' Harry said. 'Any of that sound familiar to you?'

'Oh, no.' Annie's hand went to her mouth.

'Someone's killing people,' Harry continued. 'Someone who knew Culver. Someone who knows Culver's friends. It could be someone who knows *you*.'

'Stop it!' Annie cried.

Harry moved to the sofa beside her. 'You've got to tell me everything you know about all this, Annie You've *got* to.'

'I *have*! If she met Gerald here, then I knew nothing about it!' Her eyes widened. 'And neither do the *police*,' she said. 'Or they'd have been here. I'll have to tell them now,' she said, going towards the phone. 'They've got to—'

'Hang on,' Harry said, catching her arm. 'Before you do anything rash.'

She stopped, her hand on the receiver. 'What now?' she asked, her voice afraid.

'They might ask you some awkward questions,' Harry said. 'You are what these two dead bodies have in common, after all.'

'I don't know her from Adam!'

'But she was *here*.'

Annie sat down again.

'So they would be very interested in your relationship with him, and his with her . . .'

Annie frowned. 'I thought he didn't have a relationship with her,' she said.

'Probably not,' Harry said. 'But for all I know he did. And perhaps you killed them both. That's how the police will look at it anyway.'

Annie nodded slowly.

Harry handed her the photograph. 'How did he get that?' he asked, tapping the bruise.

Annie frowned. 'When was this taken?'

The first of January. The early hours. His wife thinks he got it at a football match,' he said. 'But we know better don't we? He had that shiner by the time he got home that evening. Rough tackle, was it?' He reached across her to stub out his cigarette.

She pulled away from him. 'I don't know how he got it,' she said dully.

'He had walked out on you in the summer, and then just turned up – I assume you did have a full and frank exchange of views?'

'All right, we had a row. But no one was throwing punches.'

'Someone seems to have been.'

'You don't know that. Didn't Laura ask him how it happened?'

'He said he banged his head on the train,' Harry said.

'Then he probably did,' Annie said.

'Maybe. His wife doesn't think so.' Harry put the photographs away. 'So, you had a row on New Year's Eve. What happened then?'

'Nothing. I never saw him again.' She looked at him. 'Do you believe me?'

Harry nodded. 'But the police wouldn't,' he said.

'Why not, if you do?'

'Because they're paid not to believe you,' he said. 'I've got a lot more trusting since I left.'

'What's happening?' she asked, and she was scared.

'I don't know. But whatever it is, it's a safe bet that it's happening here. And that Rosemary Wright met your boyfriend here in August, whether you knew about it or not.'

'I don't understand.'

'No. Why did he want to call it a day?'

'Do you want his reasons or my theories?' she asked.

'Both. What were his reasons?'

'It was no life for me, he couldn't spend enough time here, I should have more of a social life, etcetera.'

'And your theories?'

'We were getting busy at last. Gerald ran a bigger risk of someone recognising him every time he came here. He was worried that Laura would find out.'

'He was fond of his skin, wasn't he?'

'He was fond of Laura,' she said, her voice flat. 'He didn't want to hurt her.'

'Then what was he doing with you?'

85

Annie's cool glance made him feel a little uncomfortable.

'Oh, I think you hit the nail on the head last time you were here,' she said. 'I *was* a working-class pursuit – a holiday from Laura. I know you meant me to find it offensive, but I don't. It's true.'

'But if it was getting too risky,' Harry said, 'what made him come back?'

'He missed me,' Annie said. 'If you find that difficult to believe, tough. He missed me.'

Harry didn't find it at all difficult to believe. Laura Culver was to Annie what expensively beautiful shoes were to running barefoot in the grass.

'Missed you? Or missed playing snooker and letting his braces dangle?'

'That's what I wanted to know,' she said candidly.

'Who did he know here?' Harry asked.

'Not many people,' she said. 'Linda, Christine. That's all really. He met other people, of course, but no one else really knew him.' She thought for a moment. 'And he met Karen Grant once or twice,' she said. 'But she didn't know anything about him – who he was, or anything.'

'Who's Karen Grant?'

'The owner's wife.'

'The owner is the big guy with the Brylcreem?'

'Yes. He's staying here because she's away just now.'

'Did Culver know him?'

'No,' she said. 'He's only just found out. I told him the other day – I had no choice. God knows what he'll do if it gets in the papers.'

'Another good reason for not ringing the police,' Harry said.

Annie agreed, with a quick nod of her head.

'How come he knew Mrs Grant?'

'She gets her hair done here. She pops in for coffee and a chat. Gerald was here a couple of times.'

'Inconvenient,' said Harry. 'Did you get time added on for stoppages?' Before Annie could say anything he carried on. 'Did he know your daughter's boyfriend? I met him when I was here before.'

'Did you?' Annie looked surprised. 'You did ask around, then?'

'Man of my word,' he said. 'Pete, isn't it?'

'Pete. My future son-in-law, I'm told.'

Harry smiled. 'Do I detect a slight sneer?' he asked.

'I suppose you do,' she said. 'I think he's much too old for her, for a start. And he's carrying a torch for someone else, if I'm any judge.' She smiled. 'But she seems to get on with him, so I mustn't turn into a music-hall joke.'

'Not much fear of that,' Harry said.

'Ainsley, you are not helping things by mumbling.'

This advice was given to Pete by Detective Superintendent Webb, whom he had been very careful to avoid until now.

'Someone lent me some money,' he said, in a slightly louder voice.

'Why were you hanging round the Wellington car park?'

'I wasn't hanging around.'

'What were you doing?'

'I was probably on my way in.'

What had the Wellington to do with anything? Pete didn't like it when he didn't understand why he was being questioned.

'When?' Webb asked.

'Whenever it was you saw me.' He glanced at the constable at the door, and recognised him. 'You mean when he was there?' he asked. 'The other day?'

'Yes. And more to the point, on the morning of the thirty-first of December last year.'

'I was visiting someone,' said Pete. 'If you must know.'

Webb raised an eyebrow, and Pete wondered how many hours in front of the mirror it had taken him to perfect the gesture.

'Who?'

'The manager's daughter's a friend of mine.' Pete's voice

dared Webb to raise an eyebrow at that.

'Is she now?' he said, accepting the dare. 'You'll know her name, in that case.'

'Chrissie Maddox. Her mother runs the place.'

'She's a bit young for you, isn't she, Ainsley?' Webb tapped his chin with the cap of his pen.

'She's nineteen.'

'Are you often there? How come I've never seen you?'

'Because I've made sure you haven't,' Pete replied.

Webb rubbed his right eye. 'Thirty-first of December. You were meeting Christine?'

'Yes.'

'Then what did you do?'

'We got a lift into Harmouth.'

'To do what?'

'To see a friend of ours. And then we went for a drink—'

'To the Anchorage?'

Sitting back, Pete glanced from Webb to the constable. He couldn't be sure. They looked different out of uniform.

'The Anchorage isn't a very nice place to take a young lady,' Webb said.

'It's all right at lunchtime.'

'Then what?'

'We came back to the hotel. But you know that already, I suppose. He probably put one of those bug things on the van.'

'When did you leave?'

'Half past five. Why are you asking me these questions?'

Webb got up, and turned his back, looking out of the window. 'Did you know the owner's car was stolen while you were there?'

'Yes. We found out just before I left.'

'Worried you, did it?'

If this was about a stolen car, Pete asked himself, why was he being interviewed by a superintendent? He shifted a little in his seat. 'Why should it worry me?' he asked.

'Taking and driving away's a hobby of yours, isn't it?'

'I haven't done that since I was sixteen.'

Webb spun round. 'No!' he shouted.

If it was meant to alarm him, it failed.

'No,' he repeated, quiet again. 'You've graduated since then. Aggravated burglary – do you carry a knife, Ainsley?'

'No! And I was found not guilty, if you check.'

'So you were. My deepest apologies. Let's see what you were found guilty of, shall we? Yes, here it is.'

'I didn't use a knife.'

Webb sat down. 'And the Wellington Hotel was unlucky enough to have *two* car thieves on the premises at once,' he said. 'Out of season, too.'

'I don't know what this is all about,' Pete said. 'But if he's been watching me, you'd better call him off. I've got rights – this is harassment.'

'I wonder,' Webb mused, his eyes on the ceiling, 'who first said that? An ex-con, like you? A political agitator, maybe.' He rubbed both his eyes. 'Or a poor, overworked copper like me. Don't tell us about harassment,' he said, and stood up again. 'I take it Christine Maddox will confirm what you've told us?'

'Yes,' said Pete, but there was an uncertainty about that that showed just a little.

'Sure, are we, Ainsley?'

'I'd like to ask Sandra about Mrs Wright,' Harry said. 'She isn't on until lunchtime, though, is she?'

'I'll give you her address, if you like.'

'Good. Thanks.'

Annie found an envelope on which she wrote the address and a small, accurate map. 'There you are,' she said, handing it to him.

'*MR A. MADDOY you have been chosen from among our Amblesea customers to receive a FREE ENTRY in this year's SUPER SUMMER PRIZE DRAW. Open this envelope MR MADDOY, and find your FREE DRAW NUMBER!!!*'

'You haven't opened your envelope, Mr Maddoy,' Harry

said, as he put it in his jacket pocket. 'Amblesea's sole representative and all.' He picked up his cigarettes. 'Right, I'll be on my way. Oh – can I book a room?'

'Yes, of course. I'll see to it if you like.' She went to the door. 'Do I send the bill to Mrs Culver?' she asked mischievously.

'Oh – no.' Harry realised what he had done. 'No. I'm not working for Mrs Culver.'

'Is this some sort of hobby?'

'It beats making models of St Paul's out of used matches,' Harry said. 'But I'd forgotten I'd have to foot my own bills.'

Annie smiled. 'No, you don't,' she said quietly. 'It's on the house.'

'Why?' Harry asked.

'Because I want you to find whoever killed Gerald,' she said. 'That's why. I can't afford to employ you, but I can put you up while you're here.'

'Fine,' Harry said, with a brief smile. 'That'll be fine.'

TEN

As they went out into the foyer, Annie saw Tom Webb coming in. He stopped when he saw Harry, and frowned a little.

'Inspector Lambert!' he said, snapping his fingers. 'Right?'

'Right,' Harry said. 'It's Superintendent Webb, isn't it?' He extended his hand. 'Nice to meet you again, sir. You were based in Leicester last time we met.'

Annie's eyes widened a little.

'Countryman,' Tom said to Annie. 'Remember? Hicks from the sticks to look for rotten apples. Makes sense, I suppose.'

Annie smiled nervously.

'It's all right,' Tom said. 'He's on our side.' He laughed, then turned back to Harry. 'Are you here officially? I wasn't told to expect you.'

'Weren't you?' Harry looked astonished. 'I'm sorry, sir. I'll check with our end, of course – but I'm certain that they would have let Amblesea know.'

Annie watched, dismayed and quite speechless.

'They probably did,' Tom said heavily. 'The Amblesea lot aren't very keen on Harmouth overseers.'

She couldn't stop it. Not now.

'So – what brings you here?'

'Background,' Harry said. 'It seems Amblesea's just the job for a dirty weekend.'

He glanced at Annie; she looked away.

'Don't we know it,' Tom said. 'Annie had seven couples called Smith one Saturday night, didn't you?'

'Three,' Annie said, automatically correcting the exaggeration.

91

'That's the problem,' Harry said. 'I'm trying to find out who my man was here with – doubtless another Mrs Smith.' He pulled out the photograph of Gerald, and handed it to Tom. 'Ring any bells?'

Tom glanced at it. 'Isn't that—?'

'Yes,' Harry said, interrupting him.

'Don't tell me he's been having it away with a beautiful Russian spy in Amblesea, of all places!'

'You never know,' Harry said.

'Oh, the glamour of it all. Who gave him the black eye?'

'That's what we'd like to know,' Harry said.

Tom handed back the photo. 'Have you shown it to Annie?'

Harry actually held it out to her. 'I've seen it,' she snapped.

'No go?' said Tom. 'When's he supposed to have been here?'

Harry put the photograph away. 'The last week in August,' he said.

'Oh God, you'll be lucky. The Prime Minister wouldn't be recog—'

Harry silenced him with a disapproving look.

'Sorry,' Tom said. 'You don't want to take it all so seriously, Lambert.'

'We have to follow it up, sir.'

'I know, I know. We have to try not to look clueless. We've got one just now – a taxi driver. Robbed – probably a drunk with a knife. The driver died, so where does that leave us? No witnesses. And whoever did it was probably half-way up the bloody motorway before anyone even found the poor sod. No weapon – nothing.'

'The widow isn't very impressed,' Harry said. 'From what I hear.'

'Oh – they've been talking to you, have they? Sure, his widow thinks we should have caught him by now. She's right. We'll get him, but it means pulling in the likely lads until we get lucky, or hear a whisper.' He sighed. 'Isn't that what it always boils down to? That and paperwork.'

'Can't argue with you there, sir,' Harry said, as Grant came downstairs.

He looked across at Tom without acknowledgement, and went out.

'Another dissatisfied customer,' Tom said. 'Car nicked – from right under Annie's eye. Right, Annie?'

'Yes,' she said, barely able to raise a smile.

'We thought it might all connect up for a while,' Tom went on. 'It happened the same day.'

'No joy?'

'None whatsoever. Joker wore gloves – mind you, he would. It was bloody cold, New Year's Eve. There were only Grant's prints on the bloody car – and the time we had getting them! We had to destroy them in front of him. He's convinced the country's going to turn into a police state.' He laughed. 'Fat chance,' he said. 'No one takes a blind bit of notice of us.'

He turned to Annie. 'I'm really here to see Christine – is she around?'

Annie, still transfixed by Harry's portrayal of a career policeman, took a moment to gather her thoughts.

'Christine? Yes. It's her day off, but she's around.'

'Can you tell her I'd like a word?'

'Yes, sure. What about?' Annie asked.

'Excuse me,' Tom muttered as he walked past Harry. 'It seems she's friendly with one Peter John Ainsley,' he said.

'Yes,' Annie said.

'I'd like to ask her about that.'

'I'll see if I can get her.' Annie went up to the desk, and as she did so, Peter John Ainsley walked in.

'Too late, Ainsley,' Tom said. 'I got here first.'

Harry left, walking out past Pete, who nodded to him.

Tom frowned. 'Do you know him?' he asked Pete.

'Yes.'

'How?'

'Do I have to check with you before I say hello to people?' Pete asked.

'How come you know a Murder Squad inspector?'

'An ex-Murder-Squad inspector,' Pete said, grinning. 'Didn't he tell you? Tell Chris I'll see her later,' he said to Annie.

'It's all right,' Annie told Linda, who looked just as apprehensive as she felt. 'Don't bother getting Christine.' She walked to the corridor door, with Tom at her shoulder.

He followed her into the sitting room, and closed the door. She hadn't looked at him once.

'Did you know?' he asked.

'Yes.'

'Why the hell didn't you tell me?'

'I couldn't!' She turned to him. 'By the time I realised what he was doing it was too late – I'd have made you look—' She broke off, aware of her lack of tact.

The door opened and Christine came in. 'Just going to do some shopping,' she said. 'Do you want anything?'

'Just a minute!' thundered Tom.

Poor Christine. There was no need for Tom to take it out on her.

'Peter John Ainsley,' he said. 'He says he's a friend of yours.'

'Yes, he is.'

'You've got some funny friends, Christine.'

'I don't think so.'

Annie had never seen Christine look like that. There was something sullen, something mutinous about her that shocked Annie.

'We're making enquiries into the murder of Daniel Fowler on the thirty-first of December last year,' Tom said heavily.

'And just because Pete's been in trouble,' Christine said, 'you jump to conclusions. Just like before.'

'Can you tell us where he was at the time?' Tom asked.

Annie couldn't believe this was happening.

'When was it?' Christine asked.

'The thirty-first of—'

'What time? How do you expect me to tell you where Pete was if you don't tell me when it was?'

'Just tell me when he was with you,' Tom said. 'That's the

only time you can vouch for him, isn't it?'

Christine flushed with annoyance. 'Pete was with me nearly all day,' she said. 'We were in Harmouth in the morning, and here from about three.'

'Were you really?' Tom said, obviously not believing her.

'If Christine says that's when he was here, then it is,' Annie said.

'Did you see them?'

'Yes,' she said.

'And when was that?'

'About five,' Annie said. 'Between five and half past.'

'Could you say that he had been here all along, since three o'clock?' Tom asked, raising his voice.

'No, but—'

'Then I don't want to know,' he said.

Tom turned his attention once more to Christine.

'He had some money on him that night, didn't he?' Tom asked. 'Where did he get it from, Christine?'

Annie went to her side. 'Why are you asking her, Tom? Why don't you ask Pete?'

'We have,' he said grimly. 'Well, Christine? Where did he get it from?'

'I gave him it,' she said.

'You give him money?'

'Sometimes,' she said.

'And you're saying he was with you from three? Until when?'

'He left at about ten to six and went to his flat.'

Tom moved a step closer to Christine, and Annie instinctively put her arm round her.

'Does Sandra know Ainsley by sight?' he asked.

'Yes.'

'We asked her who had been in and out of the hotel – how come she didn't mention him?'

Annie could feel Christine relax a little. 'Because she didn't see him,' she said. 'We came in with Jimmy.'

'Jimmy?'

'The boy who did the disco that night,' Annie explained.

'He's a friend of ours. That's why Mum got him. We'd been to Harmouth to help him load up, and we came in by the basement.'

'Why does that mean Sandra didn't see you?' Tom asked.

'Because you use the service lift from the basement,' Annie said. 'The one outside my door. That's the only way to and from the basement.'

Tom nodded, but he didn't look convinced, and neither was Annie. She switched on the lights as dark clouds gathered.

Tom went to the door. 'Is Lambert coming back here?' he asked.

'I expect so,' Annie said.

The door banged behind him, and Annie turned to Christine.

'All right,' Christine said, immediately on the defensive. 'He's been in trouble. So what?'

'So *what*?' Annie repeated.

'It was a long time ago.'

Annie sat down. 'What sort of trouble?'

'Nothing like that!' Christine made for the door. 'I've got to go and see him.'

'You're going nowhere until we sort this out.' Annie's eyes met her daughter's, and she found she could still win the silent battle of wills, as she had when Christine was four. Christine edged reluctantly away from the door.

'What sort of trouble?' she asked again.

'He stole something,' Christine said.

Annie inclined her head a little. 'OK,' she said. 'But there are a lot of ways to steal something. Which did he choose?'

'A crowd of them broke into a shop,' Christine said miserably. 'He didn't hurt anyone.'

'But the others did?'

'No! They weren't going to *do* anything. They didn't know he'd be in there – the man who owned the shop. They threatened him or something. Pete wasn't found guilty of that – he just drove the car.'

'Was he really with you when this taxi-driver business

96

happened?'

'Yes!' But she turned away as she said it. 'Tom Webb's got no right to talk to me in front of you anyway.'

'It's just as well he did,' Annie said. 'Chris – if you're lying to protect Pete, you'll be in terrible trouble.' She reached over to take Christine's hand. 'Are you telling the truth?'

'Yes,' Christine said.

ELEVEN

Fowler. Harry drove along the Harmouth road where Mr Fowler had been killed. It was virtually deserted now. New Year's Eve had been a Sunday and there would have been no traffic at all along its cold, windy length. The *Harmouth Advertiser with Amblesea Bulletin*'s Amblesea office had let him see the editions he needed. Mrs Fowler, as he had correctly guessed, was the Driver's Widow of the headlines that he'd read.

Webb was investigating Fowler's death; Harry was investigating Culver's. Both had been stabbed. Both were in Amblesea on New Year's Eve, and Harry didn't believe in coincidence.

Rain began to fall as he entered Harmouth's dockland. This was where life ran a little wild and woolly; this was where you might expect trouble. Not in the quietness of a Sunday afternoon in Amblesea.

He parked on a double yellow line, and the grey buildings loomed up in front of him, old warehouses and offices that had seen better days. Some of them were closed up for good. It was mid-morning, but the inhabited buildings had lights on in the grey day, looking oddly welcoming in the hard surroundings. A ship was preparing to sail; seamen took their leave of their ladies, as they had done for hundreds of years.

The romance of the sea had always charmed Harry; sailing on the tide, making landfall, riding at anchor – the evocative phrases stirred something in his heart. The sea itself – the actual heaving, treacherous water – stirred only his stomach, and his was a landlubber's love of the ocean.

A couple stood a few feet from his car. She was crying, he was kissing her. The whole place was one enormous, romantic cliché, with its grim, square, business-like buildings framing all the frantic farewells and euphoric reunions. Heightened by long separations, private emotions were on public display, and it would be no surprise if passions ran high now and again, if knives sometimes came out, and sometimes went in. But it hadn't happened here. It had happened in Amblesea.

He started the car as a traffic warden walked purposefully towards him, and went on his way. Harry wanted to talk to Driver's Widow. Perhaps she would hit out at something more deadly than apathy this time.

A bell sounded as Grant opened the front door, and he walked quickly to the alarm and turned it off.

'Not very welcoming,' he said to Sandra. 'But necessary, these days.'

Sandra smiled doubtfully, and rubbed her hands together. 'It's even colder inside,' she said.

The house looked gloomy and unfriendly, even to Grant's eye. He opened the curtains that covered almost all of one wall, revealing the view of the sea.

'That's better,' he said.

'It's very big,' said Sandra.

Grant found her very irritating at times. 'I'm sorry it's so cold,' he said. 'There's an electric fire.' He flicked a switch on the wall. 'I just wanted you to see it,' he said.

Little sparks of dust danced along the elements as they glowed red, and the smell peculiar to long-unused electric fires hung in the cold air.

'Come and get warm,' he said.

Sandra held outstretched hands to the fire, looking out of the window.

'Did you build those?' she asked, after a moment.

She indicated the housing estate, and Grant snorted. 'No, I did not,' he said. 'And I can assure you that they would not have

99

been built there if I had.'

'But it'll be a lot less lonely,' Sandra said. She looked round the dust-sheeted room. 'I'd want some neighbours.'

You probably would, thought Grant. He wished it was Mrs Maddox to whom he was showing off his house, but that seemed a rather unlikely prospect.

'Look,' he said, and began pulling off the dust-sheets, revealing studded leather armchairs, and french-polished wood. Sandra looked unimpressed. 'It's very big,' she said again.

'I'll get some cleaners from the hotel,' he said. 'The next time you come, everything will be gleaming – there will be a log fire burning, the central heating will be on, and if we're lucky, there will be snow. This place is beautiful when it's snowing outside.'

Sandra shivered.

'It will be much better here,' he promised. 'It won't be like London. This is a beautiful house.'

'What if your wife comes back?'

He took a deep breath. 'She won't,' he said. 'And if she does – what does she expect? She walked out on all of this.'

Sandra lifted up the corner of a dust-sheet to reveal the hi-fi.

'Ah! Yes – take it off. We will have music.' He ran a finger along the rack of records, and selected one.

Red and green LED lights came on, and a moment later Mozart filled the room from concealed speakers. 'Do you like Mozart?' he asked.

'I don't know,' she said.

She would doubtless rather have Jim Reeves, like Karen. Like Lesley, come to that. He always wound up with the wrong women.

'Do you know who this man Lambert is?' he asked her.

'Lambert?' Sandra looked blank, but then she often did. Sandra's assets were her youth, and her availability. No more.

'I met him about a week ago with young Christine. He was at the hotel again this morning.'

'Oh, Lambert!' Sandra laughed. 'I thought you were talking about a composer! You mean the man who was asking questions about Gerald Culver?'

Grant stared at her. 'Culver?' he said, sounding just like she did.

'Yes – you know. The MP who was murdered.'

Grant knew all right. And he knew that Mrs Maddox had not mentioned Lambert's interest. 'Is he a reporter or something?' he asked.

'No. Christine says he used to be a policeman. He told her he resigned before they kicked him out.'

'Did he now?' Grant changed the subject. 'What do you think of my beautiful house?' he asked.

'I'm not sure,' she said. 'Once the heating's back on and all that, I'll probably like it all right.'

He drew her to him, to prove to himself that she was worth it. She was.

'My name is Lambert,' he said, to the pale young woman who opened the door. 'Would you be Mrs Fowler?'

'Yes,' she said, moving slightly so that the door wasn't quite so open, not just such an invitation to enter.

'I'd like to talk to you about your husband,' he said. 'If you wouldn't find it too distressing.'

'Why?' she asked, with the directness of a child.

'Because I think I might be able to help,' he said.

The door closed a little more. 'Are you some sort of religion?' she asked.

Harry's smile was involuntary, but his fears that he might have offended her were allayed as she visibly relaxed, and the door opened a few more inches.

During the conversation that followed, the door was a barometer; he explained who he was, and what he was trying to do. He didn't try explaining why; he couldn't fathom it himself.

Eventually, the door was pulled wide enough for him to enter.

'Go through,' she said.

He was given a cup of tea and an oddly self-aware photograph of the deceased in dinner jacket and bow tie. He learned that Fowler had been married for almost twelve years. He noticed a glossy 8 x 10 of the same photograph, and found out that Danny Fowler had sung with a jazz band until about three years ago.

He had found out from the *Advertiser* that he had been stabbed just once, and left for dead, like Culver, like Wright. But he'd had money stolen. Why try to make just one of them look like robbery?

'Do you have reason to think that it might *not* have been robbery?' he asked.

'No,' she said. 'I'm sure it was.'

'He wasn't any different from usual that day? Worried, maybe?'

'No. Anything but.'

Harry made a mental note of the 'anything but', and moved on. 'Where would he have been picking up?' he asked. 'Did he cruise, or get bookings or what?'

'He'd pick up if he was hailed,' she said. 'If not, he went to the rank.'

'The docks rank? Or the station?'

'Oh – no. Sorry, I thought you knew. Danny didn't work in Harmouth. He worked for Amcabs in Amblesea.' She shook her head. 'That was what was so—' She sighed. 'He wouldn't work here because he said it was too dangerous for cabbies. They got beaten up sometimes,' she explained. 'There's been a lot of attacks. Cabby-bashing, the papers called it. But no one was doing anything about it.'

Harry nodded. Give it a nice neat name and it stops being malicious wounding or grievous bodily harm. It all starts to be treated like some sort of rough boys' game. So that was the apathy at which she had been hitting out.

'That's why he went to Amblesea,' she said. 'But it happened to him there.'

Harry finished his tea. 'You said he was anything but worried. What did you mean?'

'He'd got a letter from his agent – he didn't get one very often,

102

not these days. But he still got the odd gig – jazz clubs that remembered him, you know.' Her eyes went to the piano, where the 8 x 10 sat.

'He was quite well known, then?'

'No. He said his claim to fame was that he once nearly sang on the radio. He did a session for them, but they never used it. The clubs knew him though, and some pubs round here.'

Harry took out his cigarettes. 'Do you smoke?'

She shook her head.

'So – he'd got a singing job, had he?'

'I don't know,' she said.

'Oh, I thought you said the letter—'

'He picked it up on his way out. He said he'd let me know – he was in a hurry, you see.'

She couldn't go on for a moment, but she took a breath. 'He put it in his wallet,' she said. 'It must have fallen out when they took the money.'

Harry frowned. 'Was there anything else in the wallet? Apart from it and the money?'

She nodded. 'Everything was still there,' she said. 'Club cards and things. But the letter wasn't *in* the wallet – not in a compartment. He just folded his wallet over it – you know?'

'Yes.'

'So I never saw the letter,' she said. 'I rang his agent, to tell him what had happened. But I couldn't ask him. I didn't want to know. I think them throwing away that letter was the worst thing. Stupid, isn't it?'

'No, pet.' He ground out his cigarette. The letter puzzled him; if it had fallen out, it would have been there when Fowler was found. But why would anyone want to steal his letter? No reason, he decided. 'Which rank did he go on in Amblesea?' he asked.

'The one at the precinct – near the conference centre.'

'The *Wellington* Conference Centre?' Harry asked, as though there were dozens.

'Yes,' she replied warily. 'Does that mean something?'

103

'Probably not,' Harry said, getting to his feet. 'I don't suppose he ever mentioned anyone called Culver, did he? Or Wright – a woman called Wright?'

'No,' she said. 'Not that I remember.'

He showed her their photographs, but she still looked blank. She told him he could keep the small version of Danny's publicity photo. 'It was taken two or three years ago,' she said. 'But he hadn't really changed.'

Harry paused for a moment, trying to get an idea of the man behind the bland publicity smile.

'So,' he said, putting it with the other photographs, in his wallet, exactly as she had described Fowler doing with the letter. 'He would have dropped a fare in Harmouth and been on his way back, you think?'

'Definitely,' she said. 'He'd have got lynched if he'd picked anyone up in Harmouth. He wasn't allowed.'

She opened the door for him. 'You don't think he was mixed up in anything, do you?' she asked.

'Do you?'

She lifted a non-committal hand.

Pete put on the radio, and put it off again. Surely Chris would come once Webb had finished with her? She wouldn't let him go on worrying, would she?

The sergeant had taken as lengthy and detailed a statement about nothing as he had dared, and Pete had tried to phone her, but his money had just fallen through. So Webb had got to her first, and he just had to hope that she was all right.

He shouldn't have gone back to the Wellington that night. He should have stayed away – gone away. Christine needed him like she needed a hole in the head, and a moment or two of Webb on the warpath had probably convinced her of that.

A rainy Wednesday lunchtime in Amblesea. Harry sat in his car, watching the precinct begin to empty of people as the shops began to close early.

The taxi rank was on this road, serving the shoppers and the conference centre. Taxis barely stopped moving as more and more people finished shopping and arrived at the rank. Harry, parked safely if illegally in someone's staff car park, wound down his window, and threw out his cigarette.

The rain was beating a tattoo on the roof, a loud unrhythmic drumming, and he closed his eyes and listened to the sounds of the town.

Somewhere a child was crying, his mother too harassed to console. Buses churned through the rain, their engines labouring up the hill to the bus station. A woman's voice nagged her husband as she passed the car – her husband didn't speak.

It wasn't like this the afternoon Danny Fowler died. Busy and wet and noisy. It must have been deserted, wet and quiet.

Images filled his head. A ship, ready to sail; the sailor and his girl. Danny, with his jazz-club background. Culver, Wright, Fowler.

At last, the queues grew shorter, until there was no one at the rank. Queue or taxi. The rain eased off, and everything dripped forlornly for a time.

A taxi appeared, its tyres hissing on the wet street, and Harry got out of the car.

'Sorry,' he said, when he got to the rank. 'I'm not a customer. I'd like to ask you some questions about Danny Fowler.' He produced the photograph.

'You the law?'

'Uh-huh,' Harry said. 'I'd like to know what he was like.'

'Like?'

'Yes. Did you know him?'

'Well enough. He was a good bloke.'

'I don't want a whitewash job just because he's dead,' Harry warned.

'Look, mate – he was an ordinary bloke with a wife and two kids.'

'Did you see him that afternoon?'

'No. I wasn't out.'

'Do you know if anyone saw who he picked up?'

'We've told you everything we know.'

Harry crouched down, his back aching from bending over. 'You've not told me,' he said.

Webb sat in the car, keeping the engine running so that he could have heat, but he had to run down the window now and then to let some air in, which rather defeated the object.

Grant had come back at one o'clock, with Sandra. He wondered a little about that. Grant had looked over at the car, and for a moment Webb had thought he was coming over. But he had just followed Sandra into the hotel.

Perhaps Lambert had been scared off – perhaps Ainsley had warned him. But then that rather depended on why he was here in the first place. And that's what Webb was going to find out.

Harry drove round to the Wellington a little wiser than when he'd started out. As the drivers had arrived back at the rank, they'd all given him snippets of information. Some he'd had to discount, but there emerged a picture of an ordinary family man with the usual impedimenta – a mortgage he could just afford, if he worked Sundays, a wife that he grumbled about no more and no less than any other man, two kids that he talked about, and who presented no especial problem.

He had picked up a man, they thought – no description worthy of the name, other than that he wasn't suspicious looking. So who was suspicious looking? Eliminate that man with the striped sweater and the bag marked swag because it wasn't him.

Fowler hadn't seemed nervous or excited. He had just been doing his job. It had happened on his way back from Harmouth, on the waste ground by the old prom. He must have been flagged down by whoever did it, the other drivers said. He couldn't pick up in Harmouth, so he wouldn't have had a passenger.

He wouldn't pick up, Harry thought. But he might have given a lift to someone he knew. Culver opened the security door to someone he knew.

Culver was in Amblesea on New Year's Eve. The taxi driver died in Amblesea on New Year's Eve.

Harry switched off his windscreen wipers as the rain died away, and drove into the Wellington car park, pulling the car over to the far side, under the canopy.

As he got out of the car, he was grabbed from behind and pushed back against a pillar with a force that left him gasping for breath. Before he could recover, a blow sent him sprawling to the ground.

He looked up to see Webb standing over him, and scrambled to his feet, his fists clenched.

'That's right, Lambert,' Webb said. 'Hit me. Assaulting a police officer in the execution of his duty as well as impersonating one.'

Harry lowered his hands.

'That's better.' Webb took a step forward. 'You tried to make a fool of me, Lambert.'

'I succeeded.'

'What are you doing here?'

Harry gingerly felt his chin. 'Private enquiries,' he said, still breathless. 'I practically told you.'

'What sort of enquiries?'

'Matrimonial.' He brushed his hair back with his hand.

'I don't believe you, Lambert. How come you've got a photograph of Culver?'

'Because Mrs Culver is my client.'

Webb shook his head.

'Ring her up,' Harry said, hoping that Mrs C. would come through if Webb took him up on it. 'Ask her.'

'The man's dead! Why would she care now?'

Harry sat down on the low wall. 'She has some property that she wants to return,' he said. 'It's private. Nothing to do with you.'

'Why didn't you just tell me that?'

'Because I was enjoying myself.'

Webb took a threatening step towards him, and Harry got to his feet.

'I don't think you should stay in Amblesea, Lambert.'

Harry sat down again. 'Are you running me out of town?' he asked. 'You've seen too many John Wayne movies.'

'You can stay here as long as you like,' Webb said. 'I can't stop you.' He started to walk away, and turned back. 'But you had better be very, very law-abiding. If I see you so much as looking as if you might be going to think about spitting in the street, I'll have you.' He walked briskly to his car and drove away.

A cloud of exhaust fumes hung in the cold, damp air, and Harry got up slowly. He walked into the hotel, straight to the bar, where he drank earnestly and steadily, ignoring the barman's overt disapproval.

The shutters were being pulled down before it had even taken effect, and he decided to take a bottle to his room for company. So, he asked for a bottle.

And that was what caused the trouble.

TWELVE

'Have you given him a lift key?' Annie asked Christine. The key that allowed you to take the lift to the basement. The key that allowed you to come in *by* the basement.

'No. What if I had? You gave Gerald one!'

'Gerald wasn't a thief! Do you make a habit of giving him money?'

'It's *my* money – I'll do what I bloody like with it!'

'Don't you use language—'

The intercom buzzed, and Annie jabbed her finger on to the button. 'Yes!' she shouted.

'Mrs Maddox?' Sandra said, shyer than ever. 'Sammy says can you please go to the bar? It's Mr Lambert. Sammy's having some trouble.'

Annie closed her eyes. She didn't believe it. 'That's all I need,' she said, snapping off the intercom. 'That's *all* I bloody need!'

She was speaking to an empty room.

Christine barely smiled at Sandra, as she went out into the wet afternoon. She needed to think. She didn't know what to say to Pete. She couldn't face him, not yet.

Harry's jacket lay draped across a bar stool, rather as though he had evaporated. Sammy the barman, agitated and flushed, spoke in a stage whisper.

'I said the bar was closed, but he kept saying he was a resident – he'd been drinking a lot. And Sandra says he isn't in the

109

register, so—'

Annie lifted up a guilty hand. 'My fault,' she said. 'I was supposed to book him in, and I forgot. Sorry.' She looked around. 'He's not here, Sammy,' she pointed out.

'In there.' Sammy pointed to the double doors leading to the games room, still speaking in a whisper. 'I told him it was closed, and there was no one in there, but he said I had to tell you that he fancied a game of snooker.'

'Did he indeed?'

'I was just closing up the bar, and he said he wanted a half-bottle of whisky. I didn't know he was a resident, and I thought – well, I said no, because I didn't want to get into trouble.'

Annie picked up Harry's jacket. 'You'd better let me have the whisky,' she said, leaning over the bar and unhooking two glasses. She walked to the double doors of the games room. 'On my bill,' she said, and pushed open the door.

Harry was standing by the open window, his back to her.

'It's too hot,' he said, without turning round.

'No it's not,' Annie said. 'It's freezing.' She put the bottle and glasses on the table by the window. 'With the management's compliments,' she said. 'And apologies. I forgot to register you.'

'So I'd gathered.'

Little drops of rain flecked the shiny paint of the window-sill. Harry still hadn't looked at her.

'I'm sorry,' she said. 'But a lot's happened since I saw you last.'

'You're telling me,' Harry muttered.

'I've said I'm sorry.'

'It's got nothing to do with that!' Harry slammed the window shut.

'What, then? What's making you so angry?'

'Nothing. It doesn't matter.' He turned, and she saw that his chin was red and slightly swollen. 'I'd better go,' he said. 'I'm not very good company.'

'I'm not expecting you to tell jokes.' She poured out two whiskies. 'What happened to you?'

'Webb,' he said.

'Oh.' Annie felt as though that had been a hundred years ago. 'I hope you don't think I told him.'

'No.' Harry pushed open the window again, and took a deep breath, releasing it slowly. 'He said he could do me for impersonating a police officer,' he said, his voice light, and so quiet that Annie could only just hear. But then he wasn't speaking to her.

'*Me*,' he whispered, turning to her. 'I *am* a police officer, Annie,' he said. 'It's *all* I am.' His eyes looked into hers, but he wasn't seeing her. When he became aware of her, he turned back to the window, embarrassed, and his head suddenly drooped down. 'You don't know what it's like,' he said. 'You can't.'

'No,' she said.

'All you have to do is say you're police, and you get a reaction,' he said. 'Sometimes it's relief, sometimes it's fear, sometimes they run away. God knows, these days, sometimes they *shoot* you, but they react. They *react*. And I can't bear not having that any more.'

Annie put out a tentative hand, wanting to comfort him, to help him. He turned, and she drew her hand back, too late.

'Does Webb make a habit of punching people?' he asked.

'I shouldn't think so,' said Annie.

'After all,' he said, picking up his whisky, 'I'm not the first person to leave Amblesea a bit bruised.'

'Tom didn't even know Gerald,' Annie said. 'But you found that out for yourself, didn't you? When you were doing your bit of acting.'

Harry grunted. 'I'm not the only one who can act.'

'That was a rotten thing to do.'

'He'll survive,' Harry said, taking a gulp of whisky.

'To *me*!'

'Yes,' he conceded. 'It was, a bit.' He pressed the glass to his lips. 'How long have you known Webb?' he asked. 'How come

111

he never met Culver? He seems very at home here.'

'Tom only came to Harmouth last May,' Annie replied, ignoring his final remark.

Harry didn't comment.

'What did you do?' Annie asked. 'How did you lose your job?'

'I hit someone too,' he said, finishing the whisky in two gulps, and pouring himself another. 'It must be an occupational hazard.'

'Someone you were questioning?' Annie asked.

'Someone whose ability I was questioning,' he said.

'A superior officer?'

'An inferior officer,' he said. 'Who happened to have a higher rank.' He took out his cigarettes. 'I knocked him down,' he said, with a sudden grin. 'And like the little gentlemen we are, we all agreed that I should resign.' He exhaled smoke. 'Mind, they'd agreed that I could resign before I ever hit him,' he said. 'I was never flavour of the month.'

'So you just made it easy for them,' Annie said.

'That's about it.' He went over to the snooker table.

'Don't smoke near the table,' Annie said, automatically.

'Sorry,' he said, bowing a little. He came back to the window-sill and stood the cigarette on its filter tip. He drank most of his whisky, and picked up the bottle. 'More?' he said to her.

'No thanks,' she said.

Harry gave himself a generous measure, and carried it to the table. He picked up the cue ball and sent it spinning up the table, scattering the reds.

'What are you going to do?' she asked.

He shook his head, picking up one of the reds as it rolled back down to him. 'I don't know,' he said, sending it gently along the green baize to join its fellows. 'I'm not taking any ex-policeman jobs.'

'Do you know about anything else?'

Harry came back, and picked up his cigarette. He didn't reply.

'What did you do when you weren't being a policeman?' she asked.

'Nothing. I was never not being a policeman.'

'You must have done something when you weren't actually working,' she said. 'A hobby, or sport, or something.'

Harry threw his cigarette out of the window. 'You mean did I open for the Murder Squad Eleven?' he asked.

'I'm trying to be constructive,' Annie said. 'I can't get your job back.'

'No,' he said, finishing his drink. He walked back over to the snooker table. 'No, you can't,' he said, taking a savage swipe at the table, sending balls everywhere. 'You can't,' he said again.

'You have to live with it,' she said, going over to him. 'What's the alternative?'

'God knows. This.' He drained his glass and waved it at her. 'Another little drink, bartender.'

It was pointless to advise against it; Annie poured a modest one, and took it to him.

'Why did you let him use you?' Harry asked.

'If you mean Gerald,' she said, 'I don't believe he did use me. No more than everyone uses everyone else.'

Harry shook his head. 'He was up to something,' he said. 'He involved Rosemary Wright. And she's dead. He involved you.'

Annie could feel the dread welling up. 'I don't believe that,' she said.

'Don't you?' Harry shook his cigarette packet disbelievingly, as he always did when it was empty. 'Then why did he come here without telling you?'

'I don't think he did – I think you're wrong.'

'Why didn't you tell me about that taxi driver?' he asked, suddenly.

'I didn't tell you because I didn't think it had anything to do with it!'

'Don't give me that,' he said. 'A town this size, and suddenly two people are stabbed to death?'

'It wasn't *like* that! Gerald didn't die here, and lots of taxi drivers had been attacked – everyone thought that this was another one. Everyone still does,' she added. 'Except you, I take it.'

113

'And you, Annie. Don't tell me you haven't thought of it, because I can tell you have. Culver took a taxi from here to Harmouth station – and his taxi would be coming back to Amblesea just when Fowler's was.'

Yes, of course, Annie had thought of it. But she had put it out of her mind. Dismissed it as a coincidence. 'Not then,' she said. 'Not when you were here before.'

'I've spoken to the drivers,' Harry said. 'Culver must have taken Fowler's taxi. And you know that.' He leant his elbows on the table. 'Was that why Webb was interested in Pete Ainsley?' he asked.

'Yes,' said Annie. 'But he was with Christine when it happened.' She wasn't sure the statement carried the conviction that it should.

'Anything else happen that I should know about?' he asked. 'The day Culver was here, I mean?'

'That you should know about?' Annie said. 'What makes you think you should know about anything?'

Harry shook his cigarette packet again. 'Do you have a cigarette machine?' he asked.

'In the bar,' she said.

'When did the car go?'

'It was in the car park at quarter past three.'

'When did Culver arrive, did you say?'

'About half past three.'

'By taxi?'

'I suppose so. I don't really know.'

'Did Culver usually come by train?' he asked.

'Quite often.' She began to retrieve the scattered balls, and set them up again, for something to do. 'Why?'

'When he did, he'd be in Harmouth before and after seeing you.'

'Yes.'

Harry nodded. The brown ball had inadvertently gone in the pocket. He fished it out, and began rolling it against the cushion again. 'So he could have dealt with any business he had in

Harmouth at the same time as coming to see you?'

Annie stopped what she was doing. 'Business?' she asked. 'Illegal business, do you mean?'

'Why not?' Harry pulled a handful of change from his pocket. 'Do you have a cigarette machine?' he asked.

'That's what you mean when you say he was using me? That I was some sort of front?'

'It would have been ideal,' Harry said. 'If anyone ever queried his trips to Harmouth, they'd find you. And they'd all be frightfully discreet, and wouldn't dream of telling tales out of school. And they'd stop asking questions.'

The booze was beginning to have an effect, and Annie watched as he tried unsuccessfully to count out his change. He shrugged, and gave up.

'It's a busy port,' he said. 'Foreign ships – Rosemary Wright's husband is a sailor.'

He tried again to count the change, making little piles of coins on the edge of the snooker table. 'Maybe he was doing a spot of drug dealing.'

'Drugs?' Annie said, astonished. 'You think Gerald was mixed up with *drugs*?'

'Rosemary Wright could have been some sort of go-between. Fowler could have sold it on the street.'

'But that's ridiculous!' She gathered up the reds. 'One day,' she said, as they jostled and clicked together, 'when thinking about Gerald doesn't make me cry, this conversation will make me laugh.'

Harry leant on the table. 'Cry?' he said. 'Why would you cry for someone like him? He was no good, Annie.'

'You don't know anything about him! And you won't listen to what people say.'

'You don't know what people have said to me about Culver.'

'That's just it! I do know. No one has told you anything bad about Gerald.'

'Nothing bad,' Harry said, picking up his piles of silver. 'Just that he was a liar, a cheat, and a coward – and you're the one who told me that.'

'That's how you choose to interpret what I've said.'

'Not one of his cronies even knows you exist,' Harry said. 'Not one. He was ashamed of you.'

'He didn't want to hurt his wife,' she said.

'Were you ever in that flat?'

She shook her head.

'It was available,' he said. 'All the time.' He poured himself yet another drink, splashing the table. 'But someone might have seen you. And he had an image to maintain. He had a wife and children, and a constituency and voters. He had a position in society. He couldn't let you bugger it all up.'

'My God,' Annie said. 'You're jealous. You're jealous of him.'

He swayed slightly. 'Do you think I want to live like that?' he asked. 'Do you think I want a flat with a security lock and a house I never see and a wife I need to escape from? Do you? Do you think I want that?'

'I think you want me,' she replied.

'I'll tell you this,' Harry said. 'If I had you, everyone would know about it. I wouldn't hide you away and try to give you up like a bad habit.' He put his drink down carefully. 'He didn't want you,' he said. 'He wanted an alibi.'

'He didn't want me,' Annie answered. 'Not the way you mean. I think he only went to bed with me because it was the convention. We were friends – he liked being here, he liked the way we were. But that would have hurt his wife much more, don't you see? Everyone understands sex – even you. But we were friends.'

'Until when?' Harry demanded. 'Until Webb came, and started drinking here? Is that when Culver suddenly got concerned about his wife?'

Annie backed away. 'I don't want to hear this,' she said.

'I know, pet. But you mentioned Webb in one of those letters, and you've got to face facts. He *was* here – Rosemary Wright saw him here. Or do you think it's just a coincidence that she

116

was stabbed to death too?'

Annie shook her head. 'No, no – but—'

'But what? He's here on New Year's Eve, and his taxi driver gets stabbed to death. St Gerald is just an innocent bystander?'

'Yes! All right, it's coincidence. Because Gerald wasn't crooked.'

'What about you?' he asked. 'Where were you when all this was going on?'

'You know where I was. I was here.'

'Were you? Maybe you were with him. Maybe you went to see him off at the station. Maybe you were in the taxi.'

There was very little fight left in Annie. 'I was *here*,' she said weakly. 'Ask Sandra if you don't believe me.' She remembered that that was why he had gone out in the first place. 'Did you see her?'

'No,' he said. 'She wasn't in. Do you have a cigarette machine?'

'In the bar!' she shouted, and he went off in search of cigarettes.

Annie couldn't make him see the Gerald she had known; the gentle, quiet man that she had loved. A little vain, a little weak. But not a crook.

The door opened, and Harry came back, stumbling a little through the door, discarding the cellophane from his cigarettes.

She didn't want to hear any more of his theories on Gerald. She looked at the table.

'Why didn't you tell Webb about me?' he asked. 'Why did you let me go on?'

Annie's shoulders drooped a little. 'I don't know,' she said.

'I do.'

She felt his hand on her breast, his lips on her neck. 'What do you think you're doing?' she asked.

'I think I'm making a pass at you,' he said.

'Then don't.'

'Oh, come on,' he said. 'That's what you came in here for.'

'Out,' she said, turning to face him.

117

'You didn't show Gerald the red card,' he said.

'Out of this hotel. Now.'

He looked at her as steadily as he could with all that scotch inside him, and nodded, just once, as though his head was too heavy.

'All right,' he said, picking up his jacket. 'All right. But you can tell your friend Webb that I'm not finished. And I'll show him which of us is impersonating a police officer.'

THIRTEEN

Harry crossed the wet tarmac, his face screwed up against the misty drizzle, his jacket over his arm. As he drew closer to his car, he could see Christine sitting on the low wall, looking at the rain.

'Are you hiding from your mother, too?' he asked.

'Yes,' she said.

'I don't blame you,' Harry said, sitting down heavily beside her. 'I don't understand her.' He was aware that the words were slurring, and that he was trying too hard to correct it. 'I don't understand her at all. Why would a woman like that be content to bury herself alive in this one-horse place just so that some smoothie could—' He finished the sentence with a dismissive wave of his hand, and a grunt.

'Gerald was all right,' Christine said.

'Oh God, not you as well,' Harry groaned. 'I thought I could rely on you if no one else.'

'Rely on me to do what?'

'Tell the truth about St Gerald,' Harry said. 'Let the cat out of the bag, spill the beans, blow the whistle.' He smiled at his own cleverness. 'Take the lid off,' he added.

'Take the lid off what?' she asked, her eyes amused. 'What *do* you think Gerald was doing?'

'God knows,' Harry said, sticking a cigarette into his mouth, and waving the packet at Christine before putting it down on the wall. He took out his lighter, and pointed it at Christine. 'People *die*,' he said, the cigarette in his mouth moving up and down with the words. 'People die when they get mixed up with St

Gerald.' He flicked the lighter. 'St Gerald,' he said carefully, 'was a very gregarious martyr.'

It hadn't been easy, given that his tongue felt as though it belonged to someone else and that he had had to stop the cigarette falling out, but it had been very telling. He'd say it again.

'St Gerald,' he began, as the lighter flared, 'was a very—' He puffed at the cigarette, but he couldn't make it light. He moved the lighter nearer, scorching the side of the cigarette. 'A very—' He broke off, blinking. What was he saying?

Christine was watching him with a smile. 'You can't think Gerald was doing something wrong,' she said.

'Why not?' Harry coughed.

'Because Gerald would never have done anything that could damage his reputation,' she said. 'Never.'

'Then why was he scr—' Harry stopped himself before using the expression that had risen to his lips. 'Seeing your mother?' he amended.

'I don't really know.' Christine shrugged. 'He didn't see her, really. Not often. I mean – it was a joke, him coming to call it off. He hadn't seen her since April as it was.'

'Why? Why did she put up with it? Huh? Why did she let him call all the shots?'

'She's like that,' Christine said. 'She has to have someone – she isn't cut out to be on her own. Dad died, and, well, I suppose Gerald came along when she needed him.'

'And you didn't mind?'

'Yes, of course I minded!' Christine picked up his cigarette packet. 'Of course I minded,' she repeated, holding his hand steady as he lit her cigarette.

She was, he thought approvingly, a very pretty girl.

'Dad had been dead a year,' she said. 'But I was hurt, I suppose. I called her names, and I told her she was being unfaithful to Dad – the usual thing.'

Harry leant forward. 'And who talked you round?' he asked. 'Tell me that. Who talked you round? St Gerald, that's who.'

120

'No one. I just came round.' She smiled. 'You couldn't object to Gerald for very long.'

'I could have.'

'Perhaps. I just grew up a bit, I think.'

Harry crushed out his unsuccessful cigarette on the stonework, smearing ash and strands of tobacco across the wall, sending a little shower of sparks over his jacket.

'What about when he called it off?' he asked, brushing his jacket sleeve, peering at it to see if it had been burned. 'In July, wasn't it? When he came and finished it? What did you think about that?'

'I just said. It was a joke.' But she wasn't laughing. 'Mum was upset,' she said. 'So for that reason I was sorry it had happened. But other than that, I didn't honestly have an opinion. I'd just met Pete – I wasn't really thinking about anyone else's love life.' She gave an apologetic smile. 'I know that sounds selfish,' she said. 'It is, I suppose. But Mum and I kind of keep out of each other's business. Usually,' she added.

'But not today?' He decided his jacket was all right.

'It's Pete,' she said. 'She's found out he's been in trouble with the police.' She looked up. 'It was a long time ago,' she said angrily.

'Don't blame me,' he said.

'Just because of that they think he had something to do with this taxi driver.'

'And that's why you're sitting out here in the rain?'

'Yes and no. I was going to go to Pete's, but I don't want any more rows. I've had enough for one day.'

'Why should you have a row with him? Do you think he did have something to do with the taxi driver?'

'No. But I think he did something else. Something stupid.' She dropped her cigarette to the ground and stood on it, while Harry lit another.

'I think he stole Mr Grant's car,' she said.

'Why would he want to do that?' Harry asked.

She looked up. 'Because of Lesley,' she said.

'Who's Lesley?'

She leaned back on the pillar, and seemed glad to have someone to talk to. 'Lesley was Pete's girlfriend before me.'

'Oh. Your Mum mentioned something . . .'

The lights began to come on in the car park, the glow just touching her face, and the soft blonde hair that framed it. She was beautiful, Harry realised, and he wondered what she saw in Pete.

'She was more than his girlfriend,' she said. 'She lived with him. She worked at Wetherill's, and then Grant advertised for a secretary, and she went to work for him. She'd been there for about three months when she walked out on Pete and got her own flat.'

'And he blames Grant?'

'He paid well,' she said. 'And she got friendly with the Grants. Mrs Grant sometimes gave her clothes and things. I think she just wanted a better kind of life than Pete was offering. But he's convinced Grant was having an affair with her.' A sad little smile appeared. 'It's quite likely – he tries it on with everyone. And she wouldn't say no, from what I've heard.' She sighed. 'Pete felt sorry for her, I think. She wasn't very happy at home, and she drifted until she met him. I think he thinks she owes him something.' Another half-hearted smile flitted across her face.

'When did she leave Pete?' Harry asked.

'Just about a year ago,' Christine said. 'And then about six months later Grant sort of retired. So Lesley lost her job, and she left Amblesea altogether. That's when I met Pete.'

'And you're telling me he still hasn't got over it?' Harry laughed. 'With you to help him? She must be quite a girl. Have you met her?'

'No,' Christine said, and gave a grudging laugh. 'I've seen a photo, though. I even look like her. I got him on the rebound, all right.'

'Why didn't you throw him back?' Harry asked.

Christine didn't rise to the bait as Annie would have done.

'You don't think much of our taste in men, do you?' she said.

'Not a lot.'

'But you've only met Pete once – and you never knew Gerald at all.'

'True. When was Pete in trouble with the law?'

'Just after he came out of the army – just after he met Lesley. She was a bad influence. She's older than him, you know.'

'Well,' he said. 'I don't know if it helps, but Pete was here this morning, looking for you.'

'Pete was?' Suddenly, she looked happy.

Because they are young and in lo-o-ve, thought Harry, sourly. He stood up. 'It's been very nice talking to you, Christine, but I'd better be on my way.'

'You're not driving?'

'Well, I've been kicked out – if I was ever in – so, yes. I'm driving.'

'I don't think you should,' she said.

Harry frowned. There was nothing wrong with him. 'Why not?' he asked.

'You've had a bit too much to drink,' she said crisply. 'Give me your keys.'

'What for?'

'I'll drive you over to Pete's. You can stay there until morning.' She held out her hand.

Harry delved in his pocket. 'I never could resist pretty women,' he said, handing her the keys. 'But won't he mind?'

'No.'

'Anyway,' he said, as he got in. 'I thought you didn't want to see him.'

'So did I,' she said, doing up her seat belt. 'What's this?' She picked up an envelope. 'It's addressed to Mum,' she said. 'Sort of.'

'Oh – it must have fallen out of my jacket,' Harry said.

'What are you doing with Mum's letter?'

'Relax,' he said. 'She wrote directions on the back for me.' She handed him the envelope.

Harry stared at it. 'It's *not* a letter,' he said.

'No. It's one of these catalogue things. Are there any rituals to perform when starting this car?'

'That's not what I mean,' Harry said. 'I mean you called it a letter, but it's not.'

'Forget it,' Christine said. 'I'll manage without your help, 'I'm sure.'

The car started, and Christine backed out. Harry dragged his thoughts away from the letter and back to Christine as she drove out of the car park.

'Sorry?' he said. 'What were you asking me?'

'Why didn't you stick one on him?' Pete wanted to know.

Christine looked across at Harry, who had sobered up at last.

'Let's say he persuaded me not to,' Harry replied.

'You'd be better off investigating him,' Pete said sourly, and Christine closed her eyes. Not this again.

'Oh?'

'Don't you know about the bribery business?'

'What – Webb?'

'No!' Christine said impatiently. She had heard Pete on this subject more times than she could count. 'Mr Grant. They were going to prosecute him – something to do with bribing councillors.'

'Going to,' Pete said heavily. 'They had it all set up. But Webb suddenly arrives in Harmouth, doesn't he? And he takes over the enquiry. Suddenly, the police offer no evidence, and the whole thing's slung out. It stinks.'

Harry nodded. 'You think he was bought off?'

'Someone was.' Pete turned to Christine. 'And you tell me your mother *fancies* him?'

Christine laughed. 'I think she fancied her chances with him, anyway,' she said. 'He's nice-looking, and single. Why not?'

'*I'm* nice-looking and single,' Pete said with a grin. 'She doesn't fancy me.'

'You're too modest for her,' Christine said.

Harry lay awake on the sofa-bed, listening to the low voices from the bedroom, as they discussed something deep into the night.

Could Culver somehow have been involved in the bribery? Did *he* call Webb off? Why couldn't he have been at the Ministry of Trade or the Home Office or somewhere? The man was always at the wrong ministry.

The murmured conversation finally stopped, and Harry drifted off into a dead, dreamless sleep.

FOURTEEN

Slowly, Annie was beginning to pick up the threads of her life.

It was a grey February afternoon, with a cold wind blowing off the sea, as she took her routine walk along the pebbled beach. It still helped to watch the world get along without Gerald's presence in it; it still reassured her to see the sun go down, to watch the tides ebb and flow.

Harry Lambert seemed to have been called off at last – or he'd called himself off, if he was to be believed that he was no longer employed by Mrs Culver. The curious coincidence of Rosemary Wright seemed to have been just that, and the police had not come knocking on Annie's door.

But Gerald's death remained a mystery, something still exercising the minds of the tabloid journalists. Annie's relief at their ignorance of her existence was qualified by the hurtful truth which Lambert had forced her to concede – that they knew nothing about her because Gerald had told no one. No one at all.

But then, she argued with herself, there were people in Amblesea who knew, and who had not cashed in on their knowledge. Who was to say that Gerald hadn't also confided in someone? Her knowledge of Gerald argued back. Gerald had kept her a secret, it told her. Gerald wouldn't have jeopardised his marriage and all that went with it by so much as telling the cat.

Still, she thought, she had chosen to accept that, and it was surely not worth getting upset about it now.

And the police seemed to have given up trying to say that Pete had been involved in that taxi driver's murder. The taxi driver was another coincidence, she told herself stoutly.

I don't believe in coincidence. Lambert's clipped Tyneside tones still echoed in her mind, but more faintly now.

And perhaps there was a slight suspicion lingering on that Christine had not told the truth. Perhaps.

'Mr Culver never brought you here?'

As promised, she was at last having dinner with Grant in a suitably exclusive, expensive restaurant in Harmouth. Annie hadn't known such prices existed outside London.

'No,' she said, sipping her wine. 'We couldn't often go out anywhere.'

'Of course not,' he said.

Annie dropped her eyes from his.

'I'm sorry,' he said. 'Does talking about Mr Culver distress you?'

'No,' she said. 'Not really.'

'I can't understand why I never met him,' he said. 'I don't miss much of what goes on at the hotel.'

Annie smiled. 'We did try to keep a low profile,' she said.

'Yes. You were very successful.'

It wasn't too difficult, Annie thought, as the waiter took their empty starter plates. Grant smiled, but it was a cold smile, Annie thought.

'Not, I think, a very satisfactory arrangement,' he said. 'I don't imagine you saw much of one another?'

Suddenly, everyone was an expert on her and Gerald. 'No,' she said. 'He couldn't often get away.'

'And yet,' he said, 'he was very important to you?'

The waiter appeared at her elbow with the next course, and Annie was rapidly losing her appetite.

'Yes,' she replied.

'It must all be very distressing for you,' he said. 'Especially in the circumstances.'

Annie smiled wanly.

'Having to keep it hidden,' he persisted.

'Yes,' she said, playing with the food on her plate. Three more courses of this and she'd be a nervous wreck.

'But Mr Lambert was here professionally, wasn't he?' Grant asked.

Annie's head shot up. 'Lambert?' she said.

'Yes – I believe he's a private enquiry agent?'

How Harry would have hated that, Annie thought. 'Yes,' she said, vindictively.

'I've been making a few enquiries of my own,' he said. 'It seems that Mr Lambert was with Scotland Yard, but resigned in inverted commas.'

Annie drank some more wine. 'Did he?' she said. She wished she had never agreed to come here.

'Not a very savoury character, I think.'

'He seemed all right,' Annie said grudgingly, annoyed with herself for feeling indignant for Harry Lambert of all people. But while he was undoubtedly insensitive and ill-mannered, he wasn't as bad as all that.

'Am I right in thinking that he knows about you and Mr Culver?' he asked.

Annie's heart sank. 'Yes,' she said. 'Is this why you invited me here?'

'No!' he said, shocked. 'Not at all. But I did want to know – you see, you said no one knew.'

'Lambert's gone,' Annie said. 'He won't be back.'

'I do hope so,' said Grant. 'But you did say that no one knew. That wasn't quite true, was it?'

Annie swallowed some of whatever it was that she was eating. It could have been cotton wool. 'It wasn't a lie,' she said. 'I meant that no one knew who would make it public.'

'Well,' he said, smiling again. 'It's a small matter. What matters is you. We must help you get over this, Mrs Maddox.'

Pete had had to tell Chris. He'd said something that had made her suspicious, and he had had to tell her what he'd been doing.

'Is that everything?' she asked, angry with him.

128

It wasn't everything. Not quite. But it was as much confession as his soul could stand for the moment. 'Yes,' he said.

They were in his flat; it was quiet and peaceful with the Magicoal fire flickering.

'Why did you tell me it was over?'

'Because it was. She wouldn't even see me.'

Christine lit a cigarette, and he didn't dare tell her off this time.

'It was over as far as she was concerned,' Christine said. 'But you still wanted her back, didn't you?'

'Yes,' he said. 'But I don't any more. I want you.'

'Because I remind you of her?'

Maybe, maybe, Pete thought. But he didn't *want* to be reminded of her, not any more.

'All I want,' he said, 'is to get a job and settle down with you, and have kids.'

She looked at him, eyebrows arched.

'It's true, Chris, honestly. That's what I want now. Not Lesley.'

'It's a fantasy,' she said. 'That isn't how it would be if we got married.'

'You don't think I can get a job, do you?'

'You'd get the odd labouring job on building sites. But I'd be the one with the job. And if we did have children, we'd be scratching round for money, all the time. And we'd have rows all the time.'

God. Women were supposed to be romantic.

'The funny thing is,' she went on. 'I don't think I'd mind it all that much. But you would.'

'It wouldn't be like that!'

'Why not? Are you going to turn into someone else?'

'I can get a job – and stick to it.'

'And hate it, and blame me.' She paused. 'And think how much better everything would have been if only Lesley hadn't gone,' she said.

'I wouldn't think that.' He sighed. 'Have you ever heard of dreams, Chrissie? They're things other people have.'

'They don't believe in them. They stay where they belong – in their heads. You're not going to turn into a pipe and slippers husband and father, Pete.'

'That doesn't mean I'd be a bad husband and father.'

'I didn't say it did! But you have to be realistic.'

'Do I?' He pulled a face. 'You said you'd marry me,' he reminded her.

'I probably will,' she said.

Grant's car still smelt new. It was cold, after the warmth of the restaurant, but its efficient heater remedied that before they were out of Harmouth.

'Is everything all right, Mrs Maddox?' he asked.

'Yes, thank you.' She tried to sound surprised, as though there was nothing wrong at all.

'You seem very quiet. And you really didn't eat very much.'

'No, really. I'm fine,' she repeated, a shade irritably. 'Sorry,' she said.

They were passing the yellow fronts of Indian take-aways, and she was feeling slightly sick.

'Do you like the car?' he asked.

'Yes,' she said. 'It's lovely.'

'It'll do,' he said. 'For the moment. I expect Karen will like it.'

Annie tried to think of more small talk, but she couldn't, and the sudden burst of conversation ceased. As the uncomfortable silence reigned again, she stared straight ahead, wishing she was at home, that this evening was over.

At last, they were pulling into the car park, and she could see the end in sight, like a mountaineer glimpsing the summit, and knowing that the worst was yet to come.

Grant ushered her through the door of the hotel, his hand resting lightly on her back.

The foyer was dark except for the night porter's dim light. He sat by the desk, reading the *Sun*, and glanced up incuriously as they passed the desk.

In the corridor, they stopped at Annie's door. Annie smiled

nervously at him.

'Thank you,' Grant said. 'It was a most enjoyable evening.'

She couldn't just let him go like that, she thought. He had gone to a lot of trouble. She cleared her throat. 'Would . . . would you like to come in for a coffee?' she asked, hearing her voice shaking, hating herself for feeling such a fool. 'Or a brandy, perhaps?' she added desperately. That might be quicker.

'Might I have both?' he asked with a smile.

'Yes, of course,' Annie said.

It didn't sound enthusiastic, but he didn't seem to notice. He chatted to her as she made coffee, but she wasn't really listening.

'Thank you,' he said, taking the cup.

Annie sat down. 'It's a lovely restaurant,' she said, inanely.

'One of my favourites,' he answered. 'Harmouth is a very interesting town,' he added. 'There are such contrasts. It has a very long history.'

'Yes,' Annie said. 'So I believe.'

'Do you know Harmouth well?' he asked.

'No – I . . . I've neglected the local—' She couldn't think of any word at all to complete the sentence. She could hear the slight stammer that had haunted her in her teens.

'You must let me take you to the interesting places,' he said. 'It was a naval dockyard in Drake's day, you know.'

Why couldn't she just talk to the man? Why did she feel like a schoolgirl on her first date? Because, she assumed, this hadn't happened to her since she went out with Eddie, and not very often then. No one had taken her out, wined and dined her, brought her home, not for twenty years. At eighteen, she had known where she stood. She had known the rules, and the conventions. She didn't know what to expect from Grant, or what was expected of her, and she was afraid of making a fool of herself.

Grant spoke about Harmouth, and Amblesea. He told her about the plans that the developers had for the promenade. He seemed easy and relaxed, and her face was burning with tongue-tied embarrassment. He drank his coffee, he smoked his cigar, and finally, he finished his brandy and got to his feet.

'Thank you again,' he said, taking her hand, and pressing it to his lips. 'It was a delightful evening.'

Annie went with him to the door. 'Thank you,' she said, as he walked to the stairs. He paused on his way up to lift his hand in salute. 'Good night,' he said.

Annie closed the door, and almost fell on to the sofa in sheer relief that it was over.

Tom Webb had paid his public relations visit to the exhibition, and left, relieved not to have bumped into Grant. He had looked around for Annie, wanting to heal the rift in his relations with her, but she wasn't around. In the fortnight since his run-in with Lambert, he'd had time to cool off, to reflect. It wasn't Annie's fault. Lambert had made a fool of him, and he had no one to blame for that but himself. But he hadn't believed that story about Culver's wife; Tom wondered just what Lambert's business was in Amblesea.

Perhaps he was working for Grant, or for one of Grant's old rivals, unhappy with the outcome of the abortive prosecution. Tom would feel a great deal happier if he knew who was really the subject of his investigations.

He remembered his first meeting with the Grants, when he had had to take over the bribery enquiry.

He had been on his best behaviour; polite, deferential, courteous. And he had been so aware of being caught in the middle of Grant's hostility and his wife's frank and flattering interest.

Karen Grant had set out to bewitch him, and she had succeeded. He had made a gaffe by remarking on Grant's accent, and Karen had told him later that he mustn't let her husband worry him. His bark, she had assured him, was much worse than his bite.

Tom had the uncomfortable feeling that he would soon be putting Karen's theory to the test.

★★★

Sandra had indeed liked the house all right once it was back in order. She wouldn't want to live there all the time, she had opined. It was not an option being extended to her, Grant decided, as, dressed and ready to leave, he waited impatiently while she attended to her face. Just like Karen. It was all they thought about.

He picked up a woman's magazine of Karen's that Sandra had left lying on the bed, and flicked through the pot-pourri of articles on dieting, fashion, multiple orgasm. He sighed.

'I am not the one who will be in trouble with Mrs Maddox,' he said, looking at his watch.

'It only takes five minutes to get there,' she said. 'Linda would hang on, anyway.'

'It's not fair to expect her to,' he said.

She clipped on the bracelet he had bought her that morning, and twisted round. 'Make up your mind,' she said. 'Do you want me in bed, or behind reception?'

'I think we would attract attention behind reception,' he said.

Grant rarely made jokes. Sandra smiled. 'See? You can loosen up when you try.'

'And you can hurry up!'

She zipped her make-up bag. 'I'm ready.'

'Good.'

Annie sat on a low rock, squinting into the bright winter sun, watching the men working on the pier.

She wondered what they were doing. The promenade development exhibition had taken place only the previous week, and now it looked as though someone was actually doing something instead of just talking about doing something. The papers had been full of it, with artist's impressions of what it was all going to look like. There was many a slip, of course, but if it did get done, it would be fun. A replica Victorian pleasure beach, with bathing machines, and ice-cream trikes – even gas lamps. Saucy postcards, fortune tellers – but with everyone in Victorian dress. A living museum. It sounded interesting.

Slowly, and a little shyly, Annie went along to the pier.

'Out for a walk, in this weather?' a strong Liverpool accent enquired.

'It's a nice day,' Annie argued. 'Just a bit cold.'

'A bit?' He came out of the gate and took out a tin of tobacco.

'Sorry,' he said, as Annie made to step on to the pier. 'It's just a temporary repair.' He was rolling a cigarette as he spoke. 'No one's allowed on it yet. They're going to see if it's worth trying to do something with it. About time,' he said. 'It's a disgrace, that.' He ran the tip of his tongue along the cigarette paper. 'It won't be all that safe when we've done,' he said. 'But they won't fall in the water if they're careful.' He lit the straggly tobacco at the end of his cigarette, and acrid smoke blew into Annie's face. 'As long as it stays like this,' he added, with a nod of his head towards the gently murmuring sea.

'It'll be nice, though,' said Annie. 'If they can do something with it.'

'I know what I'd do with it,' he said.

The big gates were standing wide open for the first time in years. The council van was parked just inside. 'Is that safe there?' she asked.

'Yes,' he said with obvious scorn at her ignorance. 'Solid, this bit.' He stamped his foot on the ground as proof. 'It's built on to the rock here,' he said. 'It's further down you're in trouble. *Apart* from the hole,' he added ominously.

Annie looked nostalgically along the pier, to the gaping hole being bridged. Before the tangle of wood and metal that marked the storm damage stood the old theatre, still relatively intact. Past the gap were the other romantic buildings of her childhood – the ice-cream parlour, the candy-floss stall, the Punch and Judy – so many memories. The very end of the pier had broken away during another storm, and there was no end of pier concert hall any more.

'We're finished for the day. My mate's in there.' He pointed to the theatre. 'He said he wanted to remember what it looked like,' he said, clearly finding this too eccentric for discussion.

The other man appeared then, shouting something, but he was too far away for them to hear. He came running with an odd, stumbling motion.

Annie and the first man glanced at each other, and back at him. Now they could see his face, his hand covering his nose and mouth.

'What the hell?'

They went to the other man, who was still half running, half falling.

'No,' he said, spreading his arms as though he could bar their way. 'Don't. Just get the police. Get the police – there's a body in there. God knows how long it's been there.'

FIFTEEN

Harry woke at lunchtime to the near-constant hangover that had become a part of his life. Drinking didn't really help, but if he drank all night it made him sleep all day, and it didn't matter so much that he had no work to go to.

Culver's puzzled but co-operative widow had told him that she had accompanied Culver during the last week of August, when he had been a member of a well publicised delegation of MPs touring the North to nod gravely at one another about inner-city decay, so he and Rosemary Wright had not met in August after all; Harry had felt his advantage over the Yard slipping away. And his sudden revelation about the letter had seemed so significant, but without the resources of the police, with no back-up or even encouragement, Harry had finally given up.

All right, he had thought. It's all just a coincidence. Bugger the lot of them.

He pulled on his clothes, and looked out at the quiet London street. He must get a job, he told himself. The money was running out, and he couldn't live like this for much longer. He ran a hand over his stubbled chin, and walked barefoot down the corridor to the kitchen, pulling the paper from the letterbox as he went. It wasn't his paper, but every now and then he struck lucky when the woman upstairs left early for work.

A packet of cigarettes lay open on the kitchen table. Harry took one and searched for his lighter, which he rescued from sliding irrecoverably down the side of the armchair. A lungful of smoke, a cough, and a cup of tea constituted Harry's breakfast

136

these days. He filled the kettle, dropped a teabag into a mug, laid the paper on the table, and scanned the headlines, turning the pages as he waited for the kettle to boil.

He made his tea. Damn Annie Maddox, he thought, then frowned, the mug half-way to his lips. What on earth made him think about Annie?

He'd seen something. He put down the steaming mug, and picked up the paper. He'd read the word Amblesea, just now. Somewhere in this newspaper there was an item about Amblesea. He turned the pages quickly, checking the headlines, but that didn't help. An advertisement? Maybe. He checked the ads quickly, then more carefully. Not an advertisement.

But damn it, he'd read the word 'Amblesea', he was sure of it. As he drank his tea, Harry started at the first page, and slowly, methodically, despite his throbbing head, he read enough of each and every item to establish that it did not mention Amblesea. And then, on page four, there it was: *Grisly Find for Workmen*.

He didn't stop to wash or shave. He barely stopped moving long enough to throw some things in a bag and put socks and shoes on. Harry was in his car, heading for Amblesea, trying not to think about what he might find.

Three thirty found Harry in the Wellington car park; the hotel was bathed in bright sunlight in the crisp, clear, cold afternoon. He heaved himself and his aching head out of the car and into the hotel.

Christine looked up with surprise, laid down her pen, and regarded him.

'You look terrible,' she said.

'Thanks.' He lifted his bag on to the desk. 'Is she in?' he asked, with a jerk of his head towards the door marked private.

Christine shook her head.

Harry rubbed his eyes. 'Well, am I allowed to wait?' he asked.

Christine sighed, and reached behind her for her handbag. 'Here,' she said, handing him a key. 'You can use my room.

Take the staff lift – third floor, third door on the right.'

'Thanks, pet.' Harry picked up his bag. 'You're a gent,' he said.

'I hope you've brought a razor,' she called after him.

Harry waved confirmation without turning round.

An hour later he was shaved, bathed, and wearing his change of clothing. Christine came in as he was getting ready to leave.

'All right?' he asked, presenting himself for inspection.

'Better,' she said candidly. 'What have you been doing to yourself?' She caught the sleeve of his jacket. 'That's hanging off you.'

'Right,' he said, ignoring her, and zipping the jacket up. 'I'm away to find lodgings now that I'm respectable.' He grinned and picked up his bag. 'Thanks, Christine, pet – I won't tell her if you don't.'

'You'd better not!' Christine said. 'She'd kill me.'

'Scout's honour.' He opened the door.

'Can I talk to you?' she asked suddenly.

Harry stopped in the doorway. 'Of course you can,' he said. 'What's up?'

She looked uncomfortable, obviously in two minds about speaking to him. 'Mum,' she said.

Harry closed the door. 'What about her?'

Christine sat down on the bed, and looked at her hands. 'You wouldn't—' She stopped and glanced up at him before dropping her eyes again, as if to check that he was still there. 'Will you talk to her?' she asked earnestly.

'What about?' asked Harry.

'Anything,' Christine said. 'Anything to stop her mooning about.'

'Annie?' he said. 'Mooning *about*?'

'Well, no, not really,' Christine began loyally, but then her lips came together in a defiant line. 'Yes, she is!' she said. 'She keeps going down to the beach and just walking about.'

'What for?' asked Harry, mystified.

'She says it helps her get over Gerald,' Christine explained. 'I can't say I've noticed.'

Harry sat down beside her. 'What do you want me to do about it?'

'You helped before,' Christine said.

'I got slung out,' he corrected.

'She'll turn into one of these loonies that walk about talking to themselves,' Christine muttered darkly.

Harry smiled. 'I doubt that,' he said.

'She was there when they found that body,' she said. 'And that's just made things worse.'

'It would,' Harry solemnly agreed. 'But I don't see what good you think I would do.'

'She's worrying me.'

'I can see that.' Harry rubbed his now smooth chin, and rather missed the stubble. 'Where is she?' he asked dubiously.

'She'll be at the beach. She really does go every afternoon, practically. Please, Harry.'

'She goes there to think about Culver, and you want me, of all people, to interrupt?'

'Yes.'

Harry stood up. 'All right,' he said. 'All right.' He picked up his bag, and walked to the door.

'Pretty women,' he muttered, on his way out.

Harry saw Annie, standing by a rock, keeping her distance from the pier, now firmly locked off with a constable on guard. He had asked around at the hotel about the body, but no one knew much. Just guesses and rumours.

Annie walked along the shore, then stopped again. He drove past and stopped, walking back down to where she stood by the sea wall.

'Hello,' he said, straddling the railing, 'I thought it was you.'

Annie didn't betray any knowledge of his presence.

'I happened to be passing,' he continued, in polite, sociable tones. 'And I thought, "Isn't that Mrs Maddox doing her Widow of Windsor impersonation?" I've always found that one particularly diverting.'

There was still no reaction.

'How are you?' he asked.

Annie shielded her eyes from the sun as she turned to look at him, and sat down on the wall. 'What are you doing here?' was her less than friendly response.

'The Grisly Find,' he said, nodding back towards the pier. 'Variously described as a skeleton, a body ...' He paused. 'Remains,' he said, his voice sepulchral.

'Stop it.'

'Well, whatever it is, it was in your pleasure pier, and it wasn't very pleasant.'

'What's it got to do with you?' she asked.

'I want to find out what's going on here,' he said.

'Lambert of the Dole Queue?'

It was meant to hurt, and it did.

She slid off the wall, and Harry lit a cigarette as she walked away over the pebbles. To hell with her, then, he thought. But Christine's worried face came into his mind, and he swung his leg over the railing, jumping with a crunch on to the beach.

'Don't you care who killed your boyfriend any more?' he called, above the sound of the surf and the gulls' cries. 'Do you just want to be in mourning for him?'

'I just want you to go away,' she said.

The freshening breeze lifted the end of her scarf, and it flapped against her face. She turned out of the wind, away from him.

'Did your husband rate all this?' he shouted.

She looked back, then walked away, going out of sight behind a cluster of rocks.

Harry zipped his jacket up further, and went after her.

'Did he?' he asked again, his voice too loud in the quiet rocky shelter. It wasn't so cold there, out of the breeze. 'Did you go into a decline for him?'

He leant against the rock, waiting for a reaction, but there wasn't one.

'Were you happily married?' he asked, after a moment.

140

'People said we were,' Annie replied.

He raised his eyebrows, surprised to have got an answer. 'But you didn't think so?' he said.

'I don't know.' She scooped up a handful of pebbles, and dropped one into a pool that had formed at the base of the rock. 'We married young.' There was a pause before she carried on. 'We grew very close,' she said. 'But I don't know that that's always a good thing.' Another pebble plopped into the water. 'Eddie and Annie,' she said. 'No one ever referred to us singly. We were Eddie and Annie, always.'

Two pebbles dropped in with tiny splashes. 'When Eddie died, I felt as though there ought to have been a physical change in me. As if I should have been walking with a limp.' Her fist clenched round the pebbles.

'Chrissie had just left school,' she said. 'We'd been running a pub in Cambridge, but the brewery wouldn't let me keep it on. Not on my own.'

Harry flicked his half-smoked cigarette into the rock pool, where it landed with a hiss.

'I saw this job advertised,' she said.

She walked past him out on to the beach and up towards the promenade, the breeze ruffling her hair. She looked over the railings at the emptiness. 'I came here when I was a little girl,' she said, and nodded across towards the waste ground. 'There was an amusement arcade there.'

He had joined her, but she still had to lift her voice against the busy, blustery breeze. 'There were penny-in-the-slot machines, and a little mechanical grab that picked up sweets.'

'If you were lucky and it wasn't fixed,' Harry said, prosaically.

'And a Test Your Driving Skill machine,' she continued. 'I was too small to reach it. By the time I was tall enough, it was gone.' She smiled. 'And pinball, and those football things with the men on rods – there was even a What the Butler Saw. And a juke-box that played Lonnie Donegan and the Everly Brothers.'

She put her hand lightly on his shoulder, and pointed. 'At the very end of the pier, there was a concert hall, and right along the end there were coin-operated telescopes,' she said, her eyes shining with memories. 'That part was lost in a storm.' She dropped her hand.

'They found the body on the pier,' she said, and turned away, walking back down to the rock. 'In the theatre.'

Harry followed her. 'Which is the theatre?' he asked.

'The big building at this end.' She pointed. 'There used to be shops and stalls, and a bandstand. But best of all,' she said, 'was the camera obscura.' She smiled. 'It was very primitive, I suppose, but it was wonderful. You went into a little dark room, and you could see the whole pier, and everyone moving about. It was magic,' she said, turning to face him. 'That's why I applied for the job, I suppose. Trying to recapture childhood security, or something.'

'And you discovered it looked like this?'

She nodded. 'But it was a good job, and I was offered it. We moved here about three months after Eddie died.'

'Christine was very fond of her father, wasn't she?'

'Yes, of course,' Annie said.

'She didn't like it much when you took up with Culver, I believe.'

'You have been busy,' Annie said. 'No, she didn't like it much. Not to start with. She was like you – she thought Gerald was using me.'

'And wasn't he?'

'No, he was not!'

'What was he offering you? What did he ever do for you?'

'He made me laugh,' she said. 'And that wasn't easy, not then.'

She had dropped her voice almost to a whisper. He moved closer to catch the words.

'The Wellington was a disaster. There was no one staying, no one wanted to know about conference rooms, and I thought I was going to lose my job. Christine was off on holiday with a friend from Cambridge – I couldn't afford it, but I'd promised.

There was me and a part-time chef who didn't speak English. I was on my own, and broke, and I was never as miserable in my life.'

The tears weren't that far away now, Harry thought. But it might just be the cold wind. 'And Culver came along when you were nicely vulnerable,' he said.

'He booked in and ordered dinner,' she said. 'He was alone in the dining room, and he started talking to me.' She rubbed the smooth surface of the rock with her fingertip, round and round, as she spoke. 'He made me *laugh*, and I didn't want him to go off to his room and me to mine. So he stayed and had a drink,' she said.

A gull soared over, crying like the damned. Harry glanced up. A star had appeared in the dark blue, a frosty halo of light round it.

'And I asked him to stay with me,' she said, leaning her elbows on the rock, and looking out at the sea, dark and restless in the wind. 'Are you shocked?' she asked.

Harry shook his head. 'No,' he said. 'Should I be?'

'I don't know,' she said. 'You seem a bit old-fashioned, sometimes.'

'Sometimes,' Harry admitted. 'But I'm not shocked.'

'Gerald was, I think,' she said. 'But he stayed.'

'Well,' said Harry. 'He would, wouldn't he?'

'Maybe,' she said. 'We came down here once or twice. But he didn't like it when I talked about how it used to be. He said you had to live in the present.'

'Then he wouldn't think much of what you're doing now, would he?' Harry asked.

'No,' she said. 'But I wish he was here.'

Harry touched her shoulder. 'I'm here,' he said.

She didn't turn round. 'And what are you offering me, Harry?' she asked.

'Not much,' he said. 'No job, no money, and no prospects.'

Another star, and another. The sun was gone, but the sky still held some light.

'Mind,' he said. 'Your sex life wouldn't depend on West Ham getting into Europe.'

She turned slowly, smiling despite the tears. 'Why do I feel so at home with you?' she asked.

When he kissed her, it reminded Harry of the sailor and his girl at Harmouth. And that stirred a thought that he couldn't catch hold of. Sailors, ships, tearful kisses.

'I'm afraid,' she said. 'I'm really afraid.'

He put his arms round her. 'No, don't be,' he whispered. 'Don't be.'

'But something terrible's happening here!'

'Looks like it,' Harry said. 'Do they know who it was that they found in the pier?'

'No.' Her voice was unsteady. 'Tom Webb says the body's been there eight or ten weeks. And that means it could have happened on New Year's Eve, doesn't it?' She was shivering as she laid her head tiredly on his shoulder. 'I have to tell him about Gerald. I know I do,' she said. 'But I'm afraid to.'

'Then don't,' Harry said quickly.

She raised her head. 'Harry – four people are dead.'

'Telling the police that you were on Culver's B-team isn't going to bring them back,' he answered sharply.

She stiffened, and stepped away. 'You never miss a trick, do you, Harry?' she said.

'What good will it do?'

'They were all here at one time or another! The police don't realise that.'

'No, they don't,' Harry said. 'But I do.'

'What can you do on your own?' she cried.

'Lambert of the Dole Queue? Bugger all!' He pushed past her, and stood in the stiff breeze, breathing in the salty air, his hands thrust in his jacket pockets. When she came to him and slipped her arm through his, he ignored her.

'I shouldn't have said that,' she said.

Harry didn't speak. She'd said it because it was true. He was trying to beat Webb and the Murder Squad and everyone else to the punch. But Barbara thought he could do it – she'd said so. He pulled his cigarettes out of his pocket, disengaging himself from Annie in the process.

'I won't tell them,' she said, in a defeated voice. 'Between you and Grant, the police don't stand much of a chance.'

'Grant? What's his problem?' Harry asked.

'He doesn't want the police asking questions at the hotel,' she said. 'He doesn't like the police.'

'Why not?'

'It was when he was a young boy, I think,' she said, linking her arm in his again as they began to walk up towards the promenade. 'During the war, and just afterwards. I think he was in trouble with the KGB or something. He had a bad time with some sort of police, anyway.'

'So did I,' said Harry, with feeling.

'No you didn't,' Annie said. 'You had a good time, and you blew it.'

'Thanks for the sympathy.'

'It was your own fault,' she said. 'Don't start comparing your life with his – terrible things happened to his family.'

'Speaking of which,' said Harry. 'His wife's been gone eight to ten weeks, hasn't she?'

Annie stopped walking. 'That's a horrible thing to say!'

'Maybe it's him you should be with,' he said, pulling away. 'If he's so deserving.' He walked quickly ahead of her, to the railings.

He looked down at the pier, remembering the new rope tying the gates together, that he had thought looked out of place. Whoever dumped the body there must have tied the gates up again. If he'd only thought. That would have taught Webb a lesson, if he'd discovered the body. But whose body?

Grant's wife seemed rather to have been mislaid, as well as his car. He was very careless with his belongings.

'He took me out,' Annie said, arriving at his side.

'Grant did?' he snapped, his new train of thought uppermost in his mind.

145

'Yes.' She stepped back a little, surprised at his reaction. 'Does that annoy you?' she asked.

'No,' Harry answered. 'You're right to stay in the First Division. It gets rough down here in the Fourth.'

'If that's how you're going to—'

'No, no – I'm delighted to hear that you slip into something more comfortable than your widow's weeds now and then.'

'Less comfortable,' she said, with a smile. 'I was scared of him,' she said. 'Silly, isn't it?'

'I don't know,' Harry said, grinding his cigarette into the pebbles. 'What did he do?'

Annie moved closer, her eyes looking steadily into his. 'He brought me flowers,' she said. 'Gave me dinner, paid me compliments, and kissed my hand when he said good night.'

'You've none of that to fear from me, pet,' Harry said quietly. 'I just want to go to bed with you.'

Harry dressed quietly, but the room was unfamiliar, and he stumbled into Annie's dressing table. He heard her stir; she sat up with a sleepy, puzzled sound, and switched on the lamp.

'Sorry,' he said.

She looked at the clock, then at him. 'It's five o'clock in the morning,' she said.

'I know.'

'Why are you dressed?' she asked drowsily. 'Are you going somewhere?'

'Not me,' he said. 'I don't have to catch the team bus.'

She frowned, her eyelids heavy. 'You don't get up at this time every morning, do you?' she asked in an appalled whisper.

'No fear,' he said, sitting on the bed to put on his shoes. 'I sleep like a log, me.'

Annie closed her eyes. 'Then why aren't you sleeping like one now?'

'I've got work to do,' he said.

The truth was that he couldn't sleep. This was when he had been stumbling off to bed for the last month, his mind fogged

146

with booze. Today, his mind was sharp, ready for anything. Ready for asking the right questions of the right people this time.

'Working's more fun, is it?' Annie's sleepy indignation made him smile.

'More fun than listening to you snoring,' he said.

'I don't snore! Do I?'

'No,' he said, with more gallantry than truth.

'We should go to the police,' Annie said.

Harry twisted round to face her. 'Look,' he said, as he slipped on one shoe. 'What'll happen if we do? They'll say that you obstructed their enquiries, and they'd be right. Next thing you know, you'll have heavy-footed coppers all over the shop, asking personal questions. How would you like that?'

A faint smile appeared, and she opened her eyes. 'I don't know how I'd cope,' she said.

'Well, you couldn't just tell *them* to sod off, believe me,' he said. 'And Webb would probably clap me in irons – and you wouldn't want that, would you?'

'I don't know,' she murmured.

'It was all right, though,' he said with a smile, as he turned back to find his other shoe. 'Wasn't it?'

'Yes,' she said, and turned over. 'It was all right.'

Harry smiled to himself. Being accepted by Annie was much more important to him than he had realised. She had told him a lot about herself, and Christine, and the hotel. It made him feel good to be part of that. She had said she was glad to have someone to listen to her problems with Grant, like the business with the Friends of the Earth, and the pier exhibition. Someone who would just say 'poor Annie' and not give her sensible advice, like Linda did.

Something occurred to him about that, and he turned to speak to her, but she had fallen asleep again. Harry tiptoed out of the room, and cleared the coffee table of its bowl of fruit, substituting an ashtray. He found some paper and a pen on the sideboard, and sat down, taking out his cigarettes. He sighed at the empty packet, and searched his pockets for change.

Creeping out to the bar past the night porter, he felt like a thief. He persuaded the machine to sell him a packet of cigarettes as quietly as it could. The night porter slumbered peacefully throughout, his head on his hand, as Harry tiptoed back. He pushed the door to the private corridor, just as the lift doors opened to reveal Grant. It was hard to tell who was the more startled.

'Can I help you?' Grant asked, frowning slightly.

'No thanks,' Harry said breezily. 'Just getting some cigarettes.' He held the packet up by way of proof.

'It's Mr Lambert, isn't it?' Grant, big and powerful, blocked Harry's progress. 'I didn't know you were a guest here, Mr Lambert.'

'In a manner of speaking,' Harry said.

Grant smiled frostily. 'Forgive me, Mr Lambert, but this part of the hotel is private.'

'I'm a guest of Mrs Maddox,' Harry said.

'Ah.' Grant didn't move out of the way. 'You're a very early riser, Mr Lambert.'

'Like you,' Harry said, full of cheerful bonhomie. 'You know what they say.'

'Yes, indeed.' Grant stood aside. 'But I do hope we're not after the same worm, Mr Lambert,' he said as Harry passed, then pushed open the corridor door, and left.

Harry watched the door as it closed slowly and silently, shrugged, and carried on into the sitting room. Lighting his first, he began to write down the sequence of events, if sequence it was. It must make sense. Somehow, it must make sense. The first thing you did when you found a body was check who was missing. Mrs Grant was missing, or, at least, no one knew where she was. This was not a revolutionary thought; his brief conversations with hotel staff suggested that this was popular opinion as to the identity of the Grisly Find.

But she had left, or disappeared, in mid-December; the taxi driver had died on New Year's Eve, Culver on the 9th of

148

January, and Rosemary Wright on the 28th. If they were connected, how? He could place Culver and Fowler in Amblesea on New Year's Eve, but not Karen Grant or Rosemary Wright. And Mrs Wright, Mrs Grant, and Fowler were probably all there in August, but not Culver. And yet they *had* to be connected. He still needed answers to questions – answers he probably wouldn't get. For them, he needed an ally. And he knew just the girl.

He drew thoughtfully on his cigarette, trying to capture the fleeting thought that kept eluding his mind's grasp. He could see the ship, getting ready to sail, its dark bulk dwarfing the harbour buildings, looking too impossibly large to move. And the sailor and his girl, locked in an agonised embrace, oblivious of him. Why were they so obstinately revisiting him? Time. The time was wrong. Arrivals, departures – it was something about *when*. Ships and sailors and long farewells. Ships. Sailors. *Sailors*.

Wright was a sailor. But he knew that – that was why he had concocted his fanciful drug theory. He sat down. Wright was home for Christmas. For *Christmas*, Harry thought. But he'd sailed again soon after, hadn't he? Mrs Thomas had said *almost* the whole holiday. He'd sailed again, and he hadn't sailed from bloody Watford. He and Rosemary had said their goodbyes somewhere, soon after Christmas.

He grabbed the phone, and dialled, impatiently waiting for it to be answered.

'Barbara?'

'Harry? Do you know what time it is?'

'Do us a favour, pet.'

'Oh, I don't trust you when you go all Geordie.'

'Wright. Your friend Wright. He was at sea when his wife died – and he left just after Christmas. Find out where from and when, there's a lamb.'

'Find out where and when Wright's ship left,' Barbara repeated, spacing the words as she wrote them down.

'Thanks, pet – and come to the Wellington Hotel, Amblesea, when you've found out.'

'Is this my story?'

'I think so, bonny lass.' He smiled. 'Don't ask me what it is yet, though. I don't have the foggiest.'

He was pacing the floor when he heard the gentle knock; it was eight o'clock, he realised, to his surprise, and opened the door.

'Oh,' Linda said, looking less surprised than she sounded. 'I thought you were Annie.'

'It's just the way I've combed my hair,' he said, but Linda wasn't amused.

'I heard you moving about,' she explained heavily. 'I thought it was Annie.'

'She's still asleep.' He moved out into the corridor, closing over the door, so as not to wake her. 'Can I give her a message?'

'You could try telling her what time it is,' Linda said coolly. 'She's normally up by now.'

'What's the good of being the boss if you can't have a lie-in?' Harry asked.

Linda shrugged. 'Suit yourself,' she said. 'She won't thank you.'

Harry smiled broadly, but skipped the retort. 'Have I done something to upset you?' he asked.

'I don't know what you mean,' she replied.

'You do.'

'I'd just like to know how you swung it, that's all,' said Linda.

'Christine asked me to have a word with her mother,' Harry said innocently. 'She thought it was high time that Gerald's ghost was laid.'

'I think you've got your wires crossed somewhere,' she said. 'When are you having a word with the ghost?'

Harry grinned. 'Don't you approve?' he asked.

'It's not up to me to approve,' she said.

'Look,' said Harry. 'While you're here. Do you know of any reason why Grant should be up and about at half past five in the morning?'

Linda shook her head. 'No,' she said. 'I didn't even know he

150

was here last night – I'd heard he'd moved back into his own house.'

'Not yet,' Harry said. He wondered what had made him change his mind. Grant seemed worth a closer look, what with his wife disappearing and his recent financial history.

'Gil might know – he might have said something to him.'

'Who's Gil?'

'The night porter.'

'Him! You could drive a Centurion tank through here and he wouldn't notice.'

'Don't you believe it,' Linda said. 'He saw you creeping about all right.'

Harry nodded. 'Of course,' he said. 'So this wasn't a social call on Annie at all? You were checking up on me?'

'I had to see it to believe it,' she said.

'Yes,' Harry said slowly. 'You did, didn't you?'

Linda worked mornings and evenings, and she would have been on duty when he and Annie arrived last night. But she hadn't seen him. No one had.

SIXTEEN

Annie opened her eyes. She could hear Harry's voice, then the door closing. She didn't know if he had come in or gone out. She didn't know why he was there at all, except that his unambiguous approach left no room for vague promises. You said yes or no to Harry, and she had said yes.

She had never before told anyone how she felt about her marriage; she felt slightly guilty for having done so now. Because the truth was that the resentment she had felt at being half of a duo had only come afterwards, after Eddie had died. When she had shouted at him, and tried to shake him back to life, feeling something much more akin to rage than grief. Their life – in the singular, always – had been one of taken-for-granted camaraderie, and he'd left without giving notice. Annie had hated Eddie for dying.

And then there had been Gerald. Surprised and flattered by her outrageous pass, he had, as he himself had pointed out, got himself into an ongoing mistress situation before you could say no comment. She smiled as she remembered the little joke. Poor Gerald, always looking at his watch, anxiously checking what time he would have been home if he'd really been to this or that. Gerald's inborn charm had made his path through life as smooth as it had to be; he had married well, and been given a safe seat and a junior ministry which required more tact than aggression. Gerald was good with people, and good to people. He had been good to her. He had been good to himself, she added, as if to beat the absent Harry to the punch.

She closed her eyes. Harry. Just meeting Harry was a bruising experience, and compounding the mischief was madness. But compound it she had, with a willingness that had taken her by surprise, though he had accepted it as his due. And even this morning he had been unable to resist a jibe.

Her dressing gown made no concession to glamour, and it served him right, she thought, as she wrapped herself in it. She would probably go out and buy some cold cream and curlers to complete the effect.

'Have you seen the time?' she demanded as she flopped into the sitting room in slippers that had seen better days.

'I thought you'd need the sleep,' he said, putting his arm round his approximation of her waist.

'I'll have to skip breakfast.' Not looking at him, brushing aside his embrace, she gave him just enough time to react before turning to catch the crestfallen look. She grinned. 'Good morning,' she said.

'Speaking about breakfast,' Harry said. 'I don't think I've eaten for about two days.'

'I'll get breakfast sent in.'

He looked at her for a moment before answering. 'Yes,' he said. 'Why not?'

Annie ordered breakfast, then turned to him. 'Why did you come back, Harry?'

'The body,' he said. 'I couldn't resist it.'

'The one in the pier, rather than mine, I take it?'

He smiled. 'There was a couple of hours when I thought they might be one and the same,' he said.

Annie felt a shiver go down her back. 'You thought I'd ended up in the pier?'

'I couldn't be sure. It just said it was a woman's body.'

'Do you think I'm in danger?' she asked.

'Not now,' he said. 'I'm here.' He kissed her. 'Why did you ask for breakfast to be sent in?' he asked.

'It's more romantic,' she said. 'But wasted on someone who gets up in the middle of the night to do some work.'

'It's not because you think we'll be in trouble?'

153

'Who with?' she asked.

'I don't know. Christine? Linda, maybe?'

'No, I shouldn't think so,' Annie said. 'They all like you better than I do anyway.'

'Linda doesn't.'

'She must,' Annie said.

'I'm telling you,' he said. 'Linda does not approve of me.'

'Well, be reasonable Harry,' Annie said sweetly. 'Who does?'

By lunchtime the rumours were flying thick and fast round Amblesea, and settling like starlings on the Wellington.

It's Karen Grant, they said.

Annie heard them first; an occasional twitter, easily ignored, or sent off with a wave of the hand. They were bound to say that. Just because Mr Grant was well known, and she'd left him suddenly like that.

It's Karen Grant. Mind you, they did say that the body had been there for a long time. But if that was the case, well – you could hardly say who it was straight off, could you? Annie didn't know much about dead bodies, but she knew they didn't keep.

It's Karen Grant. The postman – usually a very reliable source – the baker's van driver, the journalist from the *Harmouth Advertiser*. The rep from the catering firm, the man in Room 371, the commis chef.

A new flock of rumours swooped in after Grant had received a phone call, and had gone out without a word.

Webb was back in the Grant's big white house, back where he'd met Karen.

He'd read about things like that. Policemen, doctors, politicians – putting their heads on the block for some woman. Silly sods, he had thought. Why risk your career for that? But along had come Karen Grant, and he had risked more than his career.

The detective sergeant from Amblesea was in the room, lifting and laying things.

'Why is everything so clean?' the DS asked. 'If you've not been living here?'

Grant looked uncomfortable. 'I have brought a friend here once or twice,' he said, with dignity, once he had gathered his thoughts.

'I see,' said the sergeant.

Webb took a deep breath. He had to go through the motions. 'Why didn't you report your wife missing, Mr Grant?' he asked.

'She wasn't missing. She had left.' Grant stood up and went over to the electric fire. 'One doesn't report that to anyone.'

'But her clothes are still here,' said the sergeant.

'Clothes?' said Grant. She buys clothes every day. Every day! She would have needed a removal van to take all her clothes.'

'But what made you so sure she had left you?'

'She left me a note,' Grant replied.

So that was how she had chosen to tell him, Webb thought. 'Do you still have it?' he asked.

'Of course I don't! I tore it up.'

'What did it say?'

'It said, "Don't try to find me",' he said.

'Is that all?' Webb could feel perspiration on his collar; Grant stood beside the electric fire. Tension affected different people different ways.

'No,' Grant answered stiffly.

'What else did it say?' Webb knew he was skating on thin, thin ice.

'That she needed time to think. Time away from here – "away from all the pressures" I think was her phrase. I expect she copied it out of one of her magazines.'

Webb could feel the anger boiling up. 'Your wife is *dead*, Mr Grant!' he shouted, to get rid of it.

'Is she?' Grant spread his hands. 'You show me a coat – she has a dozen coats.'

'It is her coat,' Webb said.

Grant sat down. 'It looks like one of hers,' he said.

155

It was easier now that he knew what Karen had said – assuming Grant was telling the truth. 'Did you try to find her?' he asked.

'No.'

'You didn't hire anyone to look for her? A private detective, perhaps?'

'No.'

So Lambert was still a mystery.

'Had you had a row with your wife?' the DS asked.

'No, not especially.'

'Not especially? Was rowing quite normal?'

'We didn't always see eye to eye,' Grant said.

'About?'

'Lots of things.'

'You said you brought a "friend" here,' said the sergeant, and you could hear the quotation marks like gunshots. 'Would that be Sandra Palmer?'

Grant nodded. 'How do you know?' he asked.

The sergeant glanced at Webb, who had supplied Sandra as a possible source of information. 'Gossip,' he said. 'We spoke to her this morning.'

'You spoke to Sandra? About this?'

The sergeant nodded.

'But why? What could she – how could she help you?'

'Well,' he said. 'You never know. Not till you ask.'

'Have you brought anyone else here?' Webb asked.

'No. I fail to see how that can interest you.'

'Do you think there was another man involved with your wife?' asked the sergeant.

'Of course there was!' Grant snapped. 'Do you think she would have left this?' He waved his hand round the room. 'Left me? Without someone else?'

And he was looking straight at Webb.

The police were still at Grant's house, according to the paper boy, at half past four. He'd got it from his mate, who had got it

156

from his mate, who had delivered Grant's evening paper.

Annie was on reception, standing in for the absent Sandra, when this latest news was imparted. Harry, lounging over the desk, called the boy back.

'Why was he delivering there?' he asked. 'The house is empty, isn't it?'

'He says he started delivering the paper again yesterday,' the boy said. 'He was mad – that's the only house down that way. It puts twenty minutes on the round.'

'Thanks, son,' Harry said, and went back into the sitting room. Annie shrugged at Linda, who had just come on for the five o'clock shift.

'I *thought* he meant to move back yesterday,' Linda said. 'I wonder why he didn't?'

Grant sat down, unwilling to trust his legs to keep standing. Sandra's flimsy chair creaked under his weight.

'I just don't want to be involved,' Sandra was saying. 'I don't want to have any more to do with you.'

His head was spinning from the questions. Memories of other interrogations, other days, another life. But there were rules now. Laws.

'I'm not asking you to have any more to do with me,' he said. 'I'm apologising. I'm sorry you got involved. I didn't tell them about you.'

'Look – whatever's been going on, I don't want to know. I just want you to leave – I don't want to be involved.'

'Sandra. I have not murdered my wife.'

But Sandra just looked apprehensive and disbelieving. The police had no right to talk to her, Grant thought angrily. He had known she would be upset.

'Why would I want to murder Karen?' he asked gently. 'An empty-headed woman, infuriating at times. But these are reasons for slamming doors, for having affairs – for divorce, even. Not for murder.'

She relaxed, just a little, then looked at the clock. 'I'll have to

157

get ready for work,' she said.

'Mrs Maddox won't expect you in tonight,' he said. 'Not when you weren't there this afternoon.'

'I'd rather go in.' Still pale, and shivering slightly, she got up. 'I don't want to be here alone. And I don't want you here. I'm sorry.'

Grant understood that. 'You don't look well,' he said. 'Will you please let me drive you, at least?'

'Well,' she said. 'All right. But let me go in first when we get there.'

'Of course,' he said. 'I do understand.'

Annie and Harry came out of the bar. It was almost nine o'clock, and Annie was about to organise cover for Sandra's late shift, when she arrived, still looking pale. 'Sorry,' she said. 'I wasn't feeling too good this afternoon.'

'You don't look very well,' Linda said.

'I can get Christine to do your shift,' said Annie. 'If you're not well.'

'No,' Sandra said. 'I'm here now.'

Grant strode in. 'Good evening,' he said.

'Oh, Mr Grant,' Linda said. 'A Mr Johnson rang to say that the next board meeting's been rearranged – it's on Wednesday instead of—'

'Don't bother me with trivialities!' he roared, and took the wide stairs two at a time.

Linda waited until he had disappeared. 'I didn't know what to do,' she said. 'I thought I should just behave as though everything was normal.'

'It obviously isn't,' Harry said. 'Where are the board meetings held?' he asked.

'London,' said Annie. 'At the head office.'

'When?'

'Every fortnight. Mondays, usually.'

'Were there any in January?'

'Yes, there would be two. Oh – of course. The first one

158

would have been New Year's Day, so they put it back to the Friday.'

'Did he go?'

'Yes,' Annie said. 'He went on the Friday morning, didn't he, Linda? And came back Sunday night.' She wasn't sure why Harry was asking, but she was sure she wouldn't like it when she found out.

'The fifth to the eighth,' Harry said. 'And the next one?'

'They went back to Monday, so that would be ...' She counted off the weeks. 'First, eighth, fifteenth. Yes – he went to that one too, and he left on the Friday again. But of course he wasn't back until Monday night that time.'

That was when Annie noticed Sandra, whose complexion had changed from pasty white to bright pink.

Annie wondered just how good Sandra was at taking care of herself, and raised her eyebrows at Linda, who shrugged as she pushed open the corridor door.

'Good night,' she said.

'Mrs Maddox?' Sandra said, with a slight desperation. 'Could I speak to you in private?'

'I'm on my way,' Harry said, going back through to the sitting room.

Sandra waited until the door closed over. 'I'm sorry about this afternoon,' she said. 'I know I should have rung in, but—'

'Oh, that's all right,' Annie said. 'I know you're on your own.'

'It's about Mr Grant,' she said. 'We've been seeing one another for a few weeks – well, you guessed I was in London with him those weekends.'

She waited, as if to give Annie a chance to preach to her the folly of her ways. Annie felt that she was hardly in a position to do so.

'Anyway, about this morning. The police came to my flat. They asked me questions about James, and his wife – I never knew his wife. I was too upset to come in, and I wouldn't have known what to say if I'd phoned.'

159

'It doesn't matter,' Annie said. But she knew that Sandra wasn't telling her all this to excuse herself for not ringing in.

'If you'd told me this a week ago, I'd have told you to steer clear,' she said. 'I've had some of the married man bit. It isn't much fun.' She sat down. 'But this is a completely different situation.'

Sandra looked down at the desk. 'I don't think he's serious about me,' she said. 'The weekends were a disaster. I hardly saw him. He was at meetings all the time.' She gave Annie a brief smile. 'I think I just wanted to tell someone.' Her pale face looked earnestly into Annie's. 'Whatever he's done, I swear I didn't know,' she said.

'I'm sure no one thinks you did,' Annie said.

The switchboard buzzed, and Annie answered it in preference to Sandra, who really did look less than well.

'Mrs Maddox?' Grant said. 'I must apologise to Miss Benson for my rudeness.'

'She's gone off now,' Annie said. 'I'm sure she understood.'

'Would you be good enough to come up?' he said.

Annie froze for a second. 'Yes, of course,' she said professionally, but a fraction too late.

'Please don't be alarmed, Mrs Maddox. You will come down again,' he said, and hung up.

'He wants me to go up,' Annie said to Harry. 'What should I do?'

'It's up to you,' he said, unhelpfully.

'What do you think he wants?'

'You've been through it all,' Harry said. 'Maybe he wants a shoulder to cry on.'

Annie felt sick. 'Don't,' she said. 'I don't want to have anything to do with him.'

'Well, I don't think he's going to take a meat cleaver to you.'

'You're a great help.'

Harry opened a can of beer. 'I can hardly come with you,' he said.

So, she was on her own. And Harry's assurances of the morning that she was safe now that he was here seemed a little empty.

'You would have gone up to see him yesterday,' he said. 'Nothing's changed.'

She went out, slamming the door, and called the lift. When it came down, it took all of her courage to step into it.

She went past Christine's room where she and Pete were talking in muffled, low voices. What were they discussing so earnestly, for so long? Nothing had changed.

Her shoes clicked on the tiled floor until she passed through the brick archway to the guest rooms, and on to the deep-pile carpet. The sudden absence of sound made her feel more alone, more undefended.

Grant's room. He scared her at the best of times. He'd scared her in the big, expensive restaurant with its view of the sea. Nothing had changed.

He'd scared her in his big, expensive car which wasn't big or expensive enough, as he had driven her home from Harmouth, passing the pier where his wife had been lying dead all this time. Nothing had changed.

She knocked on his door so quietly that she couldn't hear it herself. She knocked again, and he opened the door so suddenly, so immediately, that she gave a little cry of surprise.

'I'm sorry,' he said, stepping back, ushering her in, his hand on her back. 'I startled you.'

She stepped in, closing her eyes as the door closed behind her.

'I have some brandy,' he said. 'Would you like one?'

Her hands were shaking too much to hold a glass. She shook her head.

'The police think I killed my wife,' he said conversationally, picking up his drink and downing it in one. Annie half-expected him to toss the glass at the radiator.

'They have been to my house,' he said. 'They have been through her clothes – they've taken away some of mine.' He smiled. 'They asked my permission,' he said. 'In this country, they ask your permission.' He put down the glass, because his hands were shaking too. 'I could not stay there tonight,' he said, and turned. 'What about you, Mrs Maddox? Do you think I killed my wife?'

'No,' Annie said, but no sound came out.

He looked less than satisfied, and sat down heavily on the bed. 'I thought you and I were friends,' he said.

'We are,' Annie told him, trying desperately not to sound as though she were humouring him.

'They didn't let me see her,' he said. 'They just showed me a coat. Perhaps it's hers. Mr Webb says it's hers.'

Annie didn't know how to react, so she just listened.

Grant rubbed the back of his neck. 'They said didn't I know where she was, didn't I want to know? But she said we should have a complete break.' He sat down again. 'She said she'd come back, though. She said she'd come back and tell me whatever she had decided.'

Annie sat down by the dressing table.

'Decided?' she repeated.

'She left a note, saying she had to decide her future, away from all the pressures. I believe she was considering another offer. Mr Webb thinks that's why I killed her.' He took another sip of brandy. 'But I did not kill her, Mrs Maddox.'

'No.'

'Any more than you killed Mr Culver,' he said. 'But it's what people think that matters, isn't it? And it's odd, that we should find ourselves in the same situation.'

'But nobody thinks I killed Gerald,' Annie said in a whisper.

'Of course not. But someone killed them. My wife, your lover.'

'Why? Why would someone do that?'

Grant sighed. 'I can think of reasons,' he said. 'And I'm sure Mr Webb can. He's very good at reaching conclusions on the flimsiest of evidence.'

He smiled, the cold smile that made Annie shudder. 'But then – the police don't know that Mr Culver was in the habit of visiting Amblesea. Do they?'

Annie shook her head.

'I thought I could trust you, Mrs Maddox.'

'Me?' Annie's voice had disappeared again.

'Oh, yes. You have invested a great deal of time and effort – a great deal of *yourself* – in this hotel. I thought very highly of you.'

His strange, precise English alarmed her. He alarmed her.

'But you can't be trusted, Mrs Maddox.'

'I don't—'

'There are a great many beds in this hotel, Mrs Maddox,' he said. 'There really is no need for the guests to share yours.'

Annie felt as though everything inside her had ceased to function. She stared at Grant, and he stared back, his heavy, implacable features frozen into immobility.

'I met Mr Lambert at half past five this morning,' he said.

Annie didn't speak.

'And I want him out of this hotel, Mrs Maddox. I want him out tonight.' He stood up. 'Or you can consider yourself dismissed,' he said.

'How do I know what to believe?' Christine said, looking at the uncurtained window, seeing her own reflection.

'That was the last time I had anything to do with her,' Pete said.

'But just the other day you said you'd had nothing to do with her since October.'

She could see Pete literally hang his head, in monochrome reflection in the glass.

'I know,' he muttered. 'But it was Christmas – I just wanted to talk to her.'

'Why didn't you tell me? When you were confessing everything else?' She turned.

'Because I'd made a fool of myself, I suppose. Because of what you'd done for me – I don't know.'

If she hadn't wanted to be told, she shouldn't have asked, she told herself sternly.

'And then when I came here, Grant was sitting there.' He lifted his eyes to hers. 'I wasn't going to come back that night,' he said. 'But not because of Lesley. Because of you – what I was doing to you.'

'Why did you come back?' she asked. 'Because you wanted me to tell lies for you?'

He didn't answer, and she knew she was right.

'I tried to ring her,' he said. 'But she hadn't gone home. Her landlady said she didn't know where she was. So she couldn't help me. I didn't want you to lie for me. I wish I'd never asked you to.'

But he had. And she had done what he had asked.

'It is all over with Lesley,' he said. 'It was over then. That's why I asked you to marry me.'

Dreams. Things other people have, he had said. But she had them too. It was just that reality kept getting in the way.

'If this promenade development thing comes off, they'll need labourers . . .' Pete began.

Christine stopped listening.

Annie finally escaped from Grant, and took the guest lift down. She saw Christine and Pete, still deep in conversation as Pete was leaving. She waited by the desk, worrying a little about Sandra, who was looking worse than ever.

Pete and Chris looked none too happy either, she thought. Given the way she herself was feeling, they weren't much of an advertisement for the hotel.

'Do you fancy a drink?' she asked, as soon as Christine came back in.

'Why not?' said Christine, with a sigh.

'Trouble?' Annie asked.

'You could say,' Chris said.

'I've just escaped from Grant,' Annie said.

Christine got the drinks. 'What were you seeing Mr Grant about?' she asked.

'He was seeing me,' Annie corrected.

She supposed that in retrospect she would think it foolish, but she couldn't lose the fear. No wonder Karen had left him.

'What about?'

'Amongst other things,' Annie said, 'he told me to get Harry out of here if I know what's good for me.'

Christine smiled, but the smile faded when she realised that Annie was serious.

'You're not going to, are you?'

'I don't know. In some ways, I agree with him.'

'It's hard to keep up with you and Harry,' Christine said.

'Isn't it, though?' said Annie bitterly.

'Why does he want Harry to leave?'

'Because he's paranoid,' Annie said.

It was easy to be brave now, with Christine. It hadn't been so easy with Grant, grey-faced, his eyes as blank as a statue's, as he asked his pedantic questions and made his unspecified threats. Though the last one had been quite specific.

'Harry has to go or else,' she said.

'Or else what?'

'Goodness knows,' lied Annie.

'I think he fancies you as the next Mrs Grant,' Christine said, and Annie shuddered at the very thought.

She and Christine were still in the lounge when the shutters went up, and Annie took the glasses to the bar.

'We won't get rich on you,' the barmaid said cheerfully. 'One drink each, and you make them last all night!'

Annie smiled. 'Would you rather you were having to put us to bed?'

The girl laughed, pulling down the last grille. 'Good night, Mrs Maddox,' she said. 'Good night, Christine.'

They returned her good nights, and left the bar. At the lift, Christine kissed Annie on the cheek in a sudden and uncharacteristic gesture. 'I'll see you in the morning,' she said.

Annie opened the door to a fug of smoke that hung in the air, walked in without speaking, and opened the window.

165

'Are you drunk?' Harry asked.

'No.'

'Pity.'

She didn't reply.

'It's cold,' he said, twisting round. He shrugged, and turned away again.

After a moment, she closed the window. 'Why did you do that to me?' she asked.

'What did I do to you?'

She walked round and stood in front of him. 'He knew you'd spent the night with me,' she said. 'Why didn't you tell me he knew?'

'What would you have done if I had?'

'I'd have thought of something to tell him!'

'Yes! Well, I didn't want you to think of something to tell him. I wanted him to know the truth, and I wanted him to hear it from you.'

'And you thought that was the right way to do it?'

'It was the only bloody way to do it!'

It was the first time he'd shouted at her. He had said things – unkind things, devastating things – but always in his throw-away style, as though they didn't matter. This mattered.

'Why was it so important?' she asked. 'Why did he have to know at all?'

'Because I'm here at your invitation,' he said. 'But you made sure you sneaked me in the tradesman's entrance, didn't you?'

'I didn't sneak you in! It's more convenient, that's all.'

'Like hell! That's what Culver's key was for – the bloody service lift! So that he could come in through the basement, and no one would see him.'

'It was only if he brought his car – in case anyone spotted it. It's a conference centre. We get other MPs here. He could park in the delivery area.'

'Well, I use the front door. And Grant can like it or lump it.'

'What about me?' she shouted. 'I already had to tell him about Gerald, and he was very good about that. Now this—' She was still shaking. Now, she didn't know if it was fear or anger.

'He was very good about that?' Harry repeated incredulously. 'You've got to stop apologising for your life, Annie. And you're not going to apologise for me. Or lie about me. Or explain me away – to Grant or anyone else!' He stood up. 'If you've been through some sort of trauma with him, that's your look-out. You should have told him to mind his own business.'

Annie took a breath. 'Oh, should I?' she said. 'You weren't there.'

'No,' he said. 'But I'm here. And *I* don't slip away like a thief in the night. I'm still here in the morning, inconveniently enough.' He strode towards the bedroom. 'Which is more than you could say for Gerald,' he said. 'Isn't it?'

And with that, he closed *her* bedroom door, leaving her with the stale smoke and the clutter that he'd created in *her* sitting room. How had he managed it? How had he twisted everything, so that she was in the wrong, when he had let her go up there – she picked up an ash-encrusted beer can, dropped it in the bin, and threw open the bedroom door.

'Of all the high-handed, unprincipled bastards, you take the biscuit!' she said.

'A reputation of which I am justly proud,' Harry answered, grinning.

'Everyone thinks they can just walk in here and take me over,' she shouted.

The grin vanished. 'Well? Everyone can,' he said. 'Can't they?'

'*No*,' she said, more to convince herself than him. 'No.'

Harry looked totally unimpressed.

'Grant wants you out,' she told him. 'Tonight.'

'I'll go then.'

'No.' She shook her head. 'I told him you were staying. It had better be worth the consequences.'

She closed the door on him, and began to tidy up. She was so frightened, and Harry and his 'I'm here' routine were scant comfort. She shivered as she thought of Grant's vague threats

167

about the police.

He's very good at reaching conclusions on the flimsiest of evidence.

It *was* the flimsiest of evidence. It was no evidence at all.

She sat down, suddenly weak. It was a long time before she moved.

SEVENTEEN

Harry lay awake, beginning to piece some of it together, perhaps, but by no means all. They all had to have been in one place at one time, or it made no sense at all. Webb's face came into his mind, and he longed to punch it. But better than that, much better, would be to resolve Webb's little local difficulty for him while he was still one step behind. Because that's what it was; he could see that now. It was him versus Webb.

Annie came in quietly, and he watched her as she undressed in the dark. His feelings for her had been clouding the issue, but his policeman's mind was beginning to reassert itself.

When he had realised that he had been smuggled into the hotel, he had felt angry. But now he had become aware that it had more significance than a mere affront to his dignity. It meant that everyone he had discounted had to be put back on the list. Even Annie.

Because she wouldn't have had to pass Sandra or anyone else on her way out. She *could* have been in Fowler's taxi that day, and she could have been the person that Culver had admitted, as his wife had suspected all along. Harry was a policeman, it was all he was, he was never not being a policeman – his own words. Now they were true again. His holiday was over.

'What consequences?' he asked, sitting up.

'Dear God!' Annie's hand flew to her throat, and she sat down on the bed with a bump. 'I thought you were asleep,' she said. 'Don't do that again.'

'Why are you so jumpy?'

'I've no idea,' she said. 'Why are you still awake? Surely a

169

simple little thing like a quadruple murder isn't preying on your mind?'

'What consequences?' he asked again.

'I've lost my job,' she said. 'He told me I was fired unless you left tonight.'

Harry touched her shoulder, but there was no response.

'I didn't tell Christine,' she added. 'I don't want you to either. It would only upset her.' She carried on in the same, beaten voice. 'And he's going to go to the police, I think,' she said. 'About Gerald being here. So I'm in trouble.'

Harry moved his hand up to her face. 'Why didn't you just do what he wanted?' he asked.

'Because I wanted you here.' Her hand touched his.

'That badly?'

'I've been *scared* that badly.' Her voice was hostile, but she clasped his hand like a child. 'I need some of your cussedness,' she said. 'This seems the quickest way to get it.'

'I don't think he'll go to the police,' Harry said.

'His wife has been murdered,' Annie said slowly, as if explaining to a dim child. 'And whoever killed Gerald killed his wife. That's what you think, it's what I think, and it's what the police will think once they know the connection.' She gripped his hand. 'And *I'm* the connection,' she said, releasing him. 'And in answer to your next question, I don't think Gerald was seeing Karen Grant.'

'But you can't be sure,' Harry argued.

'Yes I can. How could he have? Where – here? Where I might see them? Or in London, where his friends might see them? Not Gerald.'

So, she had thought about it. And St Gerald hadn't come out of it very well.

'But Grant thinks they were?' he asked.

'He might. It's hard to know what he thinks.'

'Strikes me he's the jealous type.' Harry leant over to switch on the light. He wanted to see Annie's face. 'Is he?'

'I wouldn't know.'

She looked so frightened; Harry had to make himself ignore it. 'The police think he killed his wife,' he said.

'No,' she said. 'Tom Webb thinks he did.'

'Tom Webb as distinct from the police? He's certainly being a bit over-eager, I'd say.'

'Yes,' she said. 'And I think I know why.'

Harry sat back. 'Let's have it, then.'

Annie thought for a moment or two before speaking. When she did, it was not anything that Harry might have expected her to say.

'Would you recognise Linda's coat if you saw it?' she asked.

'What?' Harry, nothing if not obedient, tried to remember Linda's coat. 'No,' he said.

'But you've seen it, haven't you?'

'I suppose I have, a couple of times. But I wasn't taking a lot of notice.'

'Would you recognise mine?'

'Yes,' he said.

'That's how Karen was recognised. By her coat.' She gave him a moment to digest that. 'You know I was there when they found her?'

'Yes. Christine said.'

'Well, we rang the police, and they asked us to stay. It was Tom who came. He came out of the theatre, and he said "she's dead", just like that.'

Harry grinned. 'Aye, well, pet – he's trained to recognise the signs.'

'That's what I mean. It was hardly a summing-up of the situation, was it? I think he knew who it was straight away. I think *he* recognised her coat. And he's not likely to have done that on the strength of a couple of interviews with her last May, is he?'

'No,' Harry said thoughtfully.

'And you never see him with anyone – he's an attractive man. I think he was involved with Karen. Maybe that's why she was leaving. She seems to have been carrying on with someone.'

Harry thought about it, and about what Pete had said about Webb being paid off. Karen Grant and Webb might just make sense.

'Anyway,' Annie said. 'I think that's why he's so certain that Grant killed her.'

'Why he's been so quick to point the finger, anyway,' Harry said. 'There could be another explanation for his knowing who it was straight away.'

He could see it was what Annie had been thinking and what she couldn't put into words. Maybe Karen Grant had double-crossed Webb.

'I didn't say that.'

'What are you saying?'

'Just that Tom's wrong. Grant didn't kill his wife.'

'What makes you so certain?'

'He's too sure of himself,' she said, switching off the light.

She was lying beside him, her body warm where it touched his, but her voice was cold.

'And you might have been able to tell him to mind his own business,' she said. 'But you weren't with him. And you weren't with *me*.'

'I'm with you now,' he said.

'You're with me because I'm scared of what's going on here, and I'm not scared of you. Right now, that's all you've got going for you.'

He wanted so much to tell her everything was all right, to take her in his arms, and love her, and chase away the fear. But it wouldn't have worked, so he said nothing at all, and didn't try to stop her when she moved away from him.

EIGHTEEN

Annie was on the desk, standing in for the cold-infested Sandra, when she came.

London, Annie thought, when she saw her come into the foyer. You could always tell. Something about the way they dressed, and wore make-up. Something about their air of being lost without tube trains. She had probably looked like that once.

'Good afternoon,' she said, approaching Annie. 'I believe you have a Harry Lambert staying here?'

'Do you?' Annie said, aware that she was being unforgivably churlish, but not caring. Harry Lambert was not number one on her charts, and any friend of Harry's could take a running jump.

The girl looked briefly puzzled, but obviously decided that people in the provinces always reacted like that.

'Am I right?' she asked. 'I'm Barbara Briggs – he is expecting me.'

'You're right,' said Annie. 'But he isn't here.' With great reluctance, she felt obliged to add, 'At the moment.'

'Is there somewhere I can wait?' she asked, determinedly polite.

Annie relented. 'You can wait in the sitting room, if you like,' she said. 'He should be back soon, I think. Through the door marked private, and it's the first door on the left, opposite the lift.'

'Oh!' Barbara smiled. 'He's friendly with the management, is he?'

'Perhaps,' Annie said. 'But the management isn't over-friendly with him right now.'

173

'I see,' she said, with a sympathetic laugh. 'Harry does take a bit of getting used to.'

Annie sent someone in after a few minutes to see if she wanted coffee. It wasn't her fault that Harry was a bastard, whoever she was.

She went back to working on the accounts, to be audited tomorrow, when she became aware of a presence.

'I feel better dow,' Sandra said.

Annie laughed. 'You don't sound better,' she said.

'I ab. I had a log sleep.'

'I should think so too,' said Annie. 'Go away and have another long sleep.'

'Do, hodestly. I do feel better.'

Annie looked at Sandra, clutching her Kleenex, one permanently held under her bright pink nose.

'Are you sure?' she asked doubtfully.

'Oh, yes. It's cub out dow.'

'Yes, I can see that. Well—' She looked over to the door, feeling a little guilty now about Harry's guest. 'I would like to get off. If you think you can hold the fort until Linda comes—'

'Yes, of course I cad.'

'It'll only be for an hour or so. But I'll be next door if you want to call it a day. All right? And Christine's doing the late shift – you probably shouldn't have come in last night.'

'I thought it was just all the trouble,' she said. 'I just felt shaky.'

'It's a hot toddy and your feet up this evening,' Annie said as the phone rang.

Sandra grabbed another hankie out of the box she had placed under the desk. 'Wellingtod Hotel,' she said. 'Cad I help you?'

Annie left her to it, and went to meet Harry's visitor, feeling almost shy as she opened the door. 'I'm Annie Maddox,' she said.

They shook hands, and Annie smiled, embarrassed by her earlier behaviour. 'I'm sorry,' she said quickly, getting it out of the way. 'I'm afraid you caught me at a bad time.'

'That's all right.' Barbara smiled, a sudden wide smile that automatically produced one in response.

The door opened, and Harry came in. 'That's some cold that Sandra's got,' he said, then beamed as he saw Barbara. 'Looking good, as ever,' he said, kissing her. As kisses went, it was just this side friendly.

'Well then, bonny lass – what have you found out for me?'

She looked pleased with herself as she reached into her briefcase.

'Wright's ship is the *Margaret Mars*,' she said. 'Named after the—'

'Come on!'

'Mr Wright had to be on board by two thirty p.m. on Sunday the thirty-first of December,' she said. 'At Harmouth docks.'

Harry's smile spread as she spoke. 'I knew it,' he said. 'I knew it. They were all here,' he said. 'On the same day. The Amblesea connection. Did you have much trouble?'

'No. I found out the easy way,' she said. 'I asked Mr Wright.'

'Good thinking,' Harry said.

'It wasn't much fun,' she said. 'It got a bit emotional.'

'Well, it would,' Harry said. 'With his wife being killed and all.'

'You're all heart, aren't you, Harry? Anyway, he says they were thinking of moving to Amblesea.'

'That's right,' said Harry. 'Her next-door neighbour said something of the sort.'

'You weren't being much of a detective, were you?' she said, much to Annie's delight.

Harry's good humour vanished. 'What does that mean?'

'If you're interested in buying a house somewhere, where do you go?'

Harry hit himself on the head. 'Estate agents,' he said. 'I never even thought about it.'

'I did,' she said, tearing a sheet off her pad.

Harry looked at the paper. 'I'll have to speak to them,' he said.

'The Wrights have been on their books since August,' Barbara said. 'She was hoping to buy one of the houses on the Harmouth Road estate.'

'Oh, yes,' said Harry. 'Luxury Homes at Realistic Prices.'

'So I understand,' said Barbara. 'Mrs Wright said that she was going to look at the show house in the afternoon.'

Harry smiled. 'We're getting somewhere,' he said, taking out his cigarettes and lighter. 'I'm just nipping out to the bar for cigarettes.'

When the door closed, Barbara smiled again at Annie. 'If it was anyone but Harry I would think he was being tactful,' she said.

Annie sat down. Barbara and Harry were obviously close; she had seen that when he'd walked in. They knew each other very well. Exposure to Harry made her more direct than she might otherwise have been.

'Are you Harry's girlfriend?' she asked.

'Ex,' said Barbara. 'Very ex.'

'But you're still friends?'

'Oh, yes. You don't lose Harry – you just gain someone who rings you up and asks you to do him a favour, pet.' She picked up Harry's cigarette packet and shook it. 'Empty,' she said. 'He had me worried for a moment. And you must be his new girlfriend.'

'I didn't know it was obligatory,' Annie said.

'You're sporting the accessory Harry gives to all his friends.'

Annie looked enquiring.

'A frayed temper,' she explained. 'He frays them himself, you know. I think he learned it at night school.'

Annie smiled. She liked Barbara.

'And,' Barbara went on, 'I don't know if it makes things better or worse, but I think he's very serious about you.'

'I think he probably is,' Annie said. 'Harry being serious about you isn't all beer and skittles.'

'I'm sure it isn't,' said Barbara. 'Thank God he was never serious about me.'

Harry came back. 'Right then,' he said. 'We've placed three of

176

them in Amblesea on Sunday the thirty-first of December.'

'Three?' Barbara repeated.

'Four, actually.' Harry sat down. 'But we don't know much about the fourth one yet, except that she's one Karen Grant, wife of the owner of this establishment. And that,' he said, 'is where you come in. There's a certain policeman I'd like you to meet.'

He began filling Barbara in on the details of the murders.

'Sorry,' he said to Annie when he'd finished. 'This must be a bit rough on you.'

'It's all been a bit rough on me,' Annie said. 'It's just taken you this long to notice.'

'Cheer up,' he said. 'You've not been arrested yet.'

Barbara looked from Harry to Annie. 'Arrested?' she said.

'Oh, Annie doesn't know, of course,' Harry said. 'Barbara's a crime reporter, Annie.'

'She's a what?' Annie stared open-mouthed at both of them, at Harry's indifference, and Barbara's discomfort.

'Don't take on, pet,' he said. 'I said she's a crime reporter, not a gossip columnist. She isn't going to be interested in Culver's uninspired extramural activities.'

'Harry!' Barbara snapped. She turned, a little flustered, to Annie. 'I don't know what he's talking about, Annie, but I really am only interested in the crimes.'

'So there you are,' Harry said. 'If you didn't do them, you've nothing to worry about, as they say in all the best nicks.'

Annie didn't trust herself to speak. She hoped her silence was dignified, but she had a horrible feeling that it was just dumbfounded.

Harry took a sheet of paper from his pocket. 'I need answers,' he said. 'So far we know that both Fowler and Wright had some sort of connection with Culver. Wright had met him, and Fowler drove him to the station.'

He lit a cigarette. 'Fowler's taxi had an accident,' he said. 'What do you do when you have an accident?'

'Swear, bleed, that sort of thing,' Barbara said.

'You swop insurance details with the other driver,' Harry

177

said. 'I went to Amcabs this morning. If one of their drivers has an accident, he gets the usual info from the other driver, of course, but he should also take the names and addresses of any witnesses. And they didn't find anything on Fowler.'

'It might not have involved another driver,' Barbara said. 'Or perhaps the other driver felt more like sticking a knife in him than swopping insurance details.' She sat back. 'Maybe it was a robbery.'

Harry nodded. 'Oh, it was,' he said. 'I'm sure of that. It was a robbery all right.'

'But you think whoever did it did the others too?' Annie asked.

'He did. There are too many coincidences, otherwise.'

'Are we using he to mean male of female?' Barbara asked.

'It's more likely to have been a man,' Harry said, putting his sheet of paper on the coffee table. 'But you never know.'

'If you think it was a robbery,' Annie said slowly, 'does that mean you think it might have been Pete?'

'It has to be considered,' Harry said. 'He'd be handy with a knife, with his army training.'

'Who's Pete?' asked Barbara.

'But why on earth should Pete do anything like that?' Annie said.

'He must have done something of the sort before, or Webb wouldn't have been questioning him,' Harry said.

Annie nodded. 'Something of the sort,' she said.

She picked up the paper, and read it.

1. Lift keys – how many?

2. Accident details.

3. KG – cause of death? When?

4. Taxi driver robbed?

5. No victim?

6. Christine

'Lift keys,' she said. 'I can tell you about them, at least.'

'Good,' he said.

'There are four. I've got one, Christine's got one, and

reception has one. Gerald had the other one.'

'Grant doesn't have one?' Harry asked.

'No. He borrowed the one from reception the day he needed to use the delivery area.'

Harry nodded. 'I've told you what's bothering me about the accident,' he said. 'The next bit's for you, Barbara – I'd like you to get an interview with a Superintendent Webb at Harmouth. Tell him who you are. I'm sure he'll like some flattering Fleet Street attention. Call him Superintendent a lot, and bat your eyelashes.'

Annie knew she ought to be flying to Tom's defence, but it was true. Tom would be enslaved. Had he been similarly enslaved by Karen Grant? She wished she hadn't told Harry now.

'No victim?' she said, continuing her perusal of the list. 'Aren't four enough for you?'

'There's a thing called victimology,' Harry said seriously. 'And it's not so far out. It says there are people who are likely to be victims. The list doesn't include too many successful and uncontroversial MPs, or hard-working, honest family men.'

'Or clerk-typists from Watford,' confirmed Barbara.

'Quite. Nor the wives of wealthy property owners living in South Coast resorts. And that's all we've got,' he said. 'We don't have a victim.'

Annie could feel her throat tightening as she asked the question. 'Why have you written Christine's name?' she asked.

'Because she hasn't told the truth,' he said baldly, and looked at his watch. 'Anyone fancy a drink?' he asked.

'What do you mean?' Annie asked, but she knew very well what he meant.

'Ainsley wasn't with her,' Harry said. 'And I can prove it.'

'Ainsley?' Barbara said.

'Pete,' said Harry. 'Pete, who was a commando. Annie's future son-in-law.'

'But why?' cried Annie. 'Why would he *want* to kill all those people?'

179

Barbara, who had got to her feet in anticipation of the proffered drink, sat down again. 'Why would anyone?' she said.

'No one did,' said Harry. 'Whoever did it just wanted to kill one person. And the others were incidental.' He sat back. 'Why hide just one body?' he asked. 'He didn't hide any of the others. Why just one?'

Annie and Barbara waited obediently to be told.

'Because she was the first,' Harry said. '*She* was the one who was to be killed, whose body was to be hidden. And the others were witnesses.'

'Three witnesses?' said Barbara. 'What was he doing? Selling tickets?'

Annie looked at him. 'So you don't really think it was Pete, do you?' she asked. 'He'd have no reason to murder Karen Grant.'

'No, he wouldn't,' Harry agreed. 'So who did have a reason?' He stood up. 'That's what we've got to find out. In the meantime, I could murder a pint.'

'I wouldn't say no to a large gin and tonic,' Barbara said.

'Yes,' Annie agreed. 'I think I could do with one too. But I'll book you in first. I take it you are staying?'

'Just try to tear me away,' Barbara said.

Annie watched as she and Harry went off, heads together, talking.

'Linda,' she said, her mind only half on what she was saying. 'Could you book Miss Briggs in? Single room.'

Linda looked over as they strolled into the bar. 'All right,' she said. 'You're the boss.'

'No.' Annie said, pulling up a chair. 'That's where you're wrong, as it happens.'

NINETEEN

'Thank you,' Barbara said, taking her drink. 'What have you been doing to Annie?'

'Why?' Harry sat down, looking aggrieved. 'What's she been saying?'

'Nothing much. I just get the impression that you're in rather bad odour there.'

'That's par for the course,' he said.

'I take it that is *she*? The one you were saving yourself for?'

'Are you jealous?' he asked with a grin.

'No,' she said. 'I find a little touch of Harry goes a long way.'

Harry couldn't think of a rejoinder, so he abandoned the conversation. 'You've been a right little clever Dick, haven't you?' he said with a grin. 'Finding out all about Mrs Wright – I don't suppose you've also worked out what Culver could have given her?'

'Given her?'

'It seems, according to your mate Mrs Thomas, that she said "He gave me", and never finished her sentence.'

'How irritating,' Barbara said.

'She got interrupted, and the conversation was forgotten,' Harry explained.

'But that could be anything,' Barbara said. 'He gave me a bunch of flowers, he gave me a headache.'

Harry nodded. 'He's given me one or two,' he said.

'He gave me to understand that he was single,' Barbara said.

'That's not impossible, either.'

181

Barbara thought. 'A funny look,' she said.

'Change of a fiver,' Harry suggested.

'A rosy glow.'

'A cold in the head.'

'His undivided attention,' said Barbara proudly.

'The impression that he might be Welsh,' Harry said, triumphantly, and they both laughed.

They stopped laughing rather self-consciously as Annie came over, carrying the evening paper.

'Room 223,' she said, handing Barbara her key. 'I hope you enjoy your stay.'

'I'm not sure enjoy is the right word,' Barbara said. 'I'm sure it will be interesting.'

Harry put his beer down. 'Culver could have been in the taxi when it had its accident,' he said. 'He had a black eye when he got home that he didn't have leaving here.'

'Well, it's more likely than Tom Webb taking a swipe at him,' Annie said. 'But Gerald couldn't have been in the taxi.'

'Why not?' A chorus from Harry and Barbara.

'Because Tom says the accident happened on the other side of the road. By the building site – he had to have been coming from Harmouth. He thinks it must have happened earlier.'

Harry picked up his pint, momentarily happy with that. 'No!' he exclaimed, with a vehemence that sent his beer over the side of his mug on to the table. 'Why would Fowler go about with a smashed indicator – risk a fine? If it had happened earlier, he'd have changed his vehicle. There were plenty of cars. Hardly any of them drive on Sundays.'

'Tom would have checked all that,' Annie said.

'He wouldn't,' Harry said, stubbing out a barely smoked cigarette in his eagerness to get hold of the idea that was forming. 'As far as he's concerned, the accident has nothing to do with it.'

Annie picked up her drink. 'Are you so sure it has?' she asked.

'I think it's got everything to do with it,' he said.

'Perhaps he skidded over to the wrong side of the road, and—'

Barbara said.

But Harry was discounting that before she had time to finish the sentence.

'Webb would have known if he'd skidded,' he said, making skid marks in the spilled beer, remembering the building site.

He picked up his beer and sat back, smiling happily. He wasn't sure where it got him, but he was pretty sure that he knew what Culver had given Rosemary Wright.

'Would you excuse me a moment?' Barbara said.

It had had to come. The moment when he was alone with Annie. He had not been looking forward to it. 'Hurry back,' he said, as Barbara made her way to the ladies' room. He felt rather like a schoolboy outside the headmaster's study.

'All right,' Annie said, as soon as Barbara was out of earshot. 'What surprise do you have up your sleeve for tomorrow?'

Harry held up a hand. 'Look,' he said. 'I did a sort of deal with her.'

'A sort of *deal*,' she said. 'Well – why didn't you say? A deal's a deal, isn't it, Harry?'

'She can help out – she can talk to Webb for us. I can hardly do that,' he said.

'She's a reporter.'

'So? You like her, don't you?'

'That's not the point!' she whispered fiercely. 'I'm only in this mess because I was avoiding reporters,' she said. 'And you invite one to stay.'

'She's only interested in who murdered these people and why,' he said. 'She's not interested—'

'I know what she's not interested in. You told me.' She picked up the newspaper and thrust it into his hands. 'Read it,' she said. 'See how uninterested they are in – what did you call it? Unimaginative extramural activities?'

Harry grinned.

'I'm glad you think it's funny!' She jumped up. 'I'm expecting the police to come walking in here any minute, and you think it's funny!'

'Did he say he was going to the police?' Harry asked. 'Did he?'

'Not in so many words,' Annie admitted. 'But he hinted. "Do the police know Mr Culver was in the habit of visiting you, Mrs Maddox?"' She mimicked Grant's precise, too-English accent.

'He was just trying to frighten you.'

'He's succeeded,' she said.

'Look, he thinks because he took you to dinner that you're his property, and it's hands off everyone else. He was just trying to get rid of me.'

'I don't think so,' Annie said. 'I don't think he's interested in me – he's taken up with Sandra. That's who was in London with him.'

'He doesn't like the police,' Harry persisted. 'He won't tell them anything he doesn't have to.'

'Like the rest of us,' Annie said bitterly. 'It must be contagious.'

'We've all got our reasons,' Harry said.

'Oh, sure.'

Barbara came back, much to Harry's relief.

'I'd like you to see Webb as soon as possible,' he said. 'You might catch him in here tonight, if you're lucky.'

'OK,' she said. 'Do I mention your name?'

Harry smiled. 'Not if you're fond of your front teeth,' he said. 'Oh – and while you're at it, ask him how whoever it was got into Grant's car.'

'How am I supposed to drag that in?'

'You can say that you're wondering if the sudden rise in the Amblesea crime rate is connected,' Harry said. 'Even Webb must be wondering that by this time.'

'His car wasn't locked,' said Annie. 'And he'd left the key in it. Tom had a few choice words to say about that.'

'Grant *says* it wasn't locked,' Harry said.

'I'm sure it wasn't,' Annie said. 'I even had to close his boot for him – that's how I know it was there at quarter past three.'

Eagerly, Harry leant forward. 'You closed his boot? Did you get a look inside?'

'No,' Annie said. 'But I think I'd have noticed if there had been a body in there, Harry.'

Harry got up and switched the television off as the drum roll began. Barbara had indeed collared Webb when he came in for his evening snifter; they must have hit it off, because they had gone off somewhere together.

'Do you think they're going to arrest Grant?' Annie asked.

'Not enough to go on.' Harry flopped back down on to the sofa. 'They need evidence. And with a bit of luck, I'll find it before Webb does.'

A sigh was Annie's rejoinder.

'Where's Grant decided to sleep tonight?' Harry asked.

'I think he's staying here,' said Annie. She waited a moment before going on. 'What about you?' she asked. 'Where were you thinking of sleeping?'

Harry leant back, and folded his arms. 'With you,' he said.

Her dark eyes rested on his face. 'I don't think I want you to,' she said.

'I don't care,' he answered. 'I love you, Annie, and I'd rather be with you, but I'll sleep on the sofa, or the floor, or a chair outside the door, if you like. Because until this gets sorted out, I'm not leaving you alone.'

Her gaze fell away from his. 'I can't be sure whether you think I've murdered everyone else, or that everyone else wants to murder me,' she said.

'That's the way it is,' Harry argued. 'You said so yourself. You're the connection.'

'Oh, sleep where you like!' she snapped, defeated.

Webb dropped Barbara at the hotel, and drove home.

He'd been glad of the diversion; she was a nice girl. He'd tried to be the friendly neighbourhood copper for her, but he wasn't sure he had succeeded.

She had had to leave some time; he couldn't delay going back to his lonely flat any longer.

If only Karen had come with him, when he had asked her to. But no, she was going to tell James. It was only right, she had said, and Grant's crack about the woman's magazine came back to him.

If only she had just come with him. It needn't have ended like this.

Where Harry liked to sleep was beside Annie, who, despite what she had said, now lay drowsily in his arms. Her lips touched his shoulder, and he smiled. He had never felt like this about anyone, and he had felt just the same during her brief inclusion on his list of suspects. He had discovered that he didn't care what she had done.

But, he reasoned, if she *had* done it – been capable of it – she wouldn't be the Annie who inspired the Sir Galahad in him. She wouldn't be the Annie whose belief that she owed the world some sort of explanation made him so angry that he would be insufferably rude to her. She wouldn't be the Annie with whom, in Barbara's words, he had been smitten from the moment that he had read those letters to Culver.

Annie wouldn't want to know that, and he would never tell her. But that was when it had started, before he'd even met her. And Harry wasn't there because his top-drawer wife got too much for him now and then, because he wanted somewhere to watch *Grandstand* and eat fish and chips. He was there because he wanted Annie.

Tonight, Annie had wanted him, and for a while life had seemed beautifully simple. All they had had to do was please one another, and that was what they had done.

Harry had felt triumphant, exalted, as if instinct's temporary eclipse of intellect had been some sort of achievement, and perhaps it had. But now the euphoria was wearing off, and Annie, cradled in his arms, was still at the centre of something he did not understand. He closed his eyes, but he didn't sleep, though his thoughts began to merge together, to become irrational, and he tried to pluck himself back from the edge of dreaming.

A gold key swung from a piece of string around Annie's waist. She undid the string, swinging the key just out of his reach. Opening a box, she dropped the key into it, then held the box out to him. But as he got closer, Annie got further away. She was wearing the coat she had worn when he met her on the beach, but Harry knew that it wasn't her coat at all. It was Karen Grant's coat, and when she took it off, she wasn't Annie any more, but Christine. Christine gave him the box, but the key had gone, and the string was now rope, still fuzzily new. And Christine was dead.

He sat up, wide awake.

'Sorry,' Annie murmured. 'Did I wake you?'

Harry frowned. 'I wasn't asleep.'

Annie moved deliciously in his arms, and kissed him, a long slow gentle kiss that should have taken his mind off his half-dream. But it remained with him, because it hadn't been a dream, not really. He must have been thinking something to trigger it off. His conscious mind had been taking a back seat, allowing his thoughts to flow and fuse and become a sequence that he so nearly understood. Perhaps it was something he'd noticed, something someone had said.

He told Annie the dream, and she listened. But he didn't tell her the end, and that was the bit that was tugging away at his mind. In a vague, superstitious way, he wished it was morning, so that he could see that Christine was alive and well.

He pulled Annie closer to him, suddenly afraid of losing her.

'What are you doing here so early?' Sandra asked.

'I just came to see if you needed anything. I didn't like to think of you all alone, not well.'

The truth was that Grant had needed something to do, something to take his mind off everything. He hadn't slept, and he had left the hotel early before anyone could ask him any questions. Sandra was the only person he knew who wouldn't be asking questions.

'I'm fine,' she said, her larynx failing her.

'I've spoken to my solicitor,' he began. 'He'll come to see you if—'

'Why would I need a solicitor?'

'No reason – I just thought you might feel better if—'

'It's not a solicitor I need – it's a doctor.'

'Do you want me to phone your doctor?'

She sighed. 'No. It's just a cold. Why are you really here?' she asked.

'Because I don't want to see people,' he said, dropping the pretence. 'I needed somewhere to go. And you said you didn't want to be alone, so I thought you'd like some company.'

'I told you,' she said. 'I'd rather you didn't come here. Please.'

So he drove around, because he didn't want to go back to the hotel, and people. And he didn't want to go home, to where the police had been into everything. Everything private.

If only he had kept Karen's note – he could still see it, propped up on the mantelpiece, and feel the contempt with which he had torn it in two and let it fall on to the flames. Contempt, and relief, perhaps, that she had gone.

Sometimes, when she was being particularly irritating, when the very things that had attracted him to her were driving him to distraction, he had *felt* like murdering her. But he hadn't.

He hadn't.

'Good morning!' Christine, alive and well.

Harry beamed as he went up to the desk. 'I'm very pleased to see you,' he said.

'Oh? Why?'

'Never mind. Isn't Linda usually on in the mornings?'

'It's her day off. I'll be working for ever if Sandra doesn't come in. She's got a terrible cold.'

'Why did you lie to the police, Christine?' Harry asked, killing her smile with the verbal slap in the face.

'I don't know what you mean.'

'Of course you do,' he said impatiently. 'You said Pete was with you when Fowler was killed.'

'He was!'

'No, Christine, he wasn't. Because you thought he'd stolen Grant's car, and that was at the same time.'

The defiance evaporated. 'I thought you were drunk,' she said. 'I'd hoped you hadn't noticed.'

'I'm quite often drunk,' Harry said. 'I always notice.'

The switchboard buzzed, and she ignored it. 'I didn't see Pete until about half past five,' she said. 'I said he was with me because he'd been on his own and he couldn't prove it.'

'What made him think he'd have to?' Harry asked.

'They'd already questioned him about another taxi driver,' Christine said hotly. 'Just because he's been in trouble – no other reason. The man said it wasn't Pete, and they had to let him go. But when he heard about Fowler, he knew they'd be after him again. It's not fair!'

The polite, muted buzz continued.

'Do you still think he nicked the car?'

'No,' she said. 'He's told me where he was now.'

Harry waited.

'It was Lesley,' she said. 'She'd told him she'd see him. He waited for her at the flat, but she didn't turn up.'

She finally answered the switchboard. 'Yes,' she said. 'He's here, as it happens. Yes, I'll tell him.' She hung up. 'Barbara,' she said. 'She says to go up in about twenty minutes.'

'Thank you,' Harry said. 'How come Sandra didn't see Pete when he finally did get here?' he asked.

'It was half past five,' Christine explained. 'It was Linda who was on the desk. And no one asked her.' She paused. 'Are you going to tell Tom Webb about me?' she asked.

'Who, me?' Harry answered, and wandered off to kill twenty minutes.

In the games room, he idly threw darts while he thought.

The dream that wasn't really a dream had been running through his mind while he had been talking to Christine, and he was trying to analyse its parts.

A key, a box, Annie, a coat (Karen Grant's coat?), Christine, dead.

Karen Grant was thought to be the body, because someone, perhaps Webb, had recognised the clothes, and Grant had confirmed that they were his wife's.

Annie took off Karen Grant's coat, and turned into Christine.

Take the coat off, and it isn't who you thought it was.

Christine dead. Christine was the body.

Why Christine? Why, in that half-conscious state, had he produced Christine?

Karen Grant's clothes, Christine's face.

His dart hit the wall beside the board. Of course. That was his mental image of her, the only information his mind had had to go on.

And Harry knew that he was beginning, at last, to see the answer. There was some more work to be done, but it was there.

'Wetherill's,' he said, handing Barbara a piece of paper with the address.

'Don't you want to know what Webb told me?'

'Yes,' he said.

'Well, to be honest, nothing very much. The body was on the pier for between eight and ten weeks. There is evidence of stab wounds, but they can't say for certain yet that that's what killed her. In the absence of any other apparent injuries, they're assuming that it is. They found some bits of old rope beside the body which—'

'Were cut off the pier gates, which the murderer then tied up with new stuff,' Harry said.

'Very good,' Barbara said approvingly. 'They think she was dumped there after she was dead. They haven't ruled out a connection with Fowler's murder. Tom says they've still got some tests to do, and think they'll get a positive ID at the end of them.'

'Tom, eh? Where did you two slope off to?'

Barbara winked, then laughed. 'Nowhere very romantic. He took me to the police station, so that I could see some other

190

people. We were there for ages – I thought he was going to arrest me.'

'Good. Keep him sweet, pet – we might need him. That place—' He indicated the piece of paper. ' – is a clothing factory in Harmouth. Find someone who knows a Lesley Osborne. She used to work there, and she must have had friends.'

Barbara glanced at the paper. 'Whereabouts is it?' she asked.

'The docks. It used to be a bonded warehouse.'

'And who is Lesley Osborne? Do you think she can help?'

Harry nodded. 'Oh yes,' he said. 'I think she can. Say you're an old friend – I want to find out where she went when she left Amblesea. Any sort of lead you can get. They're more likely to tell a girlfriend where to find her than a man, or I'd have gone myself.'

'I bet you would,' she said.

'Get going, then.'

'One condition.'

Harry's eyebrows twitched upwards.

'I get to come with you wherever it is.'

He could hardly refuse. If he did, she'd go by herself.

'Is it a deal?' she asked.

'It's a deal.'

Barbara hurried off, and Harry stayed for a moment in her room. He'd been right. The images his mind had conjured up hadn't been a dream. They were the thoughts tucked away at the back of his mind, the information in his data banks. And he had the uncomfortable feeling that the important part remained in there.

The key was the lift key, the string was the new rope on the pier gates. No mystery about that. But the box – Annie put the key in the box, and closed it.

He locked Barbara's door, and handed the key to Christine just as Annie appeared, seeing her auditor off the premises.

'I've had a thought,' he began, but as he spoke, Annie's face suddenly went quite blank, and she stood completely still, as though someone had switched her off.

Harry glanced at Christine, who stared behind him, and he turned to see a woman in the foyer. She was tall, auburn-haired, and good-looking. As good a pair of legs as he'd seen. And she was wearing a fur that would buy a good-sized semi, but even so, she wasn't striking enough to cause that effect.

He smiled. 'My name's Lambert,' he said, his hand outstretched. 'And you must be Karen Grant.'

TWENTY

Everyone seemed very pleased to see Karen Grant, once they had got over the shock of her resurrection. Harry would have been better pleased if she could have delayed her unintentionally dramatic entrance just a little. With every moment that passed, one jump ahead of Webb seemed less and less like enough.

He was glad of the total confusion into which her appearance had thrown the hotel. People popping up from everywhere, exclaiming. Grant's whereabouts were being sought, thus far unsuccessfully. All this took time, and Webb still hadn't arrived, which suited Harry admirably, as he impatiently awaited Barbara's return.

He stayed in the foyer, craning his neck to see Barbara's car.

The intercom buzzed on reception, and Christine answered.

'Chrissie – can you find Harry and tell him that Karen would like to meet him properly?'

Harry shook his head vehemently. He couldn't get caught up with them – he had to be ready to leave.

'I'll tell him when I see him,' said Christine.

'Thanks,' Harry said.

Simultaneously the corridor door opened to reveal Karen Grant, and the outside door to admit Barbara.

'Are you avoiding me, Mr Lambert?'

'No,' he said, backing towards Barbara. 'I'm just in a rush, that's all.'

Annie appeared.

'Annie,' he said. 'I must go – I'll see you when I get back.' He waved, and grabbing Barbara's arm, steered her out of the hotel, walking to her car.

He'd left his jacket; it was cold, but he was in too much of a hurry to risk going back for it. He opened the passenger door. 'Come on,' he said impatiently.

'Where are we going?' she asked.

Harry pulled his door shut and fumbled for the seat belt. 'You're the only one who knows,' he said. 'What have you found out?'

'I've got an address,' she said. 'But it's in Bristol, and they don't think she's there any more.'

'Neither do I,' said Harry. 'Let's go.'

'To Bristol?'

'It's only about an hour and a half or so,' he said. 'We'll be there by half eleven. Providing you start the bloody car.'

'Do you really think this Lesley Osborne can help?'

'I'm sure she can now,' he said, as the car swept round the car park to the exit.

'Who was the looker?' Barbara asked. 'It was very flattering to be first choice.'

Harry grinned. 'That?' he said. 'That was the late, great Karen Grant.'

The car slowed to a disbelieving halt. 'Karen Grant?' Barbara repeated. 'Karen *Grant*? But she's supposed to be dead – I want to talk to her.'

'Leave it,' Harry said. 'What can she tell you?'

'She can tell me where she's been!'

'She can tell you later.'

'And Lesley Osborne can tell us something now?'

'No,' Harry said. 'If I'm right, she can't tell us anything at all.'

'Then why—?' Barbara stopped in mid-protest. 'It's *her*? The body?'

'Yes,' he said. 'So drive, for Christ's sake, before Webb catches on!'

Tom sat quite still, staring at the phone. All they had said was, 'Call for you, Sir. It's a bit strange – someone calling herself

194

Karen Grant.'

Then Karen. Not a hoax, not some sort of twisted joke. Karen, indignant. Karen, bewildered. Karen, alive.

Alive. And he hadn't been able to speak to her. He had just repeated her name, until someone knocked on the door and came in. He could have sent him away, but he didn't think. He couldn't think. So then, when he had found his voice, he couldn't say anything anyway.

Then, it was on to automatic pilot. Mrs Grant is alive – switch the manpower on to finding out who is dead. Make reports, alter the whole line of enquiry.

And now he was on his own again. He would see Mrs Grant personally, he had said. He would deal with that himself.

But how did you deal with it? She was at the Wellington, she had said. No clue as to her decision. And she must have come to a decision, away from all the pressures. Unaware of all this.

But it *was* Karen's coat. He was sure of it. The thought that Karen herself might have been involved in whatever had happened flitted across his mind, and was banished.

She was alive.

Barbara parked across the road from a big, substantial Victorian house with rooms to let. It looked clean and neat, and its tiny bit of ground at the front was tended.

She switched off the engine, and turned to Harry. 'That's it,' she said.

'Who'd have thought,' he said, 'that it could take so long for a policeman and a reporter to find their way about?'

'You were navigating,' she said, and checked her watch. 'It's only ten past twelve, anyway.'

Harry released his seat belt. 'Let's get on with it,' he said.

'What are you going to do?' she asked, as they crossed the road.

Harry wasn't at all sure. 'Play it by ear,' he replied.

The door was opened by a massive pink frock which wobbled as it settled. 'If you're after a room, they're all took,' the old lady inside it said, in a deep, soft West Country voice.

'No,' Harry said. 'I'd just like to ask you some questions if I may – Mrs—?'

'Miss,' she said. 'Todd's my name.'

'Miss Todd.' Harry beamed. 'You are the owner?'

'That's right. You from the council, then?'

'No.'

She leant a quite awe-inspiring forearm on the door frame. 'Who are you then, that you want to ask questions?' She took an asthmatic breath. 'Police?'

'No,' he said. 'My name's Harry Lambert, and this is Barbara Briggs. We're friends of Lesley Osborne's.'

'Oh, yes. Young woman who had my second floor front. Why are you asking questions about her, then?'

'I think something might have happened to her,' Harry said.

'Happened to her?'

'Yes, I'm afraid so. May we come in?'

'Well, I'm not standing here with my feet,' she said. 'So you'd best come in, I suppose.'

Harry and Barbara followed the bouncing ball into a living room which surprised him; the furniture was modern, there were one or two prints on the walls. He had expected clutter and bric-à-brac.

'Sit yourselves down,' she said, as she prepared to do likewise. It took a deal of preparation, as she mentally computed her trajectory and bias. Rather like the driver of an articulated lorry going round a tight bend, Harry thought.

Once down, she had to get her breath back before she spoke.

'What's happened to her, then?'

'A body was found recently, Miss Todd. And I'm very much afraid it was her.'

The old lady nodded. 'Accident, was it?'

'It looks as though someone killed her.' His hand automatically reached for his cigarettes, but he arrested it. The woman was asthmatic, for a start. And there was something cool and bright and fresh about the room that made cigarette smoke seem wrong.

'But you're not the police, you say?' She looked from him to Barbara.

'No,' Harry said. 'They'll be here, though.'

'So what do you want to know?' She shifted her bulk to a more comfortable position.

'When did she leave here?'

'She didn't, not rightly,' she said. 'She paid in advance, though – she didn't owe nothing, I'm not saying that. But she didn't say she wasn't coming back, and she left some things here.'

'Didn't you wonder what had happened?' Harry asked. 'When she didn't come back?'

'Of course I did,' she said. Her breath, slow and laboured, failed her for a moment. 'I told the police, but they said she'd taken clothes and money, and there was no reason to worry. Said it was none of their business.' She paused for a long moment.

'It is now,' she said, in a voice as slow and heavy as she was herself.

TWENTY-ONE

Annie put down the phone, light-headed with the relief and excitement of Karen Grant's sudden reappearance.

'Chris still can't find him,' she said apologetically. She poured another two cups from the inevitable pot of crisis tea which had made its appearance.

It was as if Karen's presence had made everything go back the way it was before; as if none of it had happened at all.

'I can't believe it,' she said. 'I can't believe it.'

'I can't believe that you all thought James had done away with me,' she said.

She was taking it all very calmly, thought Annie. But then she hadn't had anything to worry about, unlike everyone else.

'I didn't,' she answered truthfully. 'But I think the police did.'

Karen smiled, crossing one elegant leg over the other. 'Poor James,' she said.

'I know,' Annie said. 'But he couldn't say where you were – I think they thought that was—' She tailed off, convinced that whatever she said would give offence.

'Suspicious?' Karen Grant was almost teasing Annie. 'He didn't know where I was,' she explained. 'I was taking a sabbatical.'

'He said that, more or less.'

'I needed time on my own,' she said. 'So I went away for a while. I'm afraid your handsome policeman has rather fallen for me.' She paused. 'I'm not like James. Either I was leaving him, or I wasn't. So I wanted to get away from both of them – Tom and James. I needed time to think.'

***

The drive couldn't last for ever; Grant finally went back to the Wellington.

'Mr Grant!' Christine cried as soon as she saw him. 'Where have you been? We've been looking everywhere—'

She broke off as the corridor door opened and Karen appeared.

'Hello, James,' she said, and her voice was cool.

He bowed slightly. 'Good of you to come back,' he said.

'You don't seem wildly excited at my return from the grave.'

'I never thought for a moment that you were dead.'

Karen walked past him to the lift, and Christine's excitement at the reunion had turned into puzzled disappointment. Grant smiled at her.

'Not quite Romeo and Juliet,' he said, as the lift arrived, and he stepped in behind Karen.

The lift purred quietly upwards.

'I really am happy to see you,' he said.

'Why did everyone think I was dead?' she demanded to know.

'Apparently Mr Webb recognised your coat,' he said. 'I bowed to his superior fashion sense.'

Karen turned slowly to face him. 'You mean you knew it wasn't mine? And you let him think I was *dead*?'

Grant spread his hands. 'I didn't know,' he said. 'It could have been yours – it looked like one of yours. I'm not very good at that sort of thing.'

'That was—' She searched for a word.

'Despicable is the word you want, I think,' he said. 'But it wasn't. You and I are a match for one another. Mr Webb is an innocent. You were trying to prove that sauce for the goose was sauce for the gander, and you used him. But now it's all over, and we can get on with our lives.'

She shook her head. 'No. All right, it started that way with Tom – and perhaps you're right. Perhaps I should leave him alone. And perhaps I will. But I'm not coming back to you, James. Not now.' The lift doors opened. 'Not ever,' she said, stepping out.

If there was an O-level in paperback clichés, he thought wearily, Karen would actually pass.

Annie was surprised to see Karen again so soon. The reunion must have been short.

Karen sat down, composing herself before speaking, as if she were about to address a public meeting. She smoothed her skirt, and looked up.

'I told you I had gone away to think,' she said. 'And I had thought, very hard, about my marriage. I came to the conclusion that James really had been trying to turn over a new leaf. I decided that my marriage was worth saving.'

Annie made a non-committal noise, wondering why she had been singled out for this confidence.

'I went straight home when I arrived,' Karen carried on, and there was something remorseless about it. 'You know, we really should have replaced our daily when she left. Perhaps a daily would have tidied away the evidence.'

'Sorry?' Annie said.

'A cliché if ever there was one – I mean, lipstick on his collar would have been subtle by comparison.' She flashed perfect teeth at Annie in something that passed for a smile. 'She left the whole lipstick,' she said. 'On my dressing table.'

Sandra, of course. 'Oh,' Annie said. 'I'm sorry.'

'For what?'

Dismayed, Annie realised why Karen was visiting. 'You don't think it's *mine*?'

Karen set down her cup. 'I've had quite a morning,' she said. 'First of all I arrive home to find that James has had a house-guest, then I come here to be told I'm dead. I've no sooner got to grips with that than James is telling me that he's dismissed you.'

'Yes,' Annie said.

'Because you had some *man* staying here? Why on earth should that bother James?'

'I've no idea,' sighed Annie. 'But – I presume you have heard

200

from another source – Mr Grant did take me to dinner one night.'

'Yes,' she said. Her deep blue eyes were watching Annie closely.

'It was by way of an apology,' Annie went on. 'For interfering in the running of the hotel – which he had been – and it was entirely above board. You could have been with us.'

Karen Grant lowered black lashes, then looked up. 'I'm glad,' she said. 'I'm glad it wasn't you. But I've had enough, Annie. I don't know what James is going to do, but I'd like to book in here until I sort myself out. In a different room from James.'

Tom Webb arrived, and with him Annie's realisation that nothing at all had been resolved by Karen's return. Matters had only been made immeasurably worse.

'Well, well,' he said, breezing in. 'You gave us all a bit of a fright, Mrs Grant.'

'Annie knows,' she said bluntly.

Tom looked uncomfortable. 'Oh,' he said, and sat down. 'I thought you were dead,' he said.

Annie felt a little awkward. Clearly, they would rather be alone. But somehow it seemed even more tactless to leave.

'James let you believe it was my coat,' Karen said.

'Flash Gordon's got it outside,' he said, getting to his feet.

'Who?'

'Oh, nothing.' He smiled, and opened the door. 'Constable,' he said.

The constable hastily presented himself, carrying a dry-cleaning bag.

'We haven't had it dry-cleaned,' Tom said. 'The bags come in handy. That's the coat.'

Karen glanced at it, then looked at Tom, surprised. 'But that *is* my coat,' she said. 'At least, it used to be. I gave it away to a girl who worked for James. Lesley Osborne.'

Annie felt the colour drain from her face.

'Annie?' Tom said. 'Are you all right? Did you know her?'

'It needn't be her, Annie,' Karen was saying. 'She might have given the coat to someone else – it could even be another coat like mine.' She came over, putting her arm round Annie's shoulders. 'Did you know her very well?'

'Not me,' Annie said, in a whisper. 'Not me.'

Tom crouched down beside her where she sat. 'Come on, Annie,' he said, just like he had at the pier.

'Where's Christine?' Annie asked. 'Where's Christine?'

'She was on the desk,' Karen said, jumping up. 'Don't worry, Annie. I'll get her.'

'What's wrong, Annie?' Tom asked.

Before she had time to answer, Christine came in. 'What's the matter?' she asked, bewildered.

'Tell Tom,' Annie said. 'Tell him the truth this time.'

Christine's fair skin reddened. 'What?' she said, playing for time.

'Harry knows you weren't telling the truth,' Annie insisted. 'He told me.'

'And I told Harry,' Christine said. 'He knows all about it!'

'Wait a minute!' Tom shouted across them. 'Who's Harry?'

'Harry Lambert,' Annie said.

'Lambert! What the hell's he got to do with this?'

'He's a friend of mine,' Annie said.

'Is he now? If he's interfered in this, I promise you, I'll—' He gave up in frustration, and turned to Christine. 'The truth about what?' he demanded. 'Ainsley?'

Annie couldn't look at Christine.

'Ainsley?' Karen Grant said. 'Wasn't that Lesley's husband or whatever?'

Tom's head twisted round to her. 'Her *what*?' he roared.

'Well – she lived with him, I think.' She looked beautifully helpless as she turned her exquisite eyes towards Annie.

'Didn't she?' she asked.

TWENTY-TWO

'*Were* you worried?' Barbara was asking.

'No, not really,' said Miss Todd. 'I thought she'd gone back to her young man. He came here regular for a while, but she wouldn't see him, only the once, so he stopped coming. I thought they must have made it up.'

'Her young man?' Harry asked. 'Do you know his name?'

'Peter. She called him Pete, but I don't like that. Peter.' She clucked, and shook her head. 'She was teasing him, I'd say. Playing with fire, that is.'

'He came here?' Barbara said. 'When was he here last?'

'A long time ago now,' she said. 'He stopped coming because she'd never see him.'

'What made you think they'd got back together?' Barbara asked.

'The phone call,' she said, as if she had been talking of nothing else. 'At Christmas.'

Harry and Barbara were on the edge of their seats. The pay-phone was in the hall, strategically placed right outside Miss Todd's door.

'You overheard something?'

'It was him,' she said. 'I answered it. She wasn't going to take it, not at first. But then she said she would. She said she'd think about seeing him, it being New Year and all.'

Miss Todd clearly thought that eavesdropping was not something you apologised for, and Harry warmed to her as she found her breath, her natural delivery adding to the suspense.

'She said she had some business in – Amblesea, would it be?'

They nodded.

'She said she might see him, but if she wasn't there by five, he could forget it. She liked having him dangling, if you ask me.'

'When was she going to Amblesea?' Harry asked. 'Did you happen to hear?' he added with a twinkle.

'New Year's Eve,' she said. 'That's the last time I saw her. She told Peter she was being met at the station, and he needn't come.'

'You said she didn't owe rent,' said Barbara. 'Did she work?'

'No. But she was never short of money. Always paid regular. Gave me a nice Christmas box, too.' She drew in a long, noisy breath. 'Always had money,' she said again, thoughtfully.

'Boyfriend?'

'Could be,' said Miss Todd. 'Not that young man, though. He never had a penny, poor lad. He hitched lifts to get here.'

'Was he angry with her? When she wouldn't see him?'

'He wasn't pleased,' she said. 'Might have been angry – just seemed disappointed to me.'

Harry's hand went for his cigarettes again, and he had taken out the packet before he realised.

'Sorry,' he said, making to put it away.

'You go ahead,' she said, and to his horror began to wind herself up to leave the chair. 'I'll get you an ashtray.'

'I can get it,' Barbara said, but Miss Todd had made it to her feet.

She rolled and pitched to the sideboard. 'Can I get you something to drink?' she asked. 'Tea, coffee? Maybe a biscuit?'

'No,' Harry said, taking the ashtray. 'Nothing for me, thanks.'

'Nor me,' said Barbara, smiling.

'If you're sure,' she said. 'I don't often get visitors.' Finally, she was arranged in the chair once more.

Harry smiled. 'I don't suppose you'd do me one more kindness, would you Miss Todd?'

Miss Todd's chuckles gently shook the rolls of flesh. 'I'll bet you always get your own way, don't you, young man?'

'Not always,' Harry said modestly, grateful for the 'young man'. 'You said she left some things behind?'

'Yes,' she said slowly. 'It's all still in her room. I haven't relet it yet. I thought she'd come for her things, but she didn't. That's why I went to the police.'

'Could I see her room?'

'I don't know about that,' she said.

'She's probably not going to mind,' he reminded her.

The old lady leant forward, her prodigious breasts touching her knees. 'What do you think I should do?' she asked Barbara.

'It can't hurt,' Barbara said. 'You can come with us.'

Miss Todd breathed for a moment or two. 'All right,' she said. 'I like you.' She pulled herself to her feet. 'Second floor front,' she said, and waddling to a cupboard, took a key from a rack. 'Lock the door when you've finished.'

They climbed the steep stairs, and opened the door of Lesley's room. There wasn't much in there; the furniture consisted of a bed, a dressing table, a small three-drawer chest, a chair, and a cupboard which Harry presumed was a wardrobe.

An old-fashioned radio sat on the chest, and some magazines were stacked tidily on the floor. Lesley Osborne had lived simply.

Barbara looked round the little room. 'Poor Lesley,' she said.

'Yes,' Harry said, sitting down on the bed.

'Pete?' Barbara said, with barely a question mark. 'He must have lost his temper – got tired of being kept dangling, as Miss Todd would say.'

Harry shook his head. 'I don't think so,' he said. 'Why? He'd got the patience of Job where she was concerned. Look at the way he came here time after time when she wouldn't even see him. Why would he kill her just when he'd finally got somewhere with her?'

'But he wasn't with Christine when he said he was,' Barbara argued.

'I know,' said Harry. 'Which means that Christine wasn't with him.'

'*Christine?*'

'She didn't want Lesley keeping an appointment with Pete, did she?' Harry stood up. 'I'll tell you this,' he said. 'I just wish I'd never answered the phone to Mrs Culver.'

He turned as he heard Miss Todd's heavy progress up the stair, her laboured breathing audible from the bedroom.

'I thought I ought to be here,' she said, through tortured gasps.

'I haven't touched anything,' Harry said.

'I didn't really think you would, son,' she said. 'But just in case.'

'Quite right, Miss Todd,' said Barbara, giving Miss Todd one of her very best smiles.

'She didn't live it up, then,' Harry said.

'Oh now – I wouldn't say that. She wasn't hardly ever here,' she said with a knowing look. 'That's why I didn't worry when she stayed away. Not till she'd been gone too long for my liking.'

'What did she take with her?' Barbara asked.

'Just a little shoulder bag with her clothes,' said Miss Todd.

'May I?' Harry indicated the chest of drawers.

'You can look,' she said.

Harry wound his hankie round his hand and opened the bottom drawer. Underwear, tights. He opened the next. Blouses, folded neatly, and two sweaters which even he could see hadn't come from a chain store.

The top drawer had a mixture of things – stationery, scissors, measuring tape, sewing stuff, cassettes, a small screwdriver, buttons, some coins, and three letters. Harry badly wanted to read the letters, but the immovable Miss Todd would, he was sure, refuse permission. He glanced at Barbara, and flicked his eyes towards the door.

She frowned slightly, but complied. 'You know, Miss Todd, I think I would like a cup of tea after all,' she said brightly. 'Shall I give you a hand?'

'If your young man's finished in here,' she said slowly, 'we'll

206

go down and have one.'

Harry pushed the drawers in, and opened the cupboard.

'Wow,' said Barbara.

'I told the police,' Miss Todd said. 'I said her clothes weren't the kind you'd just leave, but they said she wasn't a minor, and she wasn't in danger, so they could only put her down as missing. And not look for her,' she added.

Harry felt obliged to come to their defence. 'There isn't the manpower,' he said. 'Not to look for everyone who decides to take themselves off. And most of them would be very upset if they did. You'd be amazed the things people walk away from.'

The old lady's eyes narrowed. 'I thought you weren't police,' she said.

'He's not,' Barbara assured her.

'But they'll be here,' Harry said. 'So just leave the room as it is, if you don't mind, Miss Todd.'

'I don't mind,' she said, waddling back out on to the landing. 'I just give it a dust every day.'

Harry screwed up his hankie and put it in his pocket. 'Couldn't you have told me that before?' he said.

'Where did you think the dust had gone, then?' she asked, her eyes full of mischief.

Harry grinned. They followed her downstairs; a long slow job.

It was while they were drinking the now obligatory tea that Harry realised what he had seen.

Christine had caught a glimpse of Pete at the police station, but they were being interviewed separately. She told Tom Webb that Pete hadn't arrived until after five; she had been given a lecture, and now she was answering question after question.

'What kind of mood was Ainsley in when he arrived?'

Christine was frightened. She shrugged. 'I don't know,' she said. 'Just ordinary.'

'But he left twenty minutes after he'd arrived?'

'Yes.'

'Why, Christine?'

'He just went home.'

Tom leant over the desk. 'He waited for Lesley, and when she didn't turn up, he went to the Wellington to see you. What made him leave again so soon?'

Christine didn't answer. Anything she said would only make it worse.

'You can see the car park from the staff bedrooms, can't you?' She nodded.

'Did he see me arrive? Is that why he left?'

'No.'

'Why then?'

'We went in to see Mum – Mr Grant was there. Pete got upset.'

'Why should that upset him?'

'Because – because he doesn't like him.'

'Not good enough, Christine. Why did he leave?'

Lesley, Christine thought. Lesley. Why did Pete do anything? Lesley.

'Miss Todd,' Harry said, when he had finished his tea. 'Would you let me take something from Lesley Osborne's room? I'd give you a receipt – anything you like.'

'I know you want to read these letters,' she said. 'And if the police do come, they can read them, I suppose. But I haven't, even if you think I have. Phone calls aren't private – not if they're made out there with this door open. But letters are, young man.'

'Not the letters,' Harry said when she had finished.

'What, then?'

'The tapes,' Harry said. 'The cassettes. They're not private, are they?'

'No, I suppose not. What do you want them for?'

Harry shrugged. 'They might help, they might not.'

'Why don't you just leave it all to the police?' she asked.

'You did,' he said. 'Look where it got you.'

'All right,' she said, handing him the key. 'I'm trusting you, boy. Don't let me find those letters gone.'

Harry had never felt so youthful, with her liberal use of 'young man' and 'boy'.

'Thanks,' he said. Then, winking, 'You're a canny lass yourself.'

'Mrs Maddox?'

Grant pushed open the door of the sitting room and called her name again. He was about to leave when he saw the note. He read it, and went back out to the lift.

He walked along the corridors to his room, and picked up the phone.

'Sandra? I don't wish to be disturbed by anything less than fire or flood. Do you understand?'

'Yes,' she said. 'James – I'm sorry. I'm sorry I said those things—'

'Sandra,' he said patiently. 'I do not wish to discuss it.' And he hung up.

'Thanks, Miss Todd,' Harry said, when he came back down with the cassettes. 'We'd best be off.'

He saw the signs, and placed a restraining hand on the soft padding of her shoulder. 'No, don't you get up,' he said. 'Not with your feet. We'll see ourselves out.'

'Thank you for seeing us,' Barbara said. 'And for the tea.'

'I like you,' she said again. 'And him. But you've an honest face.'

'That's nice,' Harry said. 'There is one other thing, Miss Todd.'

'What's that then?' she asked slowly.

'When the police do come,' he said. 'I'd be very grateful if you wouldn't mention this visit.'

'Oh?' she said, and the long West Country vowel was invested with grave doubt. 'Why's that?'

'Well – they don't take too kindly to me interfering with their

job,' he said. 'I'll tell them myself – and about these.' He held up
the cassettes. 'But it would be better coming from me.'

She thought for a moment. 'I like you,' she said again. 'So
here's what I'll do. If they don't ask, I won't tell them. How's
that?'

Harry smiled. 'Fair enough,' he said.

They saw themselves out; Barbara waited until she had pulled
the door shut behind them before speaking.

'Harry,' she said. 'You conned that old lady!'

'I didn't,' Harry said, injured. He had liked old Miss Todd.
He hadn't conned her.

'For all she knows, you could be the one who murdered
Lesley.'

'Quite,' he said. 'So I'd sooner I had the evidence than anyone
else who could talk her out of it.'

They got into the car. 'I didn't take the letters, if that's what
you think,' he said. 'I read them, mind. But they're not
important.' He took the cassettes from his pocket.

'What are you going to do with them now you've got them?'

'I thought I'd play them,' he said, inserting one in the cassette
deck.

'Harry!' she said, disapprovingly.

'And her not cold yet,' he said, pressing the play button, and
watching Barbara's face as she listened.

The sound quality wasn't good, but it was good enough. Two
men, having a conversation.

Barbara's brow furrowed as she strained to make out what
they were saying. 'What is it?' she asked.

'It's what paid Lesley's rent,' Harry said.

As the conversation went on, she nodded. 'Blackmail,' she
said.

'What else?' Harry switched it off. 'And I think blackmailers
are probably on the victimologists' lists, don't you?'

'How did you know? How did you know it wasn't the Beatles
or something?'

'She didn't have a cassette player,' Harry said smugly.

'Cassettes aren't usually much good without one.'

Barbara made to start the car, then changed her mind. 'Hang on,' she said. 'I'd better check the radiator. I think it might need water.' She looked at him. 'There's water in the boot.'

Harry groaned.

'I don't know why we're in my car anyway,' she complained.

'Because you can claim expenses,' he said, getting out.

The radiator was topped up, and Harry screwed up the can and put it back in the boot.

'I know the murderer, and the motive, and the means,' he said, slamming the boot shut. 'I just don't have any bloody evi—' He stared at the closed boot, and his hand. The box. The box that Annie handed him, that Annie closed.

'Yes I do,' he said. 'Damn it, of course I do!' He planted a kiss on Barbara's startled lips. 'Come on, pet,' he said. 'Drive!'

Barbara obeyed, and on the journey back, Harry at last began to piece it all together.

TWENTY-THREE

Annie shivered in the raw wind from the sea, and pushed her hands into Harry's jacket pockets, as she walked slowly towards the pier, remembering the old days. Better days? Perhaps not.

The tide was out, the sea far away. Ebb tide never helped as much, but at least she knew that it would turn, it would flow again, and even today couldn't last for ever. The invisible sun would set.

The cold, hard wind blew into her face, bringing with it droplets of rain. Perhaps Christine was right. Perhaps she would turn into one of these women who wandered about talking to themselves. Perhaps she had cause. Christine was with Pete at the police station, and had made it clear that Annie was not welcome. And just when she needed him, Harry was off with the vivacious and independent Barbara, who could apparently shrug him on and off like an old coat. Linda was in Harmouth, shopping. Even the Grants had shut themselves in their separate rooms, and Annie had found herself quite alone. She had picked up Harry's jacket, and gone.

'Mrs Maddox!' Annie heard Grant's voice, and stopped. Of all the people she didn't need right now, Grant had to be top of the list. She began to walk quickly towards the pier as though she hadn't heard. But his heavy tread quickened on the pebbles, and he was walking beside her.

'Not a day for the beach, I would have thought,' he said, as he caught up with her.

'Then why come here?' she asked.

'Because you're here,' he said.

They reached the pier, and Annie stopped under the shelter of the concrete buttress. The wind whistled along the pier's length, worse if anything. But at least it was dry, and Grant moved to take the brunt of the icy blast.

'There's some snow on the way, I think,' he said.

'Yes.' Annie leant against the wall, tired after fighting the wind.

'I don't think,' he said, 'that this walk is for pleasure.'

'There isn't much pleasure to be had at the moment,' she replied. 'This walk is more pleasant than most things.'

It was odd, being here with him. Above their heads a police car still stood guard on the theatre.

He stood in front of her in his sheepskin coat, his hair slicked back, black and shining with the rain.

'I wanted to apologise,' he said.

She'd seen his hair like that before. Blacker and shinier than ever, she had thought.

'When I saw you on the beach, I had to come. I can only excuse myself on the grounds that I had been through a lot. Reaction, you see. The police thought I had killed her, you know.'

That must have been awful, Annie conceded. Especially for him – having to get mixed up with the police again. Poor Mr Grant. He probably had to give them his fingerprints all over again. And not even for elimination this time.

'I would be very grateful if you would consider overlooking my bad manners – and my bad temper.'

Elimination, Annie thought. And she realised. But he'd been in his room, she argued with herself.

'It was unforgivable of me, but that's what I'm asking you to do.'

He hadn't been in his room. He'd been out in the rain. When she met him at the lift, his hair was black and shiny, just like now. He'd been out in the rain. And then the police had eliminated his fingerprints, and found no one else's.

'Mrs Maddox?' he said.

Annie stared at him. 'I have to go,' she said.

'No, Mrs Maddox.' He caught her arm. 'I can't let you go,' he said. 'You're the connection, don't you see?'

She ran, slithering on the wet pebbles, shouting for help. A policeman appeared on the pier, and vaulted the wall on to the sloping sea defences, sliding down as Grant caught hold of her.

'Stay where you are,' he said to the policeman, and Annie saw the knife.

His hand gripping her arm, Grant kept her in front of him as he pulled her up the sloping wall towards the pier.

'Get away!' he roared to the two men who were working on the repair. 'Get off the pier!'

They stopped working, and stared.

'Now!'

They walked slowly down towards them. Please God, don't let them try to be heroes, Annie thought. Her friend the Liverpudlian stopped in front of them, uncertain what to do.

'Go!' Grant shouted, and he went.

Grant pushed her towards the police car. 'Get in,' he said, opening the passenger door and pushing her down so that she fell across the two front seats. 'Behind the wheel,' he ordered, and she scrambled away from the knife, so close to her that she could feel it.

'Lock your door,' he said, as he locked his.

Annie sat with her hands by her sides, not daring to breathe too deeply with the knife almost touching her skin.

'Don't speak,' he said. 'I have to think.'

She didn't think she could speak if she wanted to. She didn't think she wanted to.

The silence was broken by the calm, measured tones of the police radio control. She couldn't take in what was being said. The jumble of call-signs and coded signals was interspersed with plain English, but she couldn't even understand that. The voice was interrupted every now and then by pips, soothingly monotonous. Suddenly, they stopped, and there was nothing.

'Start the car,' he said, moving the knife just a fraction away.

Annie found her hands on the wheel, though she had no awareness of putting them there. She looked for the ignition.

'I said, start the car.'

She couldn't.

'Mrs Maddox,' he said. 'Let us understand one another. I will tell you what to do, and you will do it. Start the car.'

'I can't.' Annie's hands gripped the steering wheel. 'I can't find the ignition.'

'This side,' he said. 'The keys are in it.'

Annie turned the ignition and the car growled into life.

'Reverse gear,' Grant said, for all the world as if he were giving her a driving lesson.

Annie stared at the gear lever.

'I will not continue to say things twice,' Grant said.

'I don't know the car. You'll have to let me find where reverse is.'

'Towards you and back.'

As Annie looked behind, unbidden but automatically, she saw cars arrive from everywhere, and stop at the pier entrance.

'First gear,' Grant amended, instantly.

Annie stared at the temporary bridge, only half-finished, some of its planks loose. Just wide enough for a car and no more.

'No,' she said, shaking her head.

TWENTY-FOUR

Harry's almost jaunty step faltered as soon as he went into the hotel. You could almost smell the crisis.

'Sandra?'

Sandra looked like death. 'There's no one here,' she said. 'It's been awful. Mrs Grant's turned up, and they've arrested Pete Ainsley.' Her hoarse voice was bewildered as she carried on. 'They've all gone, except James – Mr Grant, and he's in his room. He won't even answer the phone.'

Harry ran past her, down to Annie's sitting room.

Barbara followed him in. 'Look,' she said, pointing to the coffee table.

Harry picked up the note.

Harry

If you want me, you know where I'll be.

Annie.

PS I've borrowed your jacket.

'Oh, my God,' he said. 'She's left him a bloody note!'

As the car turned out of the waste ground on to the shore road, they could see that they were too late.

For the second time in four days, Harry thought Annie was dead.

'Sorry, miss,' a constable was saying to Barbara. 'We've had to close the road temporarily. You can get into Harmouth by going back through the town, and joining the—'

'Lambert,' Harry said, leaning across. 'I have to liaise with Superintendent Webb.'

The constable heard the jargon of authority. 'Yes, sir,' he said. 'I'll take you to him.'

Harry got out of the car, trying to remember how to divorce himself from all of this. An ambulance rattled past, and gave him a thin hope.

'Webb?'

Webb turned, his face set and angry. 'He's got her,' he said.

'What do you mean, got her?' Harry asked.

Webb looked across at the police car sitting at the entrance to the pier. 'He's in the car,' he said. 'He's got Annie, and he's got a knife. We can't make a move until he's simmered down.'

'She's not dead,' Harry said, stupid with relief.

Webb shook his head. 'I know how you feel,' he said. 'Believe me.' The suggestion of a smile went as soon as it had come. 'How long have you known it wasn't Karen's body?' he asked.

'Only this morning,' Harry said hastily. 'And only for sure once Karen had turned up.' He produced the cassettes. 'Your missing evidence on Grant,' he said. 'Lesley's keepsake.'

Webb took them. 'I thought she'd just been winding us up,' he said. 'She said she could prove it, she'd give evidence of meetings, and deals. Then at the last minute, she backs down. She'd made it all up, she said. They'd had a row, and she was just getting her own back. We'd got documentary evidence that proved that someone was fiddling something. But we needed her evidence to nail Grant, and she wasn't going to give it.' He smiled, and put the cassettes in his pocket. 'I really believed she had been making it all up,' he said, shaking his head. 'Silly girl.'

Harry looked across at the pier. He could just see Annie, sitting motionless behind the wheel, Grant beside her. 'What's he trying to do?' he asked.

'God knows. We're switching the radio to a different channel. When that's done, I'll have talk-through to him. Maybe we'll find out.'

'In the meanwhile we just wait?'

'What would you do?' Webb asked tiredly.

Harry acknowledged Webb's dilemma with a nod of his head.

'Sir!'

Webb and Harry watched, horrified, as the car kangaroo-hopped towards the gap in the pier.

'Will that hold a car?' Webb asked the council workman who stood with them.

'That?' he said, waving a deprecatory hand at his work. 'That's just for a couple of building surveyors to walk on. It's not even finished – it's got to have a hand rail. And the planks aren't all nailed down.'

'We've got talk-through, sir.'

Webb grabbed the radio from his driver's hand as the car inched its way towards the planks.

'Grant!'

Harry had the satisfaction of hearing the car cough and stall as Annie's foot slipped off the clutch.

'That is a temporary footbridge. It is not complete, and could collapse. Reverse away. I say again – reverse away.'

The car started up again, stumbling further towards the bridge.

'I suppose your radio *is* switched on?'

'Yes, sir,' said the constable.

'I'm glad you do something right, Constable.'

'Sir.'

Webb turned back to the workman.

'What can you tell me about the buildings on the pier?' he asked.

'Not much. We've been working on the platform,' he answered in a laconic Liverpool drawl. 'But the buildings look done for, if you're asking me.'

'How much repair work have you got done?'

'Not a lot,' he said. 'What with one thing and another, like.'

TWENTY-FIVE

Annie's hands shook, and slid on the wheel, as her palms grew sweaty.

'Grant,' the radio said. 'Let Mrs Maddox leave the car. We can talk. I'll tell you how to use the radio. Let Mrs Maddox out, and we can talk. Over.'

Annie looked at him.

'Mrs Maddox. I would be grateful if you would not stop driving just because they are speaking to us on the radio.'

'But it's a footbridge,' Annie said.

'Then I suggest you drive faster. That way, when we go over it, it will be less likely to collapse under us.'

'I can't,' Annie said.

'You will. Now, please. Start this car moving, *fast*, and drive straight over it.'

'Oh, Christ,' Annie said, and she may have closed her eyes as she accelerated up to and on to the rattling planks, until the noise stopped. One plank flew up and hit the car, but she was over. She braked hard, stopped, and slumped over the wheel.

'Now, you will continue to drive down the pier,' he said.

Annie was still trying to get her breath back, and he had knocked it all out again. 'But there *isn't* any pier,' she said. 'Look at it! The end's been ripped off, and what's there is dangerous.'

'These things are relative, Mrs Maddox. I can assure you that it is less dangerous than I. Drive the car.'

'Grant,' said the radio.

'Drive the car, Mrs Maddox.'

Annie drove, at a snail's pace.

219

'Grant. Let Mrs Maddox leave the car. We can talk. No one's going to rush you. But let Mrs Maddox leave the car.'

Annie bumped her way down over the creaking structure until she could see the jagged end of the pier.

'Go on,' Grant said.

'Grant. Where you are is structurally unsound. You should both leave the car immediately. If you refuse to do so, at least let Mrs Maddox leave.'

'Drive.'

Annie's head spun. 'Where to?' she said, and she almost laughed, almost sobbed. *Where to, guv'nor?* 'There's nowhere,' she said.

'There is a building on your right,' he said. 'It gives me cover.'

'But it's practically falling into the sea,' Annie whispered.

'Drive up to it, and turn right at the end of it.'

Annie let in the clutch, and the car stalled. She was annoyed. She was *annoyed*. How ridiculous. She started the engine, and the car leapt forward and stalled. She had forgotten what you did. She couldn't remember how to start a car.

Seat belt, mirror, indicator, look behind, check in— Oh, God, she was going mad. Neutral. Neutral. Where the hell was neutral?

'Start the car!'

She stared blankly at the controls, suddenly as unfamiliar as a shuttlecraft's. She looked at him, at the knife.

'I don't think I can,' she said, but she hadn't said it aloud.

The radio crackled. 'Where you are is extremely unsafe,' it said.

You're telling me, thought Annie.

She put the gears in neutral and started the engine, moving off slowly, indicating right automatically. She brought the car to a halt at the side of the building, its wheels crunching on the broken glass. As Grant opened the door, cold air blasted her, and she breathed deeply.

'Out, please, Mrs Maddox.' He grabbed her arm, pulling her as she tried to get out, making her stumble. 'In there,' he said, propelling her through the one-hinged door into the wreck of what had once been the souvenir shop, with its picture window facing the sea. The window was a gaping hole beside the door now, through which the wind howled.

'Don't talk,' he warned her. 'I have to think. No talking.'

'Grant.' They could hear the radio through the open door of the car.

'Grant. If you want to talk to me, take the microphone from its hook beside the radio. There is a button on the side. Press it in to speak, and release it when you have finished. I repeat . . .'

Grant still held on to her, and held the knife close to her.

'Where do these stairs go?' he asked.

'Up,' she said.

'Mrs Maddox,' he said threateningly.

Annie sighed. Grant had frightened her when he had taken her out to dinner. He had frightened her when he had spoken to her about Harry. He had frightened her on the horrendous car journey down the pier. But the novelty had worn off, and he didn't frighten her now. He might be going to kill her, and he might not. But he wasn't going to frighten her any more.

'I think I'm tired of you, Mr Grant,' she said.

TWENTY-SIX

Harry had blended in so successfully with the local force that he had even been handed a mug of tea which some enterprising soul had managed to acquire.

'Where did you get this?' he asked.

'Made it at Grant's house,' he said. 'I reckon he owes us.'

'I wish to God we could see them,' Harry said to Webb. All they could see was the tail end of the police car, its indicator winking, its exhaust showing in the cold air.

'Still,' Webb said, warming his hands on his mug. 'If we can't see them, he can't see us.' He put his mug down on the roof of the car. 'They reckon we're safe to take men down this far,' he said, indicating about a third of the way down on a rough sketch. 'After that, they only allow two workmen at a time. And where they are,' he said, 'is bad news.' He was talking to his inspector, but he was holding the plan to include Harry. 'But if he's right down there, we can at least get men quite near – near enough to see what's going on, if we're lucky.' He broke off and mopped his brow. 'How can you freeze and fry at the same time?' he asked.

'Grant?' he said again, in the same quiet voice. 'Did you hear my instructions on how to use the radio? Over.'

Nothing. Harry borrowed the binoculars, and focused on the building at the end. There weren't any windows in the wall facing, and only a high louvred window in the wall at right angles. The building rose into an odd sort of box shape, high above the other buildings, but there were no windows up there.

Through the binoculars, the car looked as if you could touch it. He didn't think he could have borne to have seen Annie. He

222

handed them back.

Webb was preparing a small group of men to go on to the pier. 'It's bloody cold,' he said to Harry. 'What's Annie wearing?'

Harry smiled wearily. 'My jacket,' he said.

'That's women all over,' Webb said, with a grim cheerfulness.

'It's never kept me very warm,' Harry muttered.

'If he's planning to stay there we might be able to do some sort of deal,' Webb said. 'He might want hot soup or cigarettes or something.'

'I could do with a cigarette,' Harry said.

'Grant. I will repeat the instructions on how to use the radio. Take the microphone . . .'

As Webb spoke, Harry felt his sleeve being nudged, and looked down to find him holding out cigarettes and matches.

'Cheers, mate,' he said, lighting one. He had never felt so useless. Webb was doing all he could, but nothing brought a response from Grant.

The inspector had been shepherding the men on to the pier, and came back to join Webb as they began to make their way down.

'The weather might beat us,' he said, after a few moments.

'Webb!' The radio suddenly came to life.

Webb grabbed the mike. 'Go ahead, Grant. I'm listening, over.'

'Get those men off the pier, over.' Grant said, deliberately mocking Webb's radio style.

'How the hell does he know they're *on* the bloody pier?' Webb asked, grabbing the binoculars. 'There's no way he can see this end of the pier from where he is.'

'You have one minute,' Grant's voice went on. 'One minute. If they are still there in one minute, I will kill Mrs Maddox. She understands that. I hope you do.'

'What's he got?' Webb was asking no one in particular. 'A bloody crystal ball?'

Harry suddenly remembered.

'Magic,' he said.

TWENTY-SEVEN

He had dragged her back up to the darkness of the camera obscura. Annie watched the group of fuzzy, indistinct figures turn and leave the pier to join the mass of images at the far end. The light wasn't good, the mirrors had oxidised, and the image being thrown on to the table in front of him had meant nothing to Grant at first, but he had soon seen its advantages.

He had his arm round her neck, the knife in his hand. 'See?' he said. 'They do as they're told.'

Annie said nothing.

He waited until the last figure was no longer discernible. 'I have to think,' he said. 'I have to think how best to use you.' He tightened his grip on her.

The room was tiny, meant only for one viewer at a time. It was stuffy and damp, with a cold clinging dampness that was seeping through to Annie's bones.

'Perhaps I should have married you, Mrs Maddox,' he said. 'You are an attractive woman – and you have a brain. You don't always use it, but you do have one.'

He released her, and she rubbed her neck. In the dim, eerie light, she could just see the knife.

'Karen is very beautiful,' he said. 'But she has no brain. Lesley, now – Lesley had a brain. But she couldn't be trusted, Mrs Maddox.'

Annie shuddered.

'Karen will probably leave me,' he said. 'Sandra is very careless.'

A gust of wind made the exposed tower tremble, and he made

224

a grab for her. 'Down,' he said, pushing her in front of him down the twisting stair. Her foot slipped, and she pitched forward, breaking away from him. She crashed against the wall and looked up at him. Evading the wild grab he made at her, she launched herself down the rest of the stairs into the shop, picked herself up, and ran.

TWENTY-EIGHT

'A camera obscura?' Webb said. 'And it's still working?'

'Nothing much to go wrong,' Harry answered. 'A little hole and a couple of mirrors.'

Suddenly, there was a flurry of movement, and Annie dashed out from the corner of the building, only to be caught and dragged back out of sight.

'Hell's bells, Annie,' Harry breathed. 'Don't start getting self-reliant now, pet.'

Webb picked up the microphone. 'Grant. If you let Mrs Maddox leave, you and I can talk. I'll listen. No tricks – just let Mrs Maddox leave. Now.'

There was no response.

Webb leant on the car, and took a cigarette out of the packet. 'I wish you were a double scotch,' he told it. 'If we could just get him on the radio and keep him there, he wouldn't be able to watch us. Even a camera obscura doesn't let you be in two places at once.'

Harry dropped his cigarette on the ground as thin snow began to fall. All around were police vehicles, lights flashing, radios chattering, except for theirs. A small crowd had gathered. Harry saw Christine, and looked away, helpless.

But then a thought occurred to him. 'I know I'm only here on sufferance,' he said. 'But he doesn't like police. I think I could get his attention. And keep it.'

'All right,' Webb said. 'We'll try again. But just three of us. The weather's getting worse, and I don't want a disaster on my hands.'

'I'm quite nifty with a half-nelson, sir,' the sergeant said.

'OK. Take your personal radio, and keep in contact with the inspector. I want to know if there's the least chance that he's back up in that thing,' he told the inspector, who acknowledged the instruction with a grim nod.

'Could I go, sir?' The constable whose car Grant had taken.

'Done. Follow me, and don't go anywhere except where I go or I direct you.'

'You, sir?' said the sergeant.

'Me, Sergeant. I can still hold my own in a fight. Right, Lambert?'

'Right,' Harry said. Providing you have an unfair advantage, he thought to himself.

TWENTY-NINE

Grant dragged her over to the gaping hole where the window used to be, and under which ran an old-fashioned radiator.

'This may be a little uncomfortable, Mrs Maddox,' he said, pulling off his tie with his free hand. 'But you can't be trusted.'

He pulled her arm behind her back, and held the knife in his mouth as he grabbed the other, with which she was hitting him. 'Now,' he said, as he secured her tightly to the radiator. 'Now I must think.'

Annie felt the snow begin to soak through the thin material of Harry's jacket, as the wind blew it unremittingly into the shop. She didn't feel cold any more. Not the shuddering, painful cold. That had been fear, and she wasn't afraid now. Now, she was numb.

'Grant?' The radio outside suddenly came to life again, and there was no mistaking the flat vowel. Illogical relief flooded over her like a warm shower.

'Grant. This is Lambert. You know me. I'm the one they kicked out because I didn't pay enough attention to their rules. And I don't have to pay any attention to them now, so you'd better answer me.'

Grant looked up slowly from his cogitations. 'Well, Mrs Maddox?' he said. 'What do you say? Do I trust him?'

'You can trust him,' she said.

Grant walked slowly out to the car, and opened the driver's door. He reached in for the microphone, and turned to Annie, holding the knife to her through the window frame. 'Is he going to offer me tea and biscuits?' he asked.

228

'No,' she said. 'Not Harry.'

Grant pressed the button. 'Lambert,' he said. 'What have you to say to me?'

'Lots of things,' Harry said. 'But first I want to speak to Annie.'

'No,' Grant said.

'I want proof she's all right, Grant. And if I don't get it, I'm coming down to sort you out myself.'

Grant pulled the microphone out to its fullest extent and held it to Annie's mouth. 'Tell the man,' he said.

Annie's tongue had gone dry. She swallowed with difficulty before trying to speak. 'I'm all right, Harry,' she said.

THIRTY

Harry let out a long, slow breath, then turned to where Christine stood, white-faced, with Pete's arm around her. He gave her the thumbs-up, and she managed something approaching a smile. Linda stood with them, returning the signal. Harry turned back to the radio.

'I'm not going to ask you to let her go,' he said. 'I'm not going to ask you to do anything. I'm going to tell you a story.'

'What are you talking about, Lambert?'

Harry nodded to Webb. 'I've got him,' he said. 'You can go any time you like.'

Webb picked up the loudhailer, and moved towards the pier with his men, as the wind gusted again, almost knocking them back. Bending their bodies against the stinging flurries of snow, they began to make their way down.

'Still there, Grant?'

'Still here, Lambert.'

'Go on,' the inspector told the sergeant.

'It's a story about four people,' Harry said. 'Do you remember New Year's Eve, Grant?'

He had to get Grant to answer him whenever he could, so that they knew he was still there.

'I do,' the radio said.

'Lesley Osborne,' Harry said. 'I never met her, but Christine says she looked like her, so she must have been all right.' He paused as the wind whipped away his breath, and got into the car. 'Rosemary Wright – ordinary sort of woman. Liked Amblesea a lot – she wanted to buy a house here.'

He waited, but there was no response.

'Danny Fowler. Taxi driver, nice bloke. And another nice bloke,' he said. 'Gerald Culver. He was in Amblesea visiting someone. And they all had the misfortune to meet you. Didn't they, Grant?'

Silence.

'Wait!' the chief inspector said, and the three figures battling the wind on the pier stood quite still.

Harry took a breath, and realised he was being handed a lighted cigarette. He nodded his thanks, and did a double-take as he saw Barbara, her reporter's low cunning having got her a ringside seat. He smiled, and went back to his task.

'You almost got away with it, didn't you?'

Still nothing from the radio. On the pier, the men clung to the treacherous structure in the wind.

'Annie thinks she's frightened of you,' Harry went on. 'But that's not the way it is, is it? You're frightened of her. You've been frightened of her all along.'

Seagulls wheeled above them, calling and crying in the gathering storm.

'You tried to kill Annie before,' Harry said. 'But murder isn't easy, is it, Grant? You've learned that better than anyone. It's bloody difficult – not like it is in books at all. People interrupt you at the wrong moment. They get in the way. And when people get in your way, you get rid of them, don't you, Grant?'

Still, Webb and his men had to wait, crouching down for protection from the elements, and Grant's possible observation.

'You've made a lot of money, haven't you, Grant? And your methods were called into question, but no one could prove anything, so they dropped the charges. But Lesley Osborne had proof, hadn't she? She could send you to prison, and she knew you'd do anything to stay out. Trouble was, she didn't realise just how far you would go. Did she?'

'You have to prove it,' Grant said, suddenly, making Harry jump.

'Go,' said the inspector quietly, and Harry watched the three figures continue their slow progress down the pier.

231

THIRTY-ONE

Annie listened to Harry as he spoke, the small hard drops of snow flying into her face.

'Lesley Osborne hadn't worked since she left you,' Harry said. 'But she was never short of money. She never owed any rent. Because you were paying her to keep quiet. But she was always a danger to you, so she had to go.'

Grant looked over at Annie. He was hardly able to keep his feet in the wind howling in from the sea, and the knife moved unsteadily. Annie shrank away from it, and he moved closer to her, pulling the microphone cord taut.

'She was good at her job, wasn't she, Grant?' Harry was saying. 'You might say she had it taped. Don't you think, Grant? You might say that.'

Grant stared at the radio, lowering the knife, and sat down heavily in the front seat of the car.

'What do you mean?' he said.

'Lesley got her own flat – or you got it for her. Is that where you met your councillor buddies? Anyway, Lesley thought it would be an idea to leave the tape deck running. I've found the tapes, Grant. You couldn't risk picking them up yourself, so I've saved you the worry.'

Grant had forgotten about Annie; slowly, with her mind groping through a fog of fear and fatigue and cold, Annie realised that Harry was buying time. Time for the police to do something. Time, she realised, for her to do something. There was broken glass everywhere. They did it in films. They cut themselves loose in films.

232

'It was all planned, wasn't it? She said she had a bit of business in Amblesea that she expected would be over by five. She even made another appointment. But she didn't keep it.'

'What has this to do with me?'

'It would hardly take any time at all. You'd leave the hotel at three thirty, to arrive at the station by three forty-five. You'd pick Lesley up, drive along the coast road, kill her, dump her body in the pier, and be back in the hotel before anyone knew you'd been out. Right so far, Grant?'

'This is a fairy story,' Grant said, having recovered some of his composure.

'Is it?' There was a pause, and Harry continued. 'You just had to get in and out of the hotel without being seen. Anyone can do that providing they've got a key to take the lift to the basement. And you had. You made sure you were moving stuff in from your house in the morning so that you'd be given a key. Which you handed in at lunchtime, but not before you'd made a copy.'

Annie couldn't quite reach the window-sill, just six inches above her hands. Her fingertips touched it, but she couldn't reach the glass. And anyway, she couldn't see what she was doing. She might hurt herself and then not be able to do anything.

'You walked round to the staff lift, used your key, and took it straight to the basement. And you went to pick up Lesley.'

Keep going, Harry, Annie prayed. Keep going. She could see a triangular piece of glass on the floor. If she could slide her hands down the pipe, she could get it. Keep *going*, Harry.

'And it all went according to plan.'

'*What's wrong?*'

'*I don't know. The nearside front wheel feels strange.*'

'*It feels all right to me. Let's just get to the house. Why couldn't you just bring it with you?*'

'*It's safer in the house. It's a lot of money.*'

'*If you think you'll get round me, forget it.*'

'*Perhaps I thought I might.*'

He stopped the car. 'I'll just have a look.' He got out, and walked round. 'Damn,' he said. 'It's almost flat.' He went to the back of the car, taking off his coat. He rolled up his sleeves, and got to work on the wheel.

He undid one wheelnut. 'Can you bring me the jack?' he asked.

She complained, but she didn't want to be stuck in the middle of nowhere, so she brought it.

'I can't see anything wrong with it,' she said.

'And you dumped her in the pier,' Harry said.

From down on the floor, Annie heard Grant cry out when he could no longer see her. She closed her eyes, her head against the radiator.

'Get up, Mrs Maddox.'

'I'm tired,' she said. 'I'm out of the wind here.'

'I want you where I can see you. Get up.'

She got to her feet with difficulty, having to pull the tie back up the pipe. He tested it, to make sure it hadn't loosened, and she thanked her numb fingers for not being nimble enough to pick up any glass, or she would surely be dead.

'But then the unexpected happened,' the radio said. 'You've always got to expect the unexpected in the murder game. It all started to fall apart. Didn't it, Grant?'

Grant hadn't moved from the window, hadn't taken his eyes off Annie. Harry's voice went on.

'You were on your way back, job done, when you took a bend and came face to face with a taxi.'

Grant turned slowly, and picked up the microphone.

'You're guessing,' he said. 'You're just guessing.'

He still had his eye, and his knife, on Annie.

'A taxi on the wrong side of the road.' Harry's crisp, clipped voice cut through the whine of the wind.

He jammed on the brakes, slithering to a halt, sliding on the wet surface and gently crumpling the taxi's bumper.

Run. No, no. Don't panic. Behave naturally. He got out of the car.

Argue. That's what you would normally do. Argue.

'We drive on the left in this country, I think.'

'You were going too fast – I'm parked here.'

'On the wrong side of the road – on a bend.'

'I was picking up!'

'Well, no point in standing here arguing about it.' Grant reached into his pocket. *'How much to cover the damage?'*

'What?'

'I'm in a hurry. How much?'

The taxi driver shrugged. *'Look mate, if it was up to me, I'd take you up on it. But it isn't my cab. Just let me get something to write down your particulars—'*

You have to, he told himself. He'll get the police if you don't. And he's got your number. You have to.

'And that was his fate well and truly sealed, wasn't it, Grant? Because now he was a danger to you too.'

Annie could have cried. She had been inches away from her piece of glass, and now she'd have to start again. If she got the chance.

Harry's voice went on, stopping occasionally, and Grant never took his eyes off her. The knife was at her throat, as he stood right beside the window. But the constant wind, and Harry, were getting to him.

'The next bit took a bit of working out,' Harry said. 'How could you be sure of getting him before he reported back to his boss? But he drove for Amcabs, didn't he? So there was nothing he could do in Harmouth except drop his fare and come back. You just waited.'

'You're guessing,' Grant said again, but the wind carried the words away. He sat in the driver's seat, his feet outside the car.

The knife at least no longer pointed at Annie, but Grant still watched her.

'He's making this up,' Grant said, when Harry didn't speak. He turned to the radio. 'You're making this up!' he shouted.

235

'Am I? You waited for the taxi, and you got him out of his car. He got exactly the same treatment as Lesley, except that you robbed him. I thought at first that you'd tried to make it look like robbery, but no. It *was* robbery, wasn't it, Grant? He'd written your name and address on the back of a letter that he had in his wallet, hadn't he, Grant?'

'No,' Grant said. 'No. You can't know that.' But he wasn't talking to Harry. He was talking to himself, his head bowed.

Harry's voice went on, as Annie crouched down once more, and slowly slid her hands down, jerking the tie down the pipe.

He'd have to come back. He could wait, try again. Offer him more money. No. No, it was no good. He'd remember, if they found her too soon. He'd go to jail. The thought clutched at him, and slowly, a plan evolved.

He lifted the bonnet of his car, and waited.

When the taxi appeared, he waved it down, and it stopped.

'What's up?' the driver asked.

'The bump must have done some damage, I think. Do you know anything about cars?'

'Some.' He got out of the car, and bent over the engine.

'But you had another problem, didn't you, Grant?'

There was silence, and Annie hardly dared blink.

'Didn't you?'

'Did I?' Grant said.

'Your car. You couldn't risk it being linked with the taxi, now. So it had to go. Just like Fowler. Just like Lesley.'

Annie's fingers touched the glass as Harry stopped.

'Go on,' Grant said, his voice hollow with bravado. 'Go on – I'm enjoying it.'

'You dumped the car – and bashed it into a wall a couple of times. And that's when you started making mistakes, Grant. You hadn't enough time to plan all this.'

Annie's numb fingers slid off the glass. Keep talking, Harry, for Christ's sake, keep talking.

236

'Lesley's prints were on the car. If they found her, they might connect you to her, and you couldn't risk that. So you wiped them away, didn't you? Everywhere she could possibly have touched. Including the boot, Grant. Especially the boot. She'd touched that, hadn't she?'

Everywhere.
Grant worked quickly, looking round at the dark, empty streets for prying eyes, but there were none. Everywhere, just in case. Quickly, before someone sees. But no one saw.

'No one saw,' Annie heard Grant say quietly. 'No one saw.'

'But car thieves don't give cars a polish, do they? And you'd been wearing gloves. It would look a bit odd if there weren't any prints on it at all. They'd suspect that. Yours should be on it, it was your car. So you opened the doors – and the boot. You'd been unloading stuff – your fingerprints ought to be on the boot. See what I mean, Grant? Murder gets very complicated, doesn't it? Now it was Fowler's murder you had to cover up.'

Go on, Harry, I've nearly got it. Annie's hand closed over the glass.

'You went back to the hotel on foot, and let yourself in by the basement lift.'

Annie gripped the glass with fingers numbed by cold and lack of circulation, and lifted it from the ground, twisting it round until she could hold it between her finger and thumb. She couldn't see it now that she was on the floor too, and she couldn't feel it. She just had to hope it was still there.

'And you got out at the ground floor,' Harry continued. 'You were being clever again, weren't you? I couldn't think why you'd do that, but then I realised.'

Annie struggled to her feet. The icy wind knocked her breath away, and, exhausted, she leant against the brickwork and closed her eyes. Seagulls called frantically to one another as the wind gusted even more strongly, and she could feel the whole flimsy structure tremble.

'If you got out at ground level,' Harry was saying, 'anyone seeing you would assume that you had just come down. And that's what Annie did assume, when she walked out of her room and found you. It's what I assumed too, but that comes later.'

Grant, who had been slumped in the driver's seat, suddenly remembered Annie, and looked up.

Annie tried not to look as though she was gritting her teeth as she pushed the edge of the glass back and forth across his tie. She had no idea if it was working; she couldn't even be sure it was the tie she was attacking, and not Harry's jacket. Harry was fond of his jacket.

'And you thought you were home and dry,' Harry said, dragging Grant's unwilling attention back to the radio.

Home, and dry. Annie had never really appreciated the poetry of those words before. There was a heater in that car, she thought, as she continued her sawing. She couldn't get proper purchase with her hands tied as they were, but she felt the first few strands of cloth give way. It was working. Slowly, but it was working. And she wasn't sawing her way through her left wrist, after all.

'You see,' Harry said, 'your great plan took almost everything into account. Just your prints and someone wearing gloves, you thought. That's all the police would have to go on. They wouldn't find Lesley's prints. And you thought then that they wouldn't find Lesley, didn't you? Why should they? No one had been near the pier for twenty years – you thought you were safe for another twenty. But it wasn't to be, Grant. Murder is bloody difficult.

'You waited for ten days before you moved on to your next victim,' Harry said. 'And I know why, Grant. Believe me. I know why.'

Annie kept pushing the glass up and down, up and down, in tiny, wrist-breaking movements.

THIRTY-TWO

Harry gulped tea as Barbara's pencil flew over the page.

He trained the binoculars on the pier. They were only half-way down, moving slowly over the treacherous platform.

Sweat trickled down his back. It seemed like hours since Grant had spoken. He may be talking to thin air. Maybe Grant had seen Webb and his men, and Annie was already dead. But if he did have an audience, he couldn't chance breaking the spell by asking to speak to Annie. He had to carry on.

'Annie got a letter about the promenade development exhibition,' he said. 'They said they'd booked the room in January. They had spoken to you. And you had realised then that Lesley's body would be found. No one had even glanced at the place for years, and now they were going to *inspect* it. Oh, well – you have to laugh, don't you?'

'Yes,' Grant answered. 'It is a very humorous story.'

'Carry on,' the inspector told his man on the pier once Grant had spoken, and the three, battling wearily against the wind blasting off the sea, carried on.

The tide rolled further and further in with every minute and dark clouds gathered. Harry rubbed his eyes.

'So now two other people were a danger to you. Lesley's discovery might excite some media attention – and it did, Grant. You were right. That's why I'm here.'

'You're here because you have a vivid imagination.'

'Two other people,' Harry repeated. 'The ones I told you about at the beginning. Rosemary Wright who was seeing her husband off at Harmouth. She popped into Amblesea to have a

239

look at the show house on the building site – she wanted one of those houses, Grant. And Culver, who was here on a flying visit. You made another mistake then, Grant. You didn't know who Culver was – you didn't know his murder would be news. But it was, and Mrs Wright remembered him. She said he gave her something. That took a while, but I think I know what he gave her, Grant.'

He cleared his throat. 'Culver was a nice man. He took Fowler's taxi to Harmouth, and when the taxi was hailed by a woman leaving the building site, he wouldn't have left her on a lonely dark road. He gave her a lift, Grant. The taxi pulled over to pick her up, and that's when you smacked into it.'

Grant didn't reply.

'Stop,' the inspector said, and through the binoculars, Harry saw the men flatten themselves on the ground. They weren't much further down.

'They were the taxi's passengers, and they had seen you. So they had to go.'

'How?' the radio growled. 'How would I know where to find them?'

'They were Fowler's witnesses too,' Harry said. 'He'd obligingly written their names and addresses for you.' He rubbed tired eyes.

'Are you all right?' the inspector asked.

'Sure.' Harry picked up the microphone. He was beginning to hate it, to see it as some sort of extension of Grant.

'If you've hurt Annie,' he said, 'I'll kill you.' But he hadn't pressed the button. It just made him feel better to say it, out loud.

THIRTY-THREE

Annie was sawing, sawing. She'd have to stop, but she couldn't, or she wouldn't be able to start again. Her right forearm ached with the effort, and she switched hands, but it didn't work at all in her left hand. Maybe she didn't have a left hand any more. She couldn't tell. The wind howled through the gaping building, and her ear ached.

'He can't know all this,' Grant said, staring at her. 'How does he know all this?'

Annie just stared back.

'She lived in Watford,' Harry said. 'He gave his London address. Which was fine for you, because you had a reason for going to London. But the dates didn't tally. That puzzled me. But of course, you had to do a recce. Old soldiers know how to do these things. You were back behind enemy lines, weren't you, Grant?'

'You talk of enemy lines,' Grant shouted. 'What do you know?'

'I know that it would take a couple of days to establish their movements,' Harry said, and his voice was tired. 'The board meeting wasn't excuse enough. You had to be there a few days, for a reason that no one would think twice about. A woman, of course. Someone once told me that everyone understands sex.'

Annie was grateful for the little message.

'So that was the answer. Take along a friend. She didn't see much of you, though, did she?'

'Where've you been?'
'I told you I'd be busy.'

241

'But you're never here. What was the point in my coming?'

'I'm here now,' he said, kissing her. 'I'm here now.'

'You sussed Culver first. Living alone in a flat in a place where everyone minds his own business. Easy. So one night, you let yourself out of the hotel by your usual route, and you took yourself off to London, and killed him. You were back before anyone even surfaced. It was as simple as that.'

'What? Yes, who is it?' Culver, sleepy.

'My name is Grant, Mr Culver. You and I were involved in an accident recently.'

'Accident?'

'In Amblesea. You were in a taxi.'

Silence.

'Mr Culver?'

'What do you want? It's the middle of the night.'

'I have to speak to you, Mr Culver. It's very important, or I wouldn't be here.'

'I don't understand.'

'I'll explain everything.'

'All right.'

A buzz told Grant to open the door. Into the lift, up to Culver's flat. Out, into the corridor. He could see Culver standing by his door.

'Mr Culver?' he said softly.

'Shush,' he said, coming out. 'What is it? What's happened?'

'It's this,' he said, putting his hand in his pocket.

'Catch them when they're asleep, eh, Grant? It's a police trick, too, you know. Dawn raids. That's when people are at their most vulnerable, isn't it? Their thoughts aren't clear. It had worked. So off you went to Watford next.'

'You don't understand—'

'Yes, I do. Prison. You couldn't go to prison. You don't even like to lock your car. You'd go mad in prison. But you had already gone mad, Grant.'

242

Up, down. Up, down. Up, down. Annie cried tears of frustration. Up, down. She'd have to stop. This was a crazy way to spend your last moments.

'Mrs Wright was on her own too. Terrorist tactics this time. Knock on her door, and kill her. Just like that.'

Just like that. She fell to the ground, and he closed the door, slipped back down the path, and into his car. She was gone too. It was all over.

'It was over,' he said. 'It was over.'

'It should have been over,' Harry said. 'But then you found out that Culver hadn't been visiting just anyone. He'd been visiting Annie. And that made Annie dangerous.'

Grant shot a look at her just as the material ripped.

THIRTY-FOUR

'Where are they now?' Harry asked.

'Almost there,' the inspector said. 'It depends on what they find. They might have to wait for a chance.'

Aching with weariness, Harry carried on.

'So you took her out, didn't you? You wined and dined her, and asked her about Culver. She hadn't told the police, but you couldn't trust her, could you? She might. She might. She was the connection, so she had to go.'

Harry drank some more tea. 'But you overlooked the unexpected again, Grant. I was with Annie the night you tried to kill her. I couldn't sleep. I'd spent three weeks boozing all night and sleeping all day – I'd got used to it. So I got up early, and this time *I* saw you getting out of the lift. And I thought you'd come down from your room,' he said. 'Just like Annie did. Even when Linda said she thought you'd gone back to the house. Which you had, of course. You had even got them to start delivering the evening paper again. You had to be seen to be tucked up in your own house that night. And you hadn't come down from your room, had you, Grant? You'd just arrived. And you'd come to kill Annie.'

'You have to prove it,' the radio snarled.

'True,' Harry said. 'Maybe you've been too clever for us, Grant.'

He released the button on the microphone.

'Maybe he has,' the inspector said. 'All you've worked out is that someone could have done that. The tapes won't be admissible, and they don't prove he murdered anyone anyway.'

'I know,' said Harry. 'But I do have evidence. It's not proof yet, but at least it's evidence that points to him.'

The inspector frowned. 'What evidence?'

'Annie's fingerprints,' Harry said. 'On the boot of Grant's car.'

'But we didn't find her fingerprints,' he said. 'Just his.'

'Have you ever heard of the curious incident of the dog in the night?' Harry asked, and smiled. 'Annie closed his boot for him. At three fifteen, when she saw his car. She left her fingerprints, and he carefully wiped them off again.'

'But if someone did steal it,' Barbara said, 'couldn't they have wiped them off?'

'And left Grant's in their place?' Harry said. 'That's a canny trick.'

THIRTY-FIVE

Annie's hands were as tightly tied as ever. The material had ripped so far and no further.

The radio went silent. Harry had run out of things to say, and she had run out of strength. She closed her eyes as the hot tears ran down her face.

Harry, sounding desperate, carried on somehow, but it was no good.

'And this afternoon, you had another go. You're supposed to be in your room at the hotel, aren't you? Did you seriously think you could get away with it in broad daylight, with the police already here?'

'No,' said Grant.

'Still,' Harry said. 'What can we prove? Nothing. So as long as you don't hurt Annie, you're still in with a chance. She's your trump card, Grant. She's your only card. So you'd better keep her alive. Do you hear?'

'Are you crying, Mrs Maddox?'

His voice was right beside her, in the shop. Annie's eyes shot open.

'Why?' he shouted above the wind. 'You heard him. I must keep you alive.'

'Are you there, Grant?' Harry's voice, urgent.

Grant took a step forward towards her, holding the knife close to her skin.

'Grant!' This time it wasn't the radio, and it wasn't Harry. The voice, distorted by a loudhailer, came from somewhere on the pier. Grant spun round.

'Grant! Let Mrs Maddox go. It can only help you if you do.'
His voice came and went with the wind, echoing round the
empty carcasses of buildings.

Behind her back, Annie's hand found some extra reserves as
she forced it to move the glass again. Up and down.

'You got me into this,' Grant said, almost conversationally. 'I
thought you could get me out. But you can't. I am what they
call cornered, Mrs Maddox.'

'Grant. Put down the knife and we'll talk.' Every word left a
tiny part of itself behind, to tag on to the next word.

Over Grant's shoulder, Annie could see Tom Webb as he laid
down the loudhailer and crept towards the doorway. She didn't
react, because she couldn't, not because of any quick thinking.

'I panicked, Mrs Maddox,' he said. 'And panic is a cardinal
sin.'

Tom could hardly stand because of the wind; he dropped to a
crouching position, and Annie couldn't see him. She worked
desperately. Just once more. And again. One more.

'The wages of sin, Mrs Maddox, is death.'

Annie could feel a thread going. Go on, go on.

'It was *your* sin, not mine, that found me out,' he said. 'If Mr
Culver had not been visiting you, there would have been no
taxi, and none of this would have happened.'

'Lesley Osborne would still be dead,' Annie said, rising to her
own defence, forcing herself to have one more go, one last try.

'Lesley was the only one who was meant to die,' he said.

Harry's victim. Annie felt another tiny rip.

'But it would never have ended,' he said. 'It would have been
you, then Lambert, then this Briggs woman. It would never
have ended. I think I knew that. I think that's why I came here.'

Annie almost cried aloud with pleasure as she felt the last
threads go.

'Instinct,' he said. 'This way I will die. I won't go to prison.
And now, they are on the pier. I told them not to come on the
pier.'

Tom was in the doorway.

247

'I told them I would kill you if they came on the pier,' he said. 'And I meant it.'

Now, *now*. For a dreadful instant, Annie's body wouldn't move. But she gathered her strength and launched herself at him, using the surprise to push him off balance. She skidded through the doorway, hurling herself round the car, flinging herself in, as the other two ran into the shop. She grabbed the door, pulling it shut and locking it in one movement. Diving to the other side, she rammed down the lock, then twisted round to the back doors. They were locked. They were locked. She was safe.

The sergeant had Grant's knife, and it was taking all three of them to pull him away from the broken edge of the pier, despite the wind screaming off the sea, pushing them back.

'Grant.' She could hear Harry's voice on the radio, but she couldn't move.

'Grant. Are you there? Grant?'

Harry. Speak to him. Speak . . . her eyes moved slowly round the car, the rest of her body quite motionless. The curled wire from the radio lay over the driver's seat, the microphone on the floor.

'Grant. Webb? Answer the radio, for Christ's sake! Webb! What's happening?'

She reached down for the microphone with torn, bleeding hands, and stared at them, frowning. She couldn't feel them. She couldn't grip the microphone.

'Webb?'

She used her other hand, and scooped the microphone up. It took all that was left of her strength to push down the button.

'Harry,' she said. 'I'm safe.' And she watched them drag Grant away.

She looked out at the sea, dark greys and greens flecked with angry foam, as the wind sent the waves crashing on to the rocks, closer and closer. Constant and inviolable. Even as she felt the pull on the old pier, Annie was grateful for that.

It seemed a long time before anyone came. The wind buffeted

248

the car, and she closed her eyes.

She turned slowly in answer to the tap on the window, and addressed herself to the daunting task of pulling up the lock.

As she succeeded, Harry opened the door. Slowly, carefully, he helped her out, his arms supporting her. The wind howled in from the sea, and salt spray showered them as they began the long difficult walk back.

Grant was driven away, and Webb waved the ambulance up the pier entrance. Snow fell as they opened the doors and rolled out a stretcher. The crowd began to press forward for a closer look at the scene, and his men ushered them back again.

Chris clung to Pete, and he patted her like a baby. They moved towards the ambulance, pushing through the people and the cars, their heads down against the driving wet snow. A policeman joined them, bringing them through. People were pointing; they looked up. Christine tried to run to her mother, but the policeman stopped her.

Linda followed Pete and Chris, never taking her eyes off the pier. She had no coat; Tom Webb took his off, and put it round her shoulders, as he had done for Annie, when all this started.

Annie and Harry, their arms round one another, made their perilous way along the centre of the pier in an unwilling, wind-assisted jog over the loosened, rattling planks to safety, and hugs, and the waiting ambulance.

'Barbara Briggs. Ready?'

In the telephone box, raising her voice against the wind whistling through the door that wouldn't quite shut, Barbara began.

'Amblesea. Spelt A-M-B-L-E-S-E-A. 1st March.

'Wealthy businessman James Grant, spelt G-R-A-N-T, was led away by Amblesea police this evening from the South Coast resort's derelict pleasure pier COMMA after a tense siege lasting almost three hours STOP

'PARA It was on Amblesea's pier COMMA just under a

249

week ago COMMA that workmen discovered the body of a woman now thought to be thirty-year-old Lesley, spelt EY, Osborne, spelt O-S-B-O-R-N-E, STOP

'PARA That discovery seems to have been the penultimate act in a bizarre, spelt B-I-Z-A-R-R-E, and bloody sequence of events COMMA dramatically unfolded here today by ex-Yard man Harry Lambert, spelt L-A-M-B-E-R-T ...'